WHEEL OF THE YEAR

WHEEL OF THE YEAR

THE AGE OF STONE

L.E.L. DELAFIELD

PALMETTO
PUBLISHING
Charleston, SC
www.PalmettoPublishing.com

@LELDelafield

wheeloftheyearbooks@gmail.com

Hardcover ISBN: 9798822949720
Paperback ISBN: 9798822949737
eBook ISBN: 9798822949744

This book is dedicated to my daughters, Eden and Alba, who inspired the two strong women at the heart of this story.

My beautiful girls, never forget the power within you or the women who came before you: the ancestors, the angels who conspire for your life to be long, healed, and fulfilled.

Love you forever.

KEY TERMS

dowser: A person who can employ a type of divination to locate ground water, buried metals or ores, gemstones, oil, gravesites, malign "earth vibrations" and other objects and materials without the use of a scientific apparatus.

Druid: A priest in ancient Celtic tradition. Ailsa's story predates Celtic culture, but the word Druid is used here since Neolithic Cosmological Priests were their predecessors.

Enheduanna: The historically documented Sumerian cosmological priestess of Ur. She would have been a contemporary of Ailsa's first ancestors who built the stone circle on the island.

hapiru: A term used in 2nd-millennium BCE texts throughout the Fertile Crescent for a social status of people who were variously described as rebels, outlaws, raiders, mercenaries, bowmen, servants, slaves, and laborers.

kerbstone: The stone sometimes found in a megalithic structure, that is not standing, but rather lying down, often denoting an entrance or border. Often highly decorated or significant as in Knowth or Stonehenge.

Litha: Another word for the Summer Solstice

maelstrom: A powerful whirlpool in the sea, thought to be caused by tectonic plate movement

menhirs: The tall, upright stones in a stone circle

middens: Ancient trash heaps

moon cycle: This may refer to the 29 day cycle of the moon from New to Full to New again, or it may refer to the female 29 day menstrual cycle.

pollard: Neolithic practice of cutting the tops off of trees to encourage new growth

Sláinte: Means "health" in both Irish and Scottish Gaelic. It is commonly used as a drinking toast in Ireland, Scotland and the Isle of Man.

timor mortis conturbat me: Latin for "fear of death disturbs me."

triskelion: a symbol of three interlocking spirals, significant to both ancient Greeks and Celts.

Union Jack: The flag of the United Kingdom that is comprised of the Scottish flag, or St. Andrew's Cross (X), transposed over the English Flag, or St. George's cross (+).

TABLE OF CONTENTS

PROLOGUE

Hiraeth (Welsh): *A proto-Celtic word that describes a longing for one's homeland, grief for a past that's lost. A deep homesickness. It has no direct translations.*

There are times when I wake in the darkness before dawn with that familiar feeling of displacement.

Everyone has this sensation from time to time—it's a product, perhaps, of a life well traveled or shifting circadian rhythms.

Anyone roused from a deep sleep too quickly may wake with hackles raised in anticipation of some ancient predator.

But I wake in a vortex of vertigo, wondering not *where* I am but *when* I am, and no matter what princely place or quaint cottage I find myself in, my ancestral home is my touchstone—my true north.

It is the longing before I open my eyes.

But time grinds us down like grain on the quern.

We are alchemized by those who came before us, and so are these places and monuments they have touched.

What home do I have to hope for anymore?

Everywhere we look, the complex magic of nature
blazes before our eyes.

– Vincent Van Gogh

Introduction:
The Ancestors

My great-great-grandmother was born ninety-nine years before me. She was known throughout the isles as a great healer. Men came down from the highest mountains and up from the singing-sand beaches of the mainland to seek her wisdom. She refused to sleep inside her roundhouse, preferring the stars as her blanket. The stories of her told around the hearth are the tales of a wild woman with something in her older than even the stone circle she danced around. But as wise as she was, she was also feared. "Women are always feared for their knowledge," my grandmother told me.

This wild-wise woman, my grandmother's grandmother, was called Ailsa too. She died before I was born, her namesake, but she speaks to me through the whistle of wind in the trees, the chatter of the birds deep in the forest, and the practical wisdom my grandmother has raised me with. Like Enheduanna from the first civilization, she was the original astronomer priestess of our island. Our family were Druids before they were called *Druids*: me, my uncle Jord, and our first ancestor on this island, my seven times great-grandfather Ailef, who moved here carrying the stones that would become the great stone circle on the moor where I stand now.

Our descendants would eventually call themselves Druids, a name meaning "knower of the oak."

We walk barefoot, even in winter, to feel the story of the earth unfolding. It's how we tell the future—through connectedness to the earth, not divination of the heavens. This is important to remember. Often, when our eyes believe they see magic, what we actually behold are the simple laws of nature, malleable in the hands of those who share the wisdom of the earth that is available to all. As a Druid, I can wield fire, heal the sick, predict the weather and the tides, and change the future, all without breaking the laws of nature. I am a vessel for wisdom, but there are things I've seen that even I couldn't explain at first: solid rock melted, time stopped, and the true power of the standing stones.

And now, as I go about my daily routine—walking to the oak grove to pray, meeting with the other Druids for council at the stone circle, hanging fish in the smokehouse, tending the barley my father planted, and grinding grain and herbs—I feel a deeper purpose in the mundane because I can feel that the earth is preparing to change again, the way it did three hundred years ago when Ailef brought the stones here. There is another *Great Shift* afoot, and there will continue to be shifts in the earth's energy as long as time exists. It has always been the way. Long ago, this land beneath our feet was covered by ice and uninhabitable to us. The same land we live on, which flourishes now with thick forests and groves, will one day be cut away. These isles will be treeless, with rolling green hills shorn for the animals that graze them, and eventually, one day, not so far off, the ice will come back to them. It's hard to imagine, but all things are circular in nature. That's why the stones take that shape.

You see, one doesn't need to be a time traveler to see the future. Foreknowledge simply requires a different perspective.

When you enter into the Druidic Order, there is a rite-of-passage ceremony on one of the main festival days: Yule, the winter solstice; Ostara, the spring equinox; Midsummer, the summer solstice; or Mabon, the autumnal equinox. Because I was born on the summer solstice, it happened on my seventeenth birthday, the first after I bled and developed my own moon cycles that initiated me into womanhood. We all gather for the main festival days, so everyone on our island and the surrounding islands was there to bear witness to my initiation into the order. And often, on the cross quarter days, those days that fall directly in between the main festival days, we travel to nearby stone circles on other islands to bear witness to *their* ceremonies. This occurs on Imbolc, between the winter solstice and spring equinox; Beltane, between the spring equinox and summer solstice; Lughnasadh, between the summer solstice and autumnal equinox; and Samhain, between the autumnal equinox and Yule, the winter solstice. If you are chosen to become the *head* Druid one day after you have proven yourself to the order, then you have another ceremony in which you have to die to your old self and be born again on one of these cross-quarter festivals.

It is told that when my ancestor Ailef became the head Druid after the stones were erected, he disappeared into the stones as a man and came back something more. My great-great-grandmother Ailsa drowned and came back to life. Ray, the head Druid before me, lived on the snowy mountain peaks alone for seven moons and froze into a block of ice before he came back to tell the tale.

Logically, I told myself this ceremony occurred so there was not great competition over who would become head Druid. People in the village weren't lining up to die because there was truly no magic in this reincarnation, only sheer will. Death stalked us enough in this time and often found us, so no one chased it down. Only one person in each generation would be willing to sacrifice themselves to be reborn; one courageous leader would emerge. Both of my parents left this world as smoke, and I had no interest in following them any time soon, or in being the head Druid, but the ancestors had different plans. In fact, the time between my entering the Druidic Order and becoming the head Druid was the shortest on record, and this is the chronicle of those seven hundred days.

CHAPTER 1:

A WINTER SOLSTICE WEDDING

An island off the western coast of Scotland, known today as the Outer Hebrides, 1800 BC

Ailsa

We were standing among the stones for the solstice ceremony just hours ago, as the Druids called the sun to ascend her throne for the shortest day of the year. Now, under the light of the stars and the surrounding circle of peat torches, I spoke different ancient vows, but a promise just as powerful. At sunrise and sunset on the solstices, the headstone in the stone circle was illuminated, and the ancestors came down to live among us and retrieve those who had died in the past wheel of the year from their burial mounds. The stones were the symbol of eternity, and rituals that extended beyond the realm of the living were saved for the sacred circle, performed the same way for a thousand years or more. I turned seventeen and officially became a Druid at the summer solstice ceremony. And today, at the winter solstice ceremony, I became a wife.

It was an honor to have my wedding to Aric coincide with the solstice celebration, and the landscape couldn't have been a more welcome wedding guest. It was an open, windswept valley near the water that any bride from any time would have chosen as an ideal spot for her eternal vows. The fog had lifted, revealing the rugged cliff edges behind us, like ancient groomsmen standing in attendance. Any bride sound of mind would also have chosen my bridegroom, and the women in the village made that very clear, yet he was not my first choice. The more I tried to put that thought from my mind during our vows, the more it crept in, like a silent, unwelcome frost on a spring morning.

Everyone from our island and the surrounding islands attended our wedding ceremony. The people whose ancient roots were tied to the island gathered around their family symbols, primitive markings carved into the large menhirs, just as old as the blue and green-veined stones themselves. The more recently assimilated north-erners, my bridegroom Aric among them, stood out in these most sacred of ceremonies, where they were gathered between stones or on the peripheries, not having an ancient, designated footing like those of us whose ancestors moved the stones into place. In the harsh firelight, their broad foreheads, straight noses, and towering height seemed enhanced. They were the predecessors of the Viking race, and their shadows on the stones gave them such formidability, towering over us during our vows.

Despite our differences, the overwhelming atmosphere of the ceremony was a joyful one: enhanced by melodious singing, the sound of waves crashing below, and the warm faces of friends and neighbors I had known my whole life looking rapt, proud even, as they watched a Druid priestess and a renowned warrior commit their lives to one another in a blood oath. Because our culture is matrilineal, I am considered elemental to this island and its ancient stones through my mother's lineage, which goes back to the first inhabitants of the island. But my father was actually a foreigner too, and I look exactly like him. Tall and dark, heads above the other girls, I have none of the roan and honey of my mother, whose coloring was identical to my grandmother's, whom I had lived with since my parents' deaths. Until tonight. Tonight I moved out of my grandmother's house and moved into Aric's roundhouse. I felt like a plucked violet being passed around and sniffed, roots dangling in search of loamy soil I could belong to.

I don't remember my mother, but my father has never left me. Five years ago I watched his funeral boat float away, aflame, as was his people's custom. But as he gained speed and distance down the river that would empty him into the southern sea, I gathered him into me, and there he stayed. I wish he could see me tonight, in the light of the fires: my wild black hair braided neatly; the opalescent mother-of-pearl necklace that his own bride had worn catching the light, warm against my skin; my dark amber eyes reflecting the torch flames that lit up the night. He would be so proud to hear the people who said—in hushed tones, as if it were bad luck—that I looked just like him.

It's true that the way in which you miss a parent that you knew and loved in this life is different from the longing for a parent you never knew. I have wished so many times to feel the embrace of my mother or have any recollection of the few days we had together before she died, especially now as I stood at the altar of wifehood, but the way I longed for something I had never known, a mother, was a duller ache than the sharp pang of grief that burned inside me since my father left me.

As our palms were bled and bound together to complete the ancient marriage rite, I wondered if other immigrants felt the same loneliness my father must have held inside him for so many years. I tried to look into my new husband's lapis-colored eyes to reckon this, but he could hold my gaze for no longer than an instant before he darted his eyes elsewhere to meet congratulations with a smile or bowed his head in deference to Ray, the head Druid who performed our wedding ceremony. *Why wasn't he looking at me?* I squeezed his huge hands, which lightly held mine, and asked him without words, heart to heart. *Is it hard to wander the hills and river valleys of someone else's ancestral home? To hunt and kill in a strange forest? To marry someone your parents never knew?*

My father was from a land not unlike ours, and he knew that the boats were getting longer, the sails larger, and the voyages easier. Traveling from island to island was becoming our way of life, and cultures like ours were more mixed with the increased exchange of people, goods, and ideas. Despite this, my father never tried to return to his ancestral home. He acted like the only thing that had tethered him down to the earth was my mother. I often wondered why, in the twelve years I had with him after she died, he didn't pack us up and take us back to his family. I guess it was because he knew I belonged here. And here I was on this day, so much a part of that place that I didn't know if I lived in it or it lived in me.

I was called by the elder Druids when I was born because the earth sent them a sign that day. My father obeyed and agreed to rear me as a future Druid priestess. Maybe if he had gone back to his home or been allowed to take me, he wouldn't have been so sad for all those years. I looked down at my pale, bare feet in the dark peat, and my vision went blurry with tears. I had thought of what I was trying not to think of.

Do not cry, I said to myself, gathering strength and grounding from the earth through my feet and up into my heart. I took a deep breath, feeling more present, and when I looked up, there he was, walking toward me from the cliffs with a defiant look in his eyes. He was the baby I was raised at the breast with, the boy I frolicked through the grain with, and the young man I had fallen in love with: my best friend, Ros. I hadn't seen him in some time, but his presence made me feel less alone. I couldn't help but smile at him over Aric's shoulder, and in that moment, Aric smiled back at me, and our fate was sealed with a kiss.

The crowd cheered, and thoughts of my parents faded as quickly as they had overcome me. Evergreen garlands were draped around us, and winter flowers like viburnum and holly flew through the air and were tucked behind our ears and into our braids. Everyone was singing and kissing, huddled together under furs, and despite myself, a warmth crept over me. I wanted to believe it was for my marriage and the love showered on us by my people, but I knew it was because my best friend was back. I searched the crowd for Ros, instinctively, as I felt Aric's large hand slip around my waist, guiding me on a path I could have, and had, walked in my sleep, down from the stone circle to the village longhouse, where we would celebrate the rest of the long night.

CHAPTER 2:
THE WEDDING FEAST

That feeling of warmth rose considerably in the light of the hundred fires that bounced off the dark alcoves of the great hall, where our wedding celebration continued into the night. Songs filled the longhouse, with the deep heartbeat of the bodhran drum matching my own. Aric laughed with the tall, angular men from the north, and I caught only clips of their increasingly incoherent conversation since they spoke the language of my father and had been drinking most of the day. My ears stayed with my new husband, but my eyes floated around the room from cousin to neighbor to the young village girls pouring honey wine and ale in every cup.

It was the custom for the bride and groom to share one large chair, around which guests and friends gathered in a half-moon, weaving in and out, like human reeds of a basket being woven together, as they brought up small trinkets and gifts, fed us bread and sweetmeats, and toasted to our future children and to Aric's virility in general. The latter toast was especially popular among his northern comrades, each one seeking to outdo the one before.

Everyone brought us either well-wishes or leather flagons of wine except my closest friend. I watched him appear and disappear across the room, like a salmon looking for a place to lay its eggs on the swim upstream. I smiled at his ruddy complexion and that full-

6

face grin he had for everyone, especially the women. Everyone but me, lately. He embraced every girl he saw, his freckled arms, roped with muscle, glowing in the firelight, but he had no embrace for the bride or groom. He always looked unwashed and smelled salty from carving out timber and constructing boats from dawn until dusk. He loved his work and loved providing the boats that the explorers would take around to the network of islands that made up our larger community. He took pride in his impeccable boat engineering, but his pride left a bitter taste at the end when it turned to ego, and taking any drink whatsoever made him altogether unpalatable.

"*Gingers*," I said out loud with disdain for this one in particular. I had loved him my whole life, but there was a darkness behind his grin now, an emptiness in his eyes since he had become a man and realized that the village would never see him, the builder, as the hero that the warriors and explorers were. I'm sure my betrothal wasn't precisely helping that matter.

"Ailsa, hellloo?" said my younger and already married cousin, giggling.

"Sorry, Morna, I was just—"

"What gingers?" she interrupted.

"I was just lost in thought as usual, Morna—don't worry about it," I answered.

"Are you nervous about tonight?" she asked, still giggling.

Morna had been just fourteen when she had bled, beginning her moon cycle, and had quickly married. That was two years ago, and I remember thinking that she seemed even younger than that as a fifteen-year-old myself at the time. The moons had waxed and waned, and with each new moon, I had thanked the gods that I was still a girl in the eyes of my village. In many ways, I was grateful I had made it to seventeen and a half, since most of my friends and cousins were married women by now. I smiled at her from my bride chair. "Morna, I don't know how to say this, but…" I raised my eyebrows in Aric's direction for effect. "I'm not nervous at all."

I gave her a wink that I thought should scandalize her enough to go and tell the first several people she saw. As she turned to go, my new husband's breath traveled down my neck, through the wisps of curled hair falling from my garland crown. As I glanced up to my right to meet his penetrating gaze, he quickly turned to a new well-wisher, his focused, kind eyes casting a spell on every woman he encountered but me. I shook my head. *I think this great warrior is afraid of me*, I thought.

There were songs about his legacy already, and our union was an honor to me because of his travels as a warrior and explorer, just as it was to him because I was a Druid. But in our culture, warrior or not, songs or none, there was no higher status than that of the Druid. I saw them, the twelve other priests of the village, gathered soberly in a corner, discussing something apparently serious. It had only been six moons since I had become one, but I still felt I was on the outside of the circle—only figuratively now, of course.

The rest of the wedding guests danced to songs sung about heroes and many songs sung about love, but when it was our turn to dance alone, it was a song about the stones. Aric led me with his large hands to the center of the longhouse. Above us the roof was open in a perfect smoke-hole circle, and the night was black and cold outside. The cool air from above sent a shiver down my spine, the bodhran and flute began their song, and as I looked up into the circular portion of sky, tiny, soft snowflakes fell down onto my face. I smiled. "Hello, Papa," I said, and the dance began.

8

I tried to distract myself with the adoring faces of the circle that had gathered around, but Ros's hair burned like the fire's flames, and his ocean-colored eyes glowed, a strong jawline exposed by his bare face, absent his usual rust-colored beard. He was marked by this land as much as I was. I wondered if I looked as much like my beloved oak grove as he looked like the restless sea, swaying and foaming with turmoil while he watched us dance.

And though Aric had been on our island since his childhood, his dark beard and tattoos seemed more exotic than usual this night. He smiled down at me, and his crescent moon eyes creased deeply in the corners, casting reflections in the firelight, not of my people but of his own ancestral past and the paths that had led the Norse here over the years. He whispered something in my ear that I couldn't hear over the resounding rhythm of the drum, but I sensed the contrast of his gentle words and his commanding physique. I wanted him to look into my eyes when we danced, to distract me from the uncomfortable feeling of being watched, but his height enabled him to naturally look over my head at the guests around us instead.

The snow had stopped. The music had stopped. Aric led me back to our chair and dismissed himself as soon as we sat, rustling the pile of furs we were perched upon. He walked out the northern door, perhaps to urinate outside. Or maybe it was just to have a moment to himself. Who could blame him? I was craving that right now too.

Fires roared from three massive hearths in the center of the great hall. And now, six hours past sundown, covered by the shroud of night, all the people of the western isles were gathered, chaotically orbiting the festivities like fireflies.

This immense building was constructed after the stone circle, nearly one hundred years ago. Rectangular in shape, it was made of four hundred felled oak logs, each of which took ten men to carry. Hazel and birch limbs were woven into the walls and pitched roof, with three roof holes left for the smoke to escape. The rest of the roof was thatched with reeds, straw, and mud, as were the sides of the building, which blocked much of the wind, though the longhouse's position, nestled between two hillsides, protected it from both sudden invasion and sudden gales.

There were four entrances, above which the four cardinal directions were carved into the lintels, and the doorways were covered with heavy animal hides. Inside, it felt warm with the body heat of crowds dancing, singing, and mingling in gaiety. Holly and mistletoe decorated the doorways, and herbs hung from the ceiling, mixing with the smoke to create an earthy, relaxing smell of juniper, lavender, rosemary, and cedar. There were hides overlapping on the ground and mounds of hay covered in wool and leather for lounging and sleeping for the little ones (or perhaps for the drunk adults).

The longhouse always held a long table and benches for village meetings, but now the tables were filled with meats, bread, cheeses, butter, dried jerkies, oat and barley cakes, and winter fruits and berries that fed the wedding guests. Weddings were for everyone: children, young adults, and the village elders. Some of my favorite memories had been made sneaking extra sweets and wine and lying out under the stars at the weddings of fellow villagers. Since I was the last girl of my age group to be eligible to wed, I had enjoyed many a night dancing and laughing in the pure gaiety of my own freedom. It seemed almost impossible to think of being that carefree now that I had become both a Druid and wife within six short moon cycles.

After our dance, the wedding guests were mostly gathered around the feast table or by the taller ale table. Fulfilling its purpose for the living, as opposed to the stone circle, which was a location to celebrate the dead ancestors, the giant gathering space pulsed with life: music, singing, dancing, the occasional romantic foray in the shadows. Babies were at their mothers' breasts, young lovers and old couples alike embraced in dance or lounged while listening to stories. The older family members were served ale and plates full of food and found seats with back supports. I spied my own grandmother, her form hunched from working a quern daily for her whole life. She was just sixty-three but was one of the oldest among us and was given a place of great comfort and warmth by the fire, where she smiled and sipped wine, her eyes blinking heavily, her head swaying to the tunes of the bard.

Yes, this was truly a space for the living. I looked around me at the many faces I loved. It felt warm, comforting, and familiar, but it didn't have the magic of the stone circle or the peace of the oak grove, and so it didn't feel as much like a place where I belonged. Perhaps that was exactly what was on my mind when I lifted the heavy hide to duck outside and wander to the grove, but I was pulled back, a large, warm hand on my shoulder. "I'm sorry, Ailsa, it's time," he said.

The next thing I knew, I stood at the center of a large group gathered around a high table that kept the stronger barley liquor and cups out of reach of the children that were scattered, playing games and sleeping in their mothers' laps. Barely having sipped my wine, I felt drunk, the world spinning around me, unsure of what was going on. Aric stood next to me, beaming, laughing, emitting his particular magnetic energy, which attracted everyone nearby. Almost everyone. He was drinking and toasting his new nuptials with all of his male companions and female admirers as they surrounded the table, filling their horns and cups. I looked at Aric and thought he truly was happy to be married, so happy that his enthusiasm lit the room. His white teeth gleamed in the firelight as he made his toast.

"To Ailsa, her dark beauty, and our future sons."

I did feel beautiful, in fact. More beautiful than ever before. I had been dressed that morning in a wool robe, dyed in the brightest red I'd ever seen, soaked over and over in hot water, urine, and red madder to achieve the depth of hue. My grandmother had helped Ros's sisters use the roots of hundreds of flowers to achieve the madder color of the fabric, which went from just below the collarbone to the ground, where it puddled at my feet, trailing a bit as I walked. The color was made all the more alluring, I was told by the women, by its contrast with my ivory skin and long black curls, which were gathered and braided into a crown on top of my head, with tiny purple thistles and holly woven throughout. The red dress was much lower-cut than the green cloak and hemp gown I was accustomed to wearing as a Druid, and I shrugged my shoulders back in a constant, awkward motion to make sure it did not reveal too much. It was fastened below the breast with my grandmother's brooch, an owl carved from walrus ivory, with moonstone eyes that shimmered, changing color in the dim firelight, complementing the freshwater pearl necklace around my too-long neck that had once been my mother's—both the necklace and the goose neck. Finally, I wore bracelets of bone and jet up each arm that made a pleasant clanking noise whenever I raised my wine glass.

My mind escaped the occasion that my body could not, as it often did. I thought back to the spring wedding that I had dressed my friend for just eight moons ago. Ros's cousin Muirin had been married at the end of the long winter, on Beltane, the fire festival, when the revelry could continue outside until the wee hours of the morning. I had recently become a woman, having started my moon cycle at the previous full moon, and I expected Ros to announce our own engagement around the great fire where everyone danced. I just knew he would ask for my hand among the celebrations and toasts, where old stories were told, great battles remembered, warriors' songs sung, and special announcements made. I felt my palms sweating with anticipation as we sang and danced, gazing around the fire that night, waiting for him to announce to the rest of the village what I had known as long as I could remember.

I thought about first knowing I loved him at eleven, walking along the evergreen trees by the northern coast with our friends as we explored the edges of the island we were allowed to roam. At thirteen, we would steal minutes away from our chores to visit the shoreline and skip stones into the crashing waves, wondering aloud what was beyond the island, beyond the mainland, beyond the only world we knew. He promised to fashion a boat that could take us anywhere. And then, holding hands under the blankets at fifteen, when the village would gather for special ceremonies or festivities that lasted late into the night. I lay under the stars, with Reina and Rasha, Ros's sisters, cuddled up on one side of me, and him on the other, interlacing my fingers with his in secret under the wool blankets as we listened to the common village songs, studying the constellations in the sky that the Druids told stories about. Those had been the best nights of my life, when I didn't feel the absence of my parents, just the nearness of him: my heart in my throat, my stomach full of butterflies. I smiled at these thoughts, which made me appear interested in the excited toasts and resultant conversations happening in present time around me, but the smile quickly faded when my mind turned to what had actually happened on Muirin's wedding night last spring.

I had grown tired waiting for Ros to appear and make his intentions known, so I set out to search for him and found him, by my own stupidity and misfortune, under a rowan tree, drunk, kissing the bridegroom's cousin. I had turned to run as soon as they saw me and ignored him yelling after me. Rather than confront him after they skulked back to the festivities, I plied myself with barley liquor and slumped down by the fire to quietly cry, hoping to become lost in the stories of foreign lands and ancient gods and kings told by the old women and warriors. It was not my intention to find myself next to Aric. He was so big and dark, his shoulders sprawling, surrounded by so many beautiful girls. He felt like harmless shelter, a place I could go unnoticed and unembarrassed among the crowd.

Aric had taken his first wife at seventeen, my age now, lost her at only eighteen, and found himself so deep in grief that he had never remarried. When I fell asleep by the fire, he had carried me away like he would have carried a child, lifting me as if I were nothing. He put me to bed in my grandmother's house, and she thanked him with a bundle of herbs. The next day I awakened to a shadow of a memory that Aric had tucked me into bed and a much deeper feeling of despair over Ros in the pit of my stomach. I had dreamed that he threw himself off the island cliffs, near the mooring for his boats, in his despair. It was a dream that still haunted me. I shuddered at the thought of it now, memories of my father's similar death racing back.

In the weeks after the incident on Beltane, I prepared for the summer solstice ceremony, in which I would officially become a Druid. I was distracted, with little time to mourn over Ros or notice what had been going on around me. Some people actually suggested he had run off in a fit of romance inspired by his cousin's nuptials. *Not likely*, I thought. All the village girls and family members visiting from other islands were accounted for. I knew Ros had left alone on his small fishing boat, which he had done before in a desperate cry for attention. I didn't have time to worry myself with his sulking. Soon enough, the summer solstice arrived. The wheel of the year continues to turn no matter what your little life may be faced with. I had learned that long ago. On the night of the solstice, after my introductory rites as Druid were performed, I found out that as I had predicted, someone *had* declared that he would take my hand in marriage at the Beltane fires that fateful night, but it was Aric and not Ros.

The wedding toasts continued through the wee hours of the night at my own wedding, each villager, friend, and relative outdoing the last. Somehow, as toasts devolved into drunken stories, I slipped away, back through the northbound hide, hoping to feel a steely wind on my face to wake me up. The sun had set at the stones nearly eight hours ago, and I was ready for bed. Dawn was just around the corner. Even the longest night of the year had to end, I thought.

A thousand stars twinkled above me, and I lifted my face into a refreshingly icy breeze, but instead of feeling it on my face, I felt it in my gut. A hand reached around my waist, familiarly. It was strong and weathered with work, but it was not the humongous hand of a Norseman. The lips that whispered in my ear were not a head above me, reaching downward, but at the same level as mine. The words were not gentle and quiet but firm and stoic. The softness of his mouth touched my ear, and all the feelings I was supposed to have for my husband bubbled over in me before I could turn around.

"I've been waiting for you to be alone," Ros whispered, spinning me around to face him, hands still on my hips. His pale blue-green eyes were brimming with tears, and he narrowed them at me. I felt like he might shake me, but I stared him down just as menacingly, nose to nose, standing up to my full height. "You reek of wine, Ros. How much have you had to drink tonight?" I asked, pushing him away a little.

He smiled slyly, with the look of permanent mischief in his eyes that he had worn since we were very young. "Enough," he replied before kissing me.

It wasn't our first kiss. It wouldn't be our last. But it was the one that changed our future. He pulled away after a few seconds. "Don't say it, Ailsa. I know how reckless I am. I know he could kill me with one blow. I know I dishonor you and the Druids disapprove of me." He moved his hands in a circular motion, shaking his finger, mocking how I might scold him about his antics as he finished his own prepared speech, for my ears only. "But I want you to hear this now, know I mean it, and then I'll leave you to enjoy the rest of your wedding feast." He raised his blond eyebrows at me and spoke in a whisper. "I don't care," he said slowly and carefully. "Not about honor or duty or death and whatever else the other Druids threaten me with."

"That's always been your problem, hasn't it?" I asked. "Carelessness."

He pulled me in to kiss me again, but jovial voices rose in the night air, floating toward us. I thought I recognized the northern accent of my father's family, or it could have been Aric's friends.

"Maybe so." Ros smiled, his eyes growing bright. "But at least it was never a lack of passion." He winked at me knowingly. "I'll be seeing you, Ails," he said, running off in the direction of the cliffs that he had come from that evening, while I turned to greet my northern wedding guests.

CHAPTER 3:

I'VE NO SPADE

But I've no spade to follow men like them.
Between my finger and thumb the squat pen rests.
I'll dig with it.
—Seamus Heaney

Modern-day Ireland

Edie

As I stepped off the cement curb into the airport crosswalk while looking down at my cell phone, a car horn blared, and I jumped out of my skin. The bumper had stopped less than a foot from my shins, so I could clearly make out the driver. He gave me a toothy grin, and I menacingly elbowed the top of his shiny rental car as I bent to collect the bag that I had dropped when my life had flashed before my eyes just moments before. I opened the passenger side door and threw my bag into the back seat as I clambered in.

"Rule number one: don't stare at your mobile when you're crossing the street. You've got to be more aware, Edie!" This was his genial greeting after two years. "Remember we drive on the other side of the road and we're coming from ways and at speeds you're not accustomed to." He sounded like he was quoting a guidebook.

"Thank you, I did live here once," I noted. "It's a crosswalk, and I wrongly assumed the good and gentle Irish people would stop for pedestrians."

"You can't trust the logic or the sobriety of my people," Frank argued, laughing.

"Or their communication, apparently," I added. "I was looking at my phone to see if you had called me back! I've been waiting for ages," I said with a side-eye.

"I did call. You haven't switched your phone over." He laughed, shaking his head.

We were the type of friends who picked up exactly where we left off no matter the time or distance between us, and this occasion was no exception.

"Seriously, though, thanks for picking me up, my dear." I kissed his cheek, and he smiled and squeezed my right hand in his left. "Pull over at the petrol station up here. I'll gas you up, and we'll grab a..." I trailed off, and Frank picked up the conversation as I searched for a cell signal, setting my phone to European service from American.

"You lived here once, you're right, and now you live here again. I still can't believe you own a house."

"Well, I was willed a house; it's not like I bought it," I answered without looking up from my battle with technology. "Aha! there we go. OK, let me just plug in the address." The bells and whistles of my Motorola went off as it announced it was in service.

"Just up the M1 to the A1, and then we'll pick up the M2 and we're there," Frank responded, turning off the car and getting out to gas up before the journey north. I giggled at the simple way in which he delivered this information. He took out the gas pump, and I jumped out of the car after plugging my phone into the console charger to make sure we had at least three hours of battery life to get us to my new Irish home.

"I thought we could go over to the A26 coastal road by Larne so I can check the ferry timetables and have a pretty view. What do you think?"

He lowered his sunglasses to give me a look that said "You are acting like an American tourist." But instead he ignored me, saying, "I'm going in for some weird-flavored crisps like pickle or curry and a bap." I smiled at his use of the Irish vernacular for a ham and cheese sandwich, which was also slang for breasts, the equivalent of the American "boobies."

Frank lived in England, but he was first Francis from Navan, a town in the Irish Boyne valley, with both Irish eyes and an Irish sense of humor. "And yes, we can go the scenic route, ma dearie. I knew it would only be so long before you had me out puking on some ferry on the damned Irish sea!" he moaned.

"Wait for me—I'll pay for the gas while you get your food!" I called as he jogged in.

Inside, the attendant smiled at me as I dropped an armful of crisps, Frank's ham and cheese bap he had selected before running out to stop the gas, and two waters on the counter. "Can I get these and the gas—I mean petrol—on number three out there?"

"Welcome to Ireland. Is this your first time?" The attendant asked. His creased eyes twinkled as he opened the cash register to retrieve my change. I felt my pulse quicken with the excitement of having euros clinking in my palm once again.

"Uhh, no. I actually went to college here." I extended my palm.

"Ohh, lovely, what brings you back then, darlin'?" he asked.

I closed my fingers around the change and cleared my throat as I gathered the large paper sack he had pushed my way between the crook of my left arm and my hip. "Oh, you know, why does anyone come back? It's the most beautiful place in the world." I smiled at "Gerry"—as was embroidered into his shirt—and grabbed a bottle of red wine from the rack next to the newsstand at the register. "This too, please."

"Take it on the house, my love." Gerry nodded, shooing me along with a nod of his head. "It's the time to be celebratin'." He smiled beatifically at me.

I thanked him and hurried out the glass doors. "Celebrate we will, for life is short but sweet for certain!" I called, hands full with snacks, quoting Frank's favorite band to him as I walked toward him and he closed the gas cap.

The light was waning as we slinked around the curves of the coastal highway that led to my northern cabin, tucked away amid the bog and bramble of County Antrim. The quaint town of Ballycastle is nestled cozily between Derry and Belfast, with views into the Irish Sea as far as Scotland. We had passed the three-hour drive from the airport petrol station in rapt conversation about everything from Frank's new nieces and nephews who came to visit/terrorize his houseboat to his most recent French boyfriend and my failed dating attempts back home, which were essentially limited to a series of dull postdoctoral students in and around the Somerville-Cambridge area. It seemed everyone from my past had converged there once I returned from graduate school in Dublin. People from my childhood, first jobs, and college popped up like spring daffodils, bursting from among the crowds of heads bent down in concentration on Massachusetts Avenue like it was newly thawed spring ground. I would meet people for a coffee or at a bar, and we'd talk about the past but have nothing in common beyond that. We played chess in Harvard Square or ice-skated at the duck pond in the common, but my heart was never there.

I did a double take in Harvard Square one afternoon after spying my high school boyfriend, a scientist I hadn't seen in ten years, out a bus window. I guess people were drawn to the place because it hadn't truly changed in nearly 250 years. It was still a nexus of cattle paths and brilliant minds. You knew what to expect from Boston. I liked it because I could still hunker down in the corner of a pub with a pint and listen to a burly bartender with an Irish accent and feel that I was here. Boston was magnetic, like Ireland, in the way it pulled people to its center, rich with industry, education, history, and medicine. But Ireland's pull was mystical and entirely different. So here I was, pulled indeed, ready to confront the past I had left behind several years before. And while I had those "stranger from a strange land" feelings in Boston, arriving in Ireland felt more like a homecoming. Everything we passed on the road was familiar: the farmer in his tractor, waving dutifully as we passed; the modern metal windmills looking like giant alien structures in the middle of thatched roofs and slate houses; the border collies that ran along the road, herding cars; the dark pubs that looked abandoned from the outside but were filled with life on the inside. The green patterns and shapes cut by the land, parceled for sheep grazing, cow herding, and farm plots were like the puzzle pieces of my heart, each outlined with lacy stone walls comprised of stones that had been repurposed before America was even a glimmer in a patriot's eye.

"It's sort of cold for Ireland," Frank said, squinting to see the next narrow turn ahead.

"It's just the wind chill from the North Atlantic current," I responded as I searched my backpack for the key.

We turned right off the main coastal road—if you could call it that—and started up an impossibly steep and rocky road. Frank's eyes bulged out of his head. "Are you serious?" he asked. "Is this the right way?"

"It is," I quietly responded, memories from my last trip here flooding my thoughts. "You can get up it, trust me."

He gave me a heroic look and pushed onward, stalling a bit at the top.

"If it's ever raining or snowing, just go the long route. Take the main road all the way to the coastal road, and then turn right off the coastal road, up the hill. The turn is directly across from the ferry station; you can't miss it."

"I thought the Larne Ferry was forty-five minutes away?" He sounded confused.

"Oh, it is. This is a much, much smaller ferry to the islands. I don't think it even runs in winter. I didn't see any times when we rode by just now."

He started to turn green.

"Don't worry, I have Dramamine for you." I smiled. "You can stop here to park. The house is just around this corner."

Frank was already out, around the back of the house, standing on the wooden deck, and rattling the back door, as I hobbled up with all my luggage. I dropped the bags on the damp deck, and as

I did, Frank swung the door open, and there it was. All mine. For the first time since embarking on this wild adventure back to my past, I felt a little self-conscious.

"You OK, Edie? Just overwhelmed?" Frank asked from the inside of the living room, which looked, through picture windows, over a hedge and a cliff down into the quiet roar of the North Atlantic.

"I can't believe he left it to me," I said, tears filling my eyes, remembering my elderly professor and only friend in Ireland other than Frank.

In college I had struggled to fit in with the Irish crowd, the age-old story of feeling too Irish for America and too American for Ireland. Round hole, square peg, all that jazz. And I was a square. I was the girl who sat in the front row, raising my hand for every question. The other foreign students did more to fit in—attended pub quiz nights, lived on campus, bounced energetically into group work—but I mostly kept to myself and lived alone. It was a great freedom and delight: my liberation from the competition of young-adult social life that had nearly killed me in high school. But every living thing needs some sort of shared experience and sounding board, so I had become close to my favorite professor before meeting Frank.

Sixty-four and happily married, with teenagers close to my age at home, he was hardly the predatory type. I was four to six years older than his kids. His wife was twenty years his junior and beautiful. They were so in love, laughing and telling stories around the dinner table. It was the only picture I'd had of a beautiful, functional family life. It felt like a scene from a Thursday night sitcom I used to dissociate myself into as a kid. It felt too good to be true, but it was deeply true. And I felt some sense of impostor syndrome being lucky enough to inherit a small part of it, here on the edge of the world, where I belonged.

Professor O'Sullivan and I liked the same archaeology, and instead of lecturing at every class, he took his students on magnificent field trips to obscure standing stones and ancient sites we never would have seen otherwise. We saw the cairns at Loughcrew, Ceide Fields in Mayo, Knowth, and Dowth; passage tombs aligned with equinoxes; and of course, Newgrange, the world's most complex passage tomb, which aligns with the rising sun on the winter solstice. He led us, as only a boy who grew up on the Wild Atlantic Coast could, through bracken, hills, and bends to solitary stones that overlooked the ocean with ancient (and some more modern) etchings.

It was in these magnificent places, the ones where they say magnetic fields and ley lines converge, that I first became obsessed with ritual landscapes. The ancients sure had a knack for real estate, but I guess you would if you had your pick of it all. There were just one hundred thousand humans in all of Britain at the time the neolithic monuments I studied were erected. It's hard to imagine that kind of space, or that kind of intimacy, when it's possible to know everyone around you.

My professor—Sully, we called him—taught us how to decipher if something had been carved by stone or metal and urged us to expostulate in our most creative voices. It was OK to make guesses and be wrong, he said. That was never something anyone else in my life had made me feel. Perhaps the most I learned on our field trips with Sully was actually in between monuments, though. He taught those of us who didn't know a doe print from a hare how to track and identify all the animals of the Mourne Mountains. But his greatest lesson to me, personally, was in grief. He had lost his sister in a car accident as a teenager too. She had been killed by a drunk driver on a narrow mountain pass, something that happened too frequently here. He understood the preciousness of life in a way that my twenty-year-old classmates could not. But I could. I had lived it too.

Once when I went to borrow a book from him for a paper, he told me that grief was a gift to be cherished, a sign of love so profound and celestial that it felt as if life could not bear it. But while life did bear it, and he had lived many years as proof, it could never be the same. "Never as sweet to live," he had said, "but all the more sweeter living for knowin' of life's worth."

We had cried silent tears in his office that day I learned about his sister, and we were forever bonded in a grief we wished on no one. He said he wanted to offer me a place in his family, something he had desperately needed in the early stages of his grief and had cultivated with his wife, the magnanimous Mary. I spent that Christmas with his family, drinking tiny glasses of port while tutoring his sixteen-year-old son in high school French and helping his eighteen-year-old daughter with her American college admissions essays. That was eight years ago, and I wondered about them for the millionth time since Sully's death. They were surely missing their father at those ages at which life seems to be happening so fast, as people complete degrees, start careers, start families, get married. Life seemed to be happening like that to everyone I knew but me. But Sully, in his wisdom, had predicted that and had left me this house and our textbook on ritual landscapes to finish. I had a purpose, and what's more, I had hope of a research professor position if I could achieve that purpose.

"Oh God, do you think I'm absolutely crazy?" I asked out loud as I ran a finger along the top of an oak dresser. I felt the O'Sullivan family's warm presence in the cabin, despite the cold air blowing in the open doors from the North Atlantic.

"Do you want my honest answer to that question?" Frank responded, peeping his head out of the doorway of the lone bedroom like a curious little prairie dog. When I didn't reply to him, he seemed all the more encouraged. "You're fit for a straitjacket for moving to an old cabin in rural Ireland without a job, but some people like a little *crazy* because it speaks to the craziness in them. Especially around here."

"Thank you for that, Jack Kerouac. The only ones for me are the mad ones too," I quoted to my most literate friend, my only friend now, as I walked over to the large bookcase that covered the entire west wall of the cabin. "Mary said he left all his books and manuscripts here, so it will be easy for me to pick up and move forward with the research, like he asked. It's set to be published with me as coauthor, so I'll be flush when the book comes out." I smiled weakly at my best friend. "I promise I won't need any of that hard-earned freelance writing cash after I finish this textbook." I winked. I was mortgage-free and income guaranteed if I could just write like Sully for a few chapters.

Frank picked up a massive tome on rock art in Brittany, ignoring me and moving on to the next thing with ease. "So is Sully like the Irish Indiana Jones? Do you think he left us some clues about your research?" Frank started removing books, flipping through them quickly, and looking between them as if for a secret map or cryptex.

"This isn't *The Da Vinci Code*." I laughed. "It's academia. Even more boring." I winked. "I think he just expects me to read through everything he wrote, especially the unpublished stuff." I knelt down, opening the cabinets below the bookcase to reveal stacks and stacks of papers and a lockbox.

Sully had died of a brain tumor while researching the connections between local rock art and similar Scandinavian designs on standing stones around specific bodies of water. I had gone to Canada to research the same thing for a North American chapter that would be included in the book. I had been slow to send my drafts and data, and I had ignored a couple of his emails, feeling the pressure of expectation or success, something that felt too adult to me at the time. And so the longer I delayed and left him hanging, the more ashamed I felt to respond.

So imagine my even deeper mortification when I received an email from his wife inviting me for Christmas again. I would arrive on the winter solstice, and Sully would pick me up at the airport and we would go straight to Newgrange to witness the alignment of the setting sun. He had won two Newgrange lottery tickets to attend for the second time, and having already taken his wife (who hated the narrow crawl space and tight corridors), he had decided to take me instead of choosing between his children. He had given me the greatest gift of my life despite my ungratefulness and unworthiness. He had looked older and more withered on that trip, but it wasn't until we returned to his home, long past dinner, with his family sitting around the dining table drinking tea (now that I think of it, there may have been some whiskey in it), that I began to suspect.

Mary had decorated the Dublin house so beautifully, with bunting and garlands and a massive tree, trimmed to the nines, in the center of the A-frame living room. But for all the gaiety and warmth of their home, my breath caught in my throat as I walked in to red, puffy eyes and ancient, dusty photo albums sprawled across the kitchen table. That's when they told me. Not Sully—he was silent, other than asking me the next morning to coauthor and finish the book. Caitlin and Mary cried and hugged me. I guess Cian, his son, had left, probably off to the local pub.

That was over a year ago now. He had died just weeks later on a freezing January morning. I wanted to give the family some space, so I had been staying at a local inn, and that morning, when I left at daybreak to head to the library so I might have something interesting to show Sully, I saw the coroner's car stop at the light in front of me and then turn right, down the road to Sully's house. The memory would stay with me forever, and it sat like a stone in my stomach now, among his beloved books.

I ran my hand along a copy of *Shakespeare's Great Works*, nearly six inches wide, in between archaeology references. "There is a tide among men." I quoted Brutus and laughed because I couldn't cry anymore. Frank and I always argued about whether Brutus was a hero or not.

"Ahh, I've got a better one," Frank piped up. "Give sorrow words. The grief that does not speak knits up the o'er wrought heart and bids it break."

I looked over at him, simultaneously surprised and comforted. "How the hell do you know so much Shakespeare by heart?" I asked.

"Just *Macbeth*, actually." Frank's last name was Campbell, and he took his Scots-Irishness so seriously that he wouldn't even mention a MacDonald. I knew he loved the Scottish tragedy. We had debated whether or not it was in the top three tragedies on more than one occasion.

"Look, Edie, he obviously wanted you working on this. He told you where all the unpublished papers were, and his wife trusted you enough to give you his computer! I mean, you are meant to finish this for him. Look, he even left you his trowel." Frank picked up an old artifact that was too rusted and antique-looking even to have belonged to Sully, who started digging on his family farm in the early 1960s.

"I don't think I can use that." I laughed, reaching beyond him to the pretty mahogany cabinet, adjacent to the bookshelf, serving as a makeshift bar. "But I could use some whiskey." I smiled, holding the Jameson up to eye level. I pulled from the bookshelf what had first caught my eye. "Maybe tonight calls for a more...local poet than old Billy Shakespeare." I winked.

I held out a tattered, much-loved collection of Seamus Heaney poems. "I'll grab the glasses and meet you on the porch," I said.

Frank looked like a schoolboy at a candy shop and lovingly took the tattered book from my hand. "Rocks for me, please!" he called on his way out to the deck. I made a disapproving scowl in the mirror over the bar. *Everyone thinks they drink whiskey the right way,* I said to myself, *but neat with a splash of water* is best.

"We're starting with *Belderring* because it's my favorite!" I cleared my throat and called out as I walked toward Frank, who was looking out over the balcony to the sea ahead. Just before I crossed the threshold, the fine hairs on the back of my neck stood up, and I could have sworn someone brushed by me. *It must have just been the wind through the open doorway,* I told myself.

Frank turned and brandished the book, open to a page in the middle. "And we will end with *my* favorite, from our shared literature course first year *and* very apropos for an archaeologist, I might add: *Digging!*"

We snuggled on the bench under a wool blanket and read and talked and laughed, accompanied only by the roar of the ocean, the twinkling of stars, and the pungent smell of damp wool enfolding us. Frank was right: it was cold, even for February. But the company was warming. Or maybe that was the whiskey.

CHAPTER 4:

I'LL DIG WITH IT

Ailsa

I don't have any memories of my mother. She died days after bringing me into the world. All I knew of her death was that she had held me and my father and said it was the happiest moment of her life, the three of us together, knowing I was healthy and would live after she had been forced to bury so many others—some tiny, with translucent fingertips, too ethereal for this world, and others so plump and perfect my father was sure they would open their eyes and take a breath at any moment, but they never did. My grandmother says the peace my mother felt in knowing that I was strong and healthy was how she was able to let go and move on to the next world without me. But I carried my mother's anguish inside of me. I've never known much of the peace my grandmother spoke of.

All too often mother and baby died together, one following the other into the mist from sheer desperation, but I had survived my first few crucial weeks on goat's milk, my aunt's breast, and my stubborn grandmother's iron will. Or at least that's what Jord, her Druid brother, my great-uncle, often said to me. My mother's younger sister had married into the neighboring village, on another small island, so she came by boat to feed me for a while, but she was pregnant herself.

Before news traveled to her, in my first days, grandmother dropped goat's milk and honeyed water into my mouth from a soaked rag. She loved her goats, and they served us well in this instance, though I was sure they were possessed by evil spirits at other times.

But I suppose I also survived because Ros was born. At least that was the story told to us since we were babes at the breast. I had a high fever, burning from within, when just five moons had passed since my birth. My father went to my aunt, risking life and limb, guiding his own boat through torrential storms since Ros's father, the master sailor, was at home for the birth of his own baby. Father begged my mother's sister to come to my aid, but she was swollen with her own child, due soon, and naturally would not risk her baby's life to save mine. Just as grandmother had dipped me in the icy river to try to bring down my fever since I would no longer take her goat's milk dripped from a rag, Ros was born to the boat makers of the village. He was healthy, huge, and squalling.

My father had run through the newly fallen snow from the caves where we docked the boats, helpless, not knowing what had happened to his tiny daughter during the day-and-a-half nonstop journey he had taken, his beloved dog following in his plush, snowy footsteps. He was expecting, I'm sure, to find me dead, but instead he found me happy, full, and sleeping next to a red, wrinkled Ros, greedily suckling at his mother's other teat. We both fed ferociously, sometimes simultaneously, and her milk flowed like the great southern falls, she used to joke.

My grandmother always laughed so heartily at that, as if they spoke some secret "milk language" that I didn't understand. Grandmother told me that Ros's mother's milk had been nothing short of a nutritional miracle. After she nursed me back to health, quite literally, I was the picture of it. I was never sick again, and by the time fifteen moons had passed, I began drinking goat's milk and honeyed water from a cup and eating bread and butter every meal with my father, with only four teeth. Every time grandmother saw Ros's mother with a new babe at her breast, she laughed her sweet laugh and threw her silver hair over her hunched shoulders, telling the babe to drink up for it was the gods' nectar.

Ros's mother's name was Leina, and I used to think of my own mother as a slightly fairer-haired version of her. She had waist-length auburn hair, not as bright as Ros's but like the color of an oak's acorn ripe on a tree. Ros's mother was long and lithe, a dancer for the Druids, and her daughters would be too.

The first wheel of the year ceremony I can remember was my fourth birthday, the great summer solstice sunrise. I can still picture her on that night, spinning and glowing by the firelight, me kneeling at grandmother's feet. After the dance was done, I would sit in Leina's small lap, sharing the limited space with her two baby daughters, Rasha and Reina. Ros never sat in her lap with us in my memory, but he was always very nearby.

I treasured these peaceful moments, falling asleep by the fire, feeling as close to my own mother as I ever could, with my mother's mother and Ros's mother cuddling me under the stars. Sometimes I would see my mother in visions, walking toward me through the wheat or barley crop as I gathered the harvest with my father and grandmother. I had no memory of her face, but I could paint it in my mind from what everyone told me. She was fair-haired, "like the barley after it's toasted," my uncle had said, and so I had imagined multicolored strands of flaxen, golden, brown, fawn, and roan. "Your skin is like cream, just like hers," my aunt had said during one visit for a festival as she rubbed my cheek. Grandmother told me one morning after a long walk on the beach collecting mussels that my mother's laugh was like the seabird's—an infectious, happy bubbling noise that filled the house. And so, bit by bit, a picture of her came together in my mind's eye.

As children, we always esteem our mothers beyond what they could ever live up to. Mothers are mere mortals, but we paint them as gods because of their ability to heal and protect and encompass us with love. If other people's mothers were goddesses, mine was their God, supreme above all. I had never had a satisfactory answer for her eye color, though. I had done what I thought was thorough investigating from reliable sources. When I asked, Grandmother had said they were beautiful and warm, brown like mine. But so often I thought the intention of her answers was to give me personal links to my mother so I would feel connected in our shared features, somehow. So I asked a less biased source than those in my mother's family, Ros's mother, Leina. At the time I asked, I remember, she was doing wash, one of the most laborious chores of the week, while trying to keep Rasha and Reina on task with their chores. Ros had run off and not stayed to help mind them as he was supposed to.

"Gods, darling," she had said looking at me with anguish after the simple yet sad question, "I don't think I remember exactly. She's been gone so long, and me with three children of my own, whose eyes I barely remember." She giggled at herself and then looked at my serious, young face, and her heart wrenched. "But I do remember that they were beautiful, sparkling, dark pools like yours."

My father was the likeliest source of tenderness and romanticism. I had always hesitated to ask him specific questions about her because I could see the pain in his eyes when he answered or deflected my series of questions. I saved up my most important questions, putting them off or waiting until he was in just the right mood, not too happy because I didn't want to bring him down but also not too sad because I was so afraid of pushing him over the edge. I spent my childhood watching him teeter on the edge of life, and I learned to tiptoe around his moods. I lived my twelve years of life before his death with my breath held, scared that any exhale might be the wind that blew him over. And even after all that tiptoeing, I still could not wipe the guilt from my child's brow after he finally did leap to his death.

But when I found the right time, when he was in a neutral, matter-of-fact mood, we were out tilling and digging trenches for spring planting. It was a dry day, the best for digging, and the loamy soil roiled up under us with inviting minerals and moistness. It looked good enough to eat; *how enriching it must be for our barley*, I thought, as I sprinkled seeds from my pocket. I asked him the same way I had asked those before, "What color were Mama's eyes?" I said it plainly, without emotion, looking up at him as he stopped to wipe his brow, leaning gently on the long pole of the shovel made from ash wood and slate. What I saw next I would remember forever. He actually smiled, huge and blissful, as the gentle spring sun shone down on his broad, creased, olive face, and he breathed it in like it was her creamy skin.

"They were the color of the forest." He sighed. "Speckled brown like the tree trunks and autumn leaves but mossy green like the summer leaves and dark, evergreen, like the pines too. With gold flecks like the sun peeking through the branches and hints of black like the loamy soil beneath the oak."

"Wow," I had said, a child certain, in that moment, that no two people had ever loved one another as much as my parents had and also confident my mother was the goddess that father saw when he spoke.

"She looked like autumn," he continued, unexpectedly, "with that golden fawn pelt hair, the forest eyes, and milky skin. She was like a harvest herself and wore the warm shades of the earth to show it off." I had some of her old dresses, and I knew what he meant. Many of the women would repeatedly dye clothes in the darkest colors available to provide bright pigment that stood out against soil and stains, but her clothes were lighter gold and green and brown, like she was trying to blend in. "She knew what complimented her and that it was her natural beauty that made her shine. So few women are like that." He looked down at me, suddenly concerned that he had upset me. He fell to his knees in front of me, holding onto the smaller shovel that I had been using that day, an old carved spade I shared with my hunched grandmother. He brushed the black locks from my face and said, "You know, Ailsa, she wanted a child so badly. She had lost so many and suffered so deeply for it. But still all she wanted was a child, and so all I wanted was to give her what would make her happy." He looked away from me, biting his lip. "I'm so thankful that she knew you were here, safe and healthy. And such a delight." he added at the end, meeting my dreamy gaze.

I remember that moment, not just because I learned a little more about my parents' love and my mother's looks, but also because it felt like he saw me for myself and not just as a token of his wife left behind on Earth, and the only thing for him to love in her absence. I was a whole separate person to love—not loved just because I came from her. He smiled into my eyes, our shared eyes, so alike in their

darkness, finding acknowledgment and commonness in the reflection of his own gene pool, so far from his own land. Gently, he tussled
my black curls, which matched his. "She will love you forever, no
matter what, Ailsa. And I do too. That was the last thing she said."
He didn't look at me when he said it but stared up somewhere into
the clouds. "Back to digging, little one. We must finish by dinner.
Grandmother is baking us fish."

That night he picked all the bones out of my fish, slowly and
carefully. I ate it out of his huge fingertips, calloused from farmwork,
and sat in his lap, listening to grandmother tell funny stories about
her most recent healing adventures at the hearth. "Should we really talk about this while we're eating, Brigd?" my father asked her,
laughing and cracking fish bones, while she talked about setting
broken ankles and noses from a fight between two old men we knew
and a harrowing journey up Goat Fell Mountain by two mischie-
vous teenagers who claimed they were hunting. Grandmother just
laughed at that and quietly mentioned that the stags were not the
only ones rutting in this particular hunting scene.

Once the stars came out, he tucked me in, pulling the furs and
wool blankets up under my chin and brushing the hair from my
forehead in methodical, repeated strokes. That night I slept peacefully while the adults chatted by the fire into the night and fell asleep
to the sound of my father's deep voice answering grandmother's soft
and hoarse one. I held on to the edges of consciousness, not because
I could make out what they were saying but only to feel the love and
comfort of them near, in happy conversation.

We don't bury our dead; we push them off on rafts made of alder wood, set aflame, and the river, wild as it approaches the sea, carries them to the next world. Only very special or specific elders and Druids were buried in the stone circle under the altar stone. My mother's sea ceremony had been my first—I was barely a week old. The women had wailed for her in a special mourning song, as was custom, and it was said that a sadder keening was never heard.

I had been to at least a dozen funeral rites since then, and I had wept a little or sometimes not at all. Death was inescapably part of life here, in a constant way that you couldn't put out of your mind for too long. Babies died, and we wept for the life they didn't get to create; the elders died, and we wept for the life full of memories that we shared with them, not knowing how to go on without them. Warriors died in battle, but mostly in travel or hunting accidents, and young women died of disease or in childbed. When I wept, I wept in a detached way, even as a child, because I knew they weren't departing into emptiness. I knew there was love and happiness beyond the living, and I suppose that is what people who fear death fear most—the uncertainty, not the dying.

When my father died, I couldn't bring myself down to the shoreline. I couldn't celebrate, I couldn't mourn. I dared not weep; how could I have ever stopped? I felt assured my father's spirit was safe in the afterlife, but I was devastated to imagine life without him in it. Grandmother had sent everyone after me, including Uncle Jord, who could track a rabbit in a snowstorm. No one thought to look for me in our own little barley field. Instead of watching my father's burning raft drift off into the fog of forever, I took his large spade from the hook that it hung on in our roundhouse and made my way to the field to finish our family's spring barley planting like we had done that day many years before when I learned about my mother's eyes. That's what he would have wanted.

CHAPTER 5:

THE OAK GROVE

Ailsa

The blanket of green moss and clover in the forest just south of the mountains was an easy peace for the busy mind. You could talk out loud to the trees, and no one could hear you over the susurrus of the river, which rolled into a babbling brook in the oak grove, bouncing off of lichened rocks and fallen logs. The trees had their own hushing quality, their soft whisper escalating to a crackling thunder as summer turned to fall and the leaves made a satisfying crunch under bare feet. The trees in the forest are as alive to me as people. Their network of underground roots connects them all, and they respond to one another, like a community. If one is suffering, they all are. I've seen a tree change to protect itself, I've heard one cry, and I've sensed the slow-pulsing signals they communicate through their bark and branches. The trees know when change is afoot. This is why we pray here as Druids. We borrow their knowing and let it inform ours.

There were a variety of trees in the forest. Some saplings were middle-aged, while others had trunks as wide as a person was tall and had been that large for as long as anyone had known. Ashes and alders, maples and birches lined the rivers, and sunlight filtered through their pale, skeletal branches. Evergreens stood above the rest of them, sheltering the other trees like guardians. Caledonian pines with their bushy tops and elegant conifers smelling of sappy pine created a dense and dark entrance to the forest from both the northern and eastern sides. The oak grove was in the heart center, and this, along with the strength and age of the beautiful trees, is surely why this became the sacred place of the village Druids. As Druids, we were expected to start our day with prayer in the oak grove, and on the special days, those festivals throughout the wheel of the year that marked the seasons and length of the days, we would make our way from the oaks to the stone circle by the sea. Legend told that some more eccentric Druids slept and lived in the oak grove rather than living among the other villagers.

I could see why. The equanimity one must attain as a Druid is more easily achieved in a place like this. Whatever came my way in life, I felt centered and calm among the oaks. I found as a child that the grove had a similar effect on even the quickest tempers, namely Ros's. Yes, the oak trees themselves were special—in between the size of the river trees and the evergreens that guarded the wood and then climbed up the mountains in the north, these oaks were giants, sure—but with dexterity and determination, one could climb to the top in a matter of an hour. Many of the children started on the bottom limbs, gaining speed, and then stopped three-quarters of the way up as they reached the dense, delicate branches that became more fragile and cumbersome.

One must approach such physical feats without fear or the self-consciousness that becomes trapped in the body as it ages, when we go through puberty, become conscious of the opposite sex, and place our worth in the externals. The judgments creep into our psyche, creating insecurities and crippling our physical bodies. How can we move freely when we feel so trapped? So laden with the burdens of living?

Thus, I began my tree climbing very early, not long after walking. I fell many times. Once I fell from such a height that I broke my arm, and grandmother mended it with a poultice and a birch arm brace. Once I hit my head on a branch on the way down and saw stars and black intermittently for several days, and Grandmother awakened me at night to keep me from falling into a deep sleep. There was one tree in particular that I could not stay away from. The top branches stretched above any others and I loved how they swayed in the wind. Grandmother begged me to start praying at the base of the tree instead of the top, but there was something that felt closer to the gods at the top of the tree. And ever since I could remember, I had chased that feeling of closeness to the sky.

The last time I remember falling was the Beltane before I turned thirteen. At Beltane, the young ladies who would become the dancers or singers of the village performed their first ritual, and the boys who had come of age would be sent off from the Beltane fires on a ceremonial hunt by the most beautiful song and dance of the year, initiating both genders into adulthood around the age of thirteen. I was already set to be a Druid, not a dancer, so I escaped the song and dance lessons with the older women who taught them. The other girls wore white, flowing dresses with spring flowers in their hair, and plaits around their flower crowns. They were the picture of beauty and femininity, ethereal dancing ghosts that mesmerized everyone at the ceremonies. While I admired them, I was glad to have some time to myself to steal off to the Druid's oak grove and be alone while they practiced.

As I was stealing that time alone, climbing my favorite oak tree, I was thinking about many things and found myself distracted reaching for the final limb I needed to access for my view. Ros had been at the bottom watching, unbeknownst to me, and broke my fall. Perhaps he did it purposefully, or perhaps it was just another example of being in the wrong place at the wrong time, but the way in which I landed on him broke his leg. Badly. The face grandmother made when I dragged him in that evening was not one I had seen in a long time. She was quiet for several breaths before she slightly narrowed her eyes and furrowed her brow. Grandmother could be an expressive woman, but she rarely betrayed her emotion on her face. I can still feel the shiver that ran down my spine in that moment, wondering what would become of my best friend, whom I had quite literally smooshed like a berry.

Ros was a greenish-gray color, which did not improve as grandmother set his leg. My punishment for climbing so carelessly was seeing his face contorted in pain while holding a bowl for him to vomit into while she rubbed herbs and wrapped a poultice around the inflamed limb. But when Grandmother put the brace on, it was the worst. Ros's father had to lie across him to prevent him from sitting up or twisting his body in any dramatic fashion so Grandmother could make sure the bones would align and knit back together.

He lay in that brace and hopped around minimally through the rest of the spring and summer. Other boys were running and playing, growing taller and stronger while he wasted away. His other male friends were out on the extended hunting trip that Ros had planned to join for the first time that year. My birthday and the solstice passed, then came Lughnasadh, his birthday, and finally, as the first leaves began to fall from the trees and the Hunting Moon approached, he was walking with a stick. I led him around like an obedient dog, stopping with him to rest, letting him lean on my tall, narrow shoulders when he needed extra support, and looking at him with a straight face, never laughter, when he attempted to walk without the stick and fell repeatedly. Then I would just extend a long, friendly arm and a sweet, tiny smile and pull him back up with a nod to keep going. We kept at this through the fall months, using the free time we had away from our daily chores at the barley fields and fishing to practice walking.

Grandmother had said that some boys mightn't have recovered from such a fall. She had known of a boy who had taken such a fall when she was a lass, and he had used a walking stick until he was an old man, hunched and crooked from never standing up quite straight again. But Ros did stand up quite straight. And when he did, at the winter solstice celebration, he was finally taller than me. I remember it was the first time he leaned down instead of reaching up to kiss me under the mistletoe of the longhouse during the solstice feast.

As Ostara arrived and the birds began to nest their eggs and tiny buds came out on the trees, he was running and jumping with the other boys again, faster and stronger than ever. I had taken away nigh a year of his boyhood with my fall. I was certain I felt guilt for it, but there was another new feeling mingled with the guilt. It was an uncomfortable feeling, like an itch or a foreboding pit in the stomach, and it was there whenever Ros was around.

It was nearly Beltane, a week before Ros was set to leave on the hunting trip that he was supposed to go on the year before. It was only a few days before the fire festival that would send the boys away, and all of the young people were practicing for their roles in the Beltane ceremony at the stone circle just like they had been the day of the accident. I had gone to talk with Ray, the head Druid, about the ceremony, and as we walked along the coast near the circle, I only half listened to Ray's excessive description of the symbolism behind each of the rites and rituals because I was riveted by Ros's behavior. He had a new confidence as he talked with the boys who would be leaving on the hunt with him. Perhaps it was because he was the oldest, having had to wait a year beyond his time to go. Perhaps his height or having been through the hardship of the last year had made him proud or courageous. He looked like a new person, laughing and joking with them, telling them animated stories with a hand on one of their shoulders like he was already a man.

But it was not his interactions with the boys that concerned me. There was also a new way he behaved with the girls: smiling at them and waving from across the stone circle, making excuses to touch a hand or an arm as he spoke to one or showed her something. His chest seemed puffed out, like he was taking them under wing. *How peculiar*, I had thought. And then, as if my thoughts had summoned him, there he was, standing in front of us, his face pink and blotchy, cold from the whipping wind of the coast; the freckles just coming out on his nose from the abundance of sun we had had the past week of preparation for Beltane; and his seafoam eyes thickly lined with blond lashes. "Ailsa, I need to tell you something," he said matter-of-factly.

I looked at Ray for dismissal. "Ros, Alisa needs to go to the oak grove to pray. It's almost sunset, and I want her centered for the ceremony."

"Then I'll tell her on the way to the oak grove," he said.

We began the walk there; it was not much of a distance, due east. Ros was babbling on about this and that related to hunting and fishing and his impending trip. I knew the anticipation must be killing him. Most boys didn't have to wait a whole extra year. As we approached the oak grove, the conversation became a bit more stilted, and Ros's tone took on a rare gravitas. And then the wholly unexpected happened.

"I want you to understand that things will be completely different when I return." He said it and immediately went silent, expecting a response. He stared at me for a few moments before I could think of anything to say.

"Look, Ros, I'm very sorry about everything that happened last year with your leg. I had hoped I had made amends by helping you through every day and cheering you on as you remastered walking, and—"

He cut me off. "No, Ailsa, I mean because I will be a man when I return, our relationship will be different. We can't share a bed in Grandmother's house or sleep out under the stars or go swimming alone together, you know…"

"Naked?" I asked.

"Exactly," he responded.

We walked in silence for a few minutes, past the tall Caledonian pines, through the rows of evergreens, into the density of the forest. Our silence became filled with the hushed noises of the familiar woods, and it was a comfort, at least to me. Ros still looked uncomfortable.

"What does it really matter?" I asked. "I mean, I'm a Druid. You seem interested in the other girls anyway. Can't we just go on being friends without people talking?"

"It's too late, Ailsa. I can tell when you look at me, when you watch me with other girls. Everything has already changed."

"Do you really think that highly of yourself?" I asked without thinking. "I won't marry, so you have nothing to worry about. No one will expect us to be together or fall in love or whatever you're so concerned about people seeing or thinking."

We had reached my special oak tree. The one I had fallen from. It had been struck by lightning and had a huge charred hole about halfway up that made footing easy. Several mossy knots toward the bottom made good makeshift seats. Not that anyone would dare sit under a tree ever again whilst I was climbing it. I leaned against one of the knots for support and noticed I was feeling a little dizzy.

Ros had a habit of acting like he knew my mind better than I did, and it really aggravated me when he told me how I had been feeling without so much as a confirmation from me first. I turned away from him and put my hands on the tree. "Well, perhaps if you don't marry and neither do I, then we can just go on as friends the way we always have," Ros suggested.

"And how will you do that?" I exclaimed. "You follow around every girl like a dog in heat!"

"Well, kissing is one thing, Ailsa; marrying is another." He laughed at himself. At least he hadn't become too proud to do that. "I know you haven't kissed anyone, but hasn't Grandmother told you the difference yet?" he teased.

I glared at him, unimpressed. Unrattled. He started to turn a darker pink color in his cheeks, and I rolled my eyes and took my leave. "I'm going to pray, Ros," I said. "Better move out of the way so you don't get smooshed again." I started up my tree and did not look back during my ascent. By the time I made it down, he had already turned to leave and was nearly past the edge of the woods. I could just make out his shadowy figure. I started to run after him, but something stopped me. My breath caught in my chest, and I watched him make his slow, purposeful way though the fields back to the stone circle for the Beltane ceremony. What if harm befell him on this hunt because of his injury? What if he died while he was gone, and I had left things this way between us?

That night at the fire, after the ceremony and before the send-off, I was able to track him down to embrace him and say goodbye. I hugged him, flames of fire and embarrassment hot on my cheeks, tears streaming down.

"Don't hate me, Ros," I croaked. But he just hugged me tighter. "I'll think of you every day that you're gone. Just come back safely," I managed to get out.

"I'll come back, don't worry." He patted the back of my intricately braided hair and kissed my forehead. "Ailsa, the way you see me with the other girls, like a dog in heat…" He laughed and trailed off. "It's different with you. I would die for you, Ailsa. It's so much more than just kissing." Then he backed away slowly, smiling his intoxicating smile, glowing in the firelight, young, alive, and determined to preserve our friendship—and I was thankful. It was the most constant thing I had in my life.

When he returned for harvest at the end of the summer, everything *was* different. He no longer wanted to frolic on the beaches and explore the mountain paths with me. He didn't bring his little sisters to Grandmother's roundhouse when he was supposed to be minding them and then steal off with me to collect animal bones. He didn't make me flower crowns or lay his head on my lap during gatherings. We didn't swim naked in the sea at night, looking up at the stars and calling them by name. He didn't sneak up behind me, snorting with laughter, to topple me over as I peed on a tree in the grove before heading home for supper. But he also didn't fight for me. And he absolutely didn't die for me like he had said.

He paid attention to the other girls now. He kissed them, carved them dolls, carved their names into tree trunks, and if I walked by when he was vying for the attention of another lass, he would act as if he didn't notice me at all. It was painful, but in a new and different way from the pain I had experienced before. Losing my father was raw and earth-shattering. This was maddening, like a betrayal. Never knowing my mother was hollow and lonely, but this was bitter and cruel, like a knife cutting me.

I stood out from the other girls because I didn't play their games or giggle enticingly. I embraced my complexity, my Druidness, in a way that made the other young people uncomfortable. I liked being a bit of an outsider to the group, though my best friend was now quintessentially on the inside of it. The truth was that I loved Ros, deeply, in the sort of way that doesn't come around every lifetime. But equally, I could not be reduced to that alone, and I wouldn't give up who I was meant to be to fit the image of a fourteen-year-old ready to be a wife like my cousin Morna. There was no choice but to stand firm in this decision and declare it.

One particularly irksome day, after I saw him fawning after a betrothed girl two years our senior, I had gone to Ray and asked him to use his preferential Druid rights to block any marriage contract for me. He just laughed and said, "We will see what the gods have to say about that." Unsatisfied, I asked if he would take me on my Druid Quest a little early that summer. "How old are you, almost fifteen now?" I nodded. "I believe that will do." He patted my head and smiled his frog-like grin, and destiny was done.

We left the next month for the great stone circle on Orkney, which is still the most incredible man-made structure I have ever seen. Even the four warriors who escorted the three of us—since my uncle Jord came along with us as well—were impressed and astounded by the standing stone complex. The circle was the largest one we had ever seen. It stretched across a broad emerald-green plain adjacent to the northernmost sea. The wind was stinging, but one hardly noticed, surrounded by twelve giant standing stones, some of which appeared to reach the clouds, the height of five men stacked on top of one another. What made the feature so incredible to behold was the juxtaposition of these giant stones with the flat peninsula on which they rested, and the calm of the surrounding sea. I had been around giant stones my whole life, but they were surrounded on one side by jagged cliffs, on another by wild forest which gave way to craggy mountains, and finally by a roiling sea that never rested. The temple complex was sophisticated beyond anything known to us. Orkney was a Druid hub, and we came here to learn ritual practices like purifications, cosmology, and stone-building techniques.

Ray's renown preceded us in the local Druid community, and we were welcomed, provided food and shelter, and witnessed the calling of the sun on the summer solstice. I felt like I was on the very edge of the earth there, like I could see it bend. There was barely any night that time of year, and when night did fall, the green and purple lights danced in the sky instead of the blanket of black and stars that we had at home. It was the most beautiful thing I had ever seen.

The people there stayed up on those nights lit by the fires in the bright sky, telling stories, dancing, singing, and rejoicing in being alive. When it got too cold, we huddled inside their subterranean round stone houses, warmed by fire and spirits and song. I felt like a fox, cozy and safe in my burrow, me against the world, plotting my next move. I was invigorated by my travels, by these new people and experiences, but a part of me ached for my southern island. I missed Grandmother, her gentle hands braiding my hair or feeding me oysters. I missed Ros and his sisters and mother, people who understood me. But most of all, I missed the oak grove. Sure, there were some trees here, but the salt winds of the ocean were destructive and blew the leaves off the limbs before they could absorb any precious nutrients. They had trees, but not lush forests like we had. As beautiful as it was at the edge of the world, I needed my home. When we left at Mabon, the fall equinox, in time to return home before the snow, I had so many emotions. I was sad to leave my new friends, excited to return home, and terrified to see Ros.

At fifteen, with so much swirling inside of me, I decided I needed to bring a part of the peace of Orkney back home with me. I wanted to be the person I had been in Orkney, connected to its spirit, vibrantly alive and engaged in the community, feeling intuitive and capable of delivering important messages. I spent the morning at the great stone circle on the edge of the world by myself, vowing to fulfill my Druidic destiny and to put that above all else in my life. My Druid ceremony, in which I became a member of the order, would not be for nearly two years, but this moment was my own personal commitment. I looked down at my palm, at the scar from making blood oaths with Ros since we were nine. I took my knife from the pocket tied around my waist and opened the scar back up. It bled quite a lot. I put my palm on the stone, closed my eyes, and promised that I would find peace like this in my homeland by always putting my duties as a Druid first. Little did I know how much this vow would come to mean to me over the next few years and how hard it would become to keep in the year after I was married.

CHAPTER 6:

SAMHAIN

Ailsa

"Raspberry leaves. Steep them in a tea every night when the moon is waxing."

I cupped my hands together, and she dropped the gift into my open palms—enough dried raspberry leaves to make a month's worth of tea, tied tightly into a hemp bag. "Thank you, Grandmother." I smiled.

"You're not afraid, my darling, are you?" she asked as she crossed the small roundhouse to her hearth. She continued grinding herbs on her stone table and dividing them among the wooden bowls lined up along the edge.

"No," I answered.

"What happened to your mother in childbed is not your destiny," she said as I dropped the hemp bag into the larger hide pocket I wore tied around my waist, under my Druid cloak, for gathering.

"I know. The gods just haven't blessed us in these last ten months," I answered quietly, rubbing my sweating palms on my wool cloak. And that was true, for the most part. Aric had spent most of the recent warm months traveling for necessary trades and exploration, as was his role, just like when he had escorted us to Orkney two years earlier. The winter after our wedding had of course kept him here for a long honeymoon, but we had been timid to get to know one another in those first few months, and I could easily count the number of times we reluctantly and delicately lay together.

"Well, then you'll know what the village gossip is about the healer's granddaughter not conceiving?" She laughed without looking up at me, but it didn't sound like she thought it very funny. "Now everyone wants to know what a strong concoction you must be taking to prevent being with child by a man like Aric?"

I flushed the color of the raspberries that she had separated from their leaves for the tea and involuntarily put my hand to the pocket tied around my waist.

"Well, everyone knows Aric is capable of making a child because his first wife was pregnant when she succumbed to her illness, so maybe it's me. Maybe I'm incapable." Something invisible grabbed my throat and would not let go. I could barely swallow.

Grandmother looked up at me then and smiled. "You will give him happiness, Ailsa, I'm sure. As soon as you are done with your little stockpile of dauco seeds. I suppose they will buy you some time to be ready."

I wanted to ask her how she knew that I was taking wild carrot seeds to stifle my fertility. Had she seen me gathering? Did she go through my pocket when it was untied while I was bathing or sleeping? I had been spending much of my time at Grandmother's house since moving into Aric's roundhouse. I felt lonely with him gone so much through the summer, when the weather was warmer for boating to the nearby islands. He came back every six weeks or so with gifts for me—new seeds to plant, pretty seashells from the beaches he had landed on, and exciting stories about the people he had met.

But now I was regretting the decision to stay with her, wondering if a bit of solitude might be beneficial. So instead of acknowledging her accuracy and admitting she had me figured out with the dauco seeds, I decided to avoid it altogether while I gathered my thoughts.

"I'm going to go check on the smokehouse, but I'll be back for dinner. That stew smells too good to miss, and Aric won't be back until until Samhain tomorrow." Grandmother nodded, smiling her knowing smile. "Men aren't meant to be still, I suppose."

"Neither am I." I mumbled mostly to myself as I took off to see that all our fish was being properly smoked for the coming winter. Ocean fishing would still be available to the brave souls who ventured out in the weather, but the lakes and river would deep-freeze this winter. All the Druids said so, and I could feel it in the chill that had finally begun take hold after an unusually warm harvest season.

Wearing clothes into a smokehouse is a very unwise decision if one does not want to smell like a smoked trout for the rest of eternity, so I took advantage of being alone, and I stripped down and hung my cloak, pocket, and dress on a nearby tree limb. I slipped out of my shoes, which I rarely wore, except on the coldest of nights, just before entering the little wooden house to stoke the embers of the smoke source. The heat felt wonderful, and my shoulders relaxed in comfort. I crouched, looking into the glowing embers, thinking about the sauna sessions Ray, Jord, and I had had with the northerners on Orkney Island. They had seen things in the smoke and embers, things that felt so real at the time, and now it all felt like a dream.

On the way back from Orkney, Ray and Jord had told me that I would need to marry to continue the pure Druidic lineage I had come from. If I didn't have an idea of who that should be, they offered for the counsel to choose for me. That was two years before, and I was finally coming to terms with the future that was decided on that trip. I was a Druid, and Druids weren't typically expected to have children like the rest of the village, so it was never something I had considered. But Druids were also not bound to chastity, and marrying Aric was a great honor. He was a humble warrior who had lost his first wife when they were both very young. I had come to see my relationship with Aric as a duty intertwined with my Druidic rites, and I had come to terms with what it meant to honor that duty through marriage. I had not yet come to terms, after less than a year of marriage and just over a year of leading our ceremonial rites, with the fact that having and raising his child was also part of that. Regardless of my hesitation in becoming a mother, I wanted to do both of these duties well, mothering and leading the Druids, and in this moment that seemed practically impossible.

I longed for the androgyny that some of the other Druids enjoyed. Not being tied to the gendered expectations of a wife and mother made spiritual focus much easier, I surmised. I was seventeen and a half when Aric and I had married the previous winter, but I had been raised to Druidism longer than I could remember. That part of me felt easier and more accessible than "wife" and "mother." And it carried less past trauma. I hadn't grown up with a mother, nor had my father ever remarried before his own death, and grandmother's husband had long perished before I came along, life expectancy being what it is here. I hadn't really been part of a functioning mother/father/child family of my own, other than Ros's. But that wasn't mine. He wasn't mine. Druidism was less complicated in some ways. It was what I understood, what I felt was not only my purpose but also my family.

I felt drops of sweat form underneath my shoulder blades and on the small of my back as they began to trickle down. I wiped my watering eyes to try to clear my blurry vision. "It's just the smoke," I told myself out loud. It was. But then I really wanted to cry. I felt it bubble up in me for the first time in ages. I couldn't remember the last time I had cried, though I searched for it in my memory. At that moment the sweat dripping down my back turned cool and a shiver went down my whole body as icy hands wrapped around my waist.

"Found you!" Ros whispered in my ear. "I've been pacing around peeking in every doorway, and I had given up tracking you until I saw your old, tattered shoes sitting right outside the smokehouse." He smiled, laughing into my face, just a hair's breadth away, our noses practically touching. "What's the point in wearing those? They can't keep your feet warm."

I stared at him in disbelief, after months of another long absence from the island, testing new sail technology on the open sea, my mouth slightly agape. He gave me a worried look and continued, "I couldn't really see your skinny little back because of all the smoke when I walked in, but then I heard you sniffling by the fire." He started to cough. You can't really talk in a smokehouse, or you end up inhaling too much smoke. I saw him realize this as he coughed and spit out a black residue. He noticed me shaking my head, silently laughing at him, and he bent toward me, hand on my lower back, and whispered, "I don't know if this some Druid ritual, but the fish look like they need some more time, so come outside and talk to me."

He was out of the door in a dash but not before planting a lingering kiss next to my earlobe. His touch felt so refreshingly cool, like the ocean on a hot day. This felt too familiar, a piece of our childhood, yet startling at the same time. I hadn't seen Ros much in the ten months since my wedding. He had been out testing boats and exploring further shores for both ideas and hard materials for his boat building. It was a convenient time for him to be gone. I felt my body and soul ache for my best friend, the one person who really knew me, and I realized for the first time that maybe his long and impeccably timed absence was a part of the loneliness I had been feeling for the last year. Ray had stepped in fully as my confidant lately, and truly his presence was so full of warmth and wisdom that it had sufficed as my only friendship through the winter, spring, and summer that had passed.

I slipped out of the smokehouse, covering my breasts with sweaty palms, and Ros wrapped my green Druid cloak around me immediately while carrying my dress in his hands, even picking up my disintegrating shoes and holding them in the crook of his arm because he knew I would prefer to be barefoot. How many times had he seen me naked throughout our lives together? Babes at the breast together, children without clothes during summer play, teenagers skinny-dipping in the ocean. But it was different now. Now I *felt* naked in front of him.

"You know, your parents were the closest example of a husband and wife I had as a child," I told him, flatly and very much out of the blue for him. He seemed blown away by this information but took it in stride.

"I guess that's true," he said matter-of-factly, "but I *am* wondering what made you think of it just now." I was walking at my usual fast clip, and Ros picked up his pace a bit to reach mine. "Are we headed to the oak grove?"

"Yes," I answered.

We walked in companionable silence until we reached the edge of the woods. The night was cooling quickly. The first frost was upon us. I could smell it in the air. It was the smell of the trees preparing for it, reaching way down to their roots to gain strength for it.

"I think I'm maybe not as good a wife as I am a Druid," I explained.

"Well, the talk among the sailors is that Aric is quite pleased with you, my dear," Ros responded. I blushed, but he continued. "And let me tell you how much I enjoy working on their boats while they talk about you like that."

We walked in silence for a moment. "It's hard for you to think of me like that?" I asked him.

He looked back at me puzzled, then smiled his sly and perfect smile. "What? No. All I do is think about you like that, Ailsa. In fact, that's why I've been looking for you."

We approached my oak tree, and as Ros moved back a heavy branch laden with golden leaves for us to walk under, we were showered with shades of orange, yellow, and gold that matched his hair. I knew that Ros's feelings about us had grown complicated, but my mind was filled with enough confusion at the moment. I decided on more avoidance. "I need to talk about me right now. And what I'm going through. Not you. It's my turn to say how I feel. You spoke at my wedding, now let me."

He looked down, abashed, but to his credit, breathed deeply once and looked up to meet my deliberate stare. He saw that, after many months of his prolonged absence, I needed my friend. The

friendship that he had had no choice over since birth. I was once a
starving three-month-old, thrust on him by his loving mother and
my stubborn grandmother. And now, eighteen years later, I was
asking him to put me first again. I had never dared ask that before,
but he accepted with grace belying his years. It was the grace of
true friendship, a chord that struck deeper than love, and I would
never forget how he was there for me that night, when I needed to
be heard. So we sat under the great oak, and I rested my head on the
huge knot just below the hole created by the lightning strike, and
we talked for hours that felt like no time at all.

Dark was approaching quickly as we exited the wood; it was on our
heels as we headed toward my grandmother's house. I asked Ros to
stay for dinner as I took my shoes from him, the night air having
grown too cold to walk without them. He still held my dress in
his hands, though I was wrapped tightly in my green wool Druid's
cloak, which flowed behind me, long enough to drag the ground.
As we came to Grandmother's house, a dark figure came into view
in the doorway, filling up far more of it than grandmother would
have. It ducked to fit inside, and I gasped, realizing it had to be Aric.
"Oh, good," I heard Ros say sarcastically. I sped up and ran toward
grandmother's door, wide-eyed.

"I thought you were arriving tomorrow," I said as I walked under the hide right behind him. Aric smiled down at me but quickly
caught sight of Ros behind me and realized that I was clutching my
cloak closed, naked underneath.

"The gales were in our favor this time and pushed us toward home with haste," he said, stroking the smooth back of my black hair. He made eye contact with Ros, who had joined us by grandmother's hearth, clearly not excited to see my husband. When grandmother turned around from the stew pot and saw Ros come up and stand behind me, her eyes bulged out of her head "Oh, I can see why the wind was in a hurry." she jabbed, and I cut my eyes at her.

"I figured you would be sleeping over with Grandmother," Aric added, "And so here you are. I guess I do know my wife." He said without taking his eyes off of Ros.

He grabbed my dress out of Ros's grasp with one huge fist. "Let's go home and go to bed, my love; it's late, and I'm weary from my travels." He said this without looking at me, looking down at my dress, holding it in one hand.

"But I don't have anything for you to eat," I rebutted quickly, not willing to be dragged away from the warmth of my grandmother's hearth and my best friend's listening ear. I felt a tad conspicuous and continued, "There's some fish in the smokehouse. I guess I could—"

"No, no." Grandmother cut me off. Thankfully. "There's plenty of stew. Please stay." She hesitated and then added, "All of you." She shot Ros a hot look but could not deny her own hospitality.

"The fish isn't ready anyway," Ros added, placing a hand on my shoulder and massaging it lightly. "Remember, Ailsa, we just checked it?"

I felt Grandmother's eyes bulge again and I wiggled out of Ros's grasp.

"Shouldn't you see to the boats that have just arrived?" Aric asked him in an unusually irritated tone.

"First thing in the morning," Ros retorted as he smiled, bent down, kissed my grandmother, who looked annoyed yet charmed by his escapades, and made his way toward the hearth.

Grandmother's hearth was in the center of the roundhouse, as was traditional in the older homes of the village, with mounds of hides and furs piled up around us and a multitude of pillows filled with goose feathers and wrapped in thick furs so that the pointy ends didn't stick out and poke you. Everything was soft and comfortable with age, treated with the sweetest smelling oil of rose, clary sage, and lavender, which made you want to drift right off to sleep. But the senses were aroused by the botanical smell of the dozens of herbs hanging overhead in various states of drying, mingled with the earthy smell of grain on the quern and chicory tea and meat stew on the fire.

Ros leaned on a giant mound of hides across the fire from me; his flint spade used for digging out boats was laid, ever so suggestively, over his lap, his legs extended and crossed at the ankles, his arms stretched out in full wingspan across the back cushions. He had seated himself in the perfect place to watch me, and so I found myself feeling self-conscious, seated cross-legged on a black fur, several pillows propped up behind me and Aric leaning back, one arm spread behind my back and the other hand on his ale cup. Suddenly not knowing how to be, utterly aware of myself in the presence of these two men in a way I had never been before, I found myself feeling awkward, trying to casually lie back against Aric's arm, as if it were natural to be held by my husband like this. I looked at him and smiled, into the fire, over at Grandmother, anything to avoid Ros's piercing gaze. Grandmother seemed not to notice any of it, humming away, stoking the fire, and stirring the pots over it. She offered each of us an herbal tea concoction from her earthenware and then sat cross-legged with us, her eyes creased in satisfaction at this impromptu gathering around her fire.

The tea was strong and soothing, and as I sipped it in silence, I felt the house darken and close in around me, as if we were in a cozy cave. The voices of my husband, my best friend, and my grandmother seemed to echo around me to amplify this effect. I stopped wondering whether my head was sitting neatly erect over my body or whether it was cupped in the curve between Aric's bicep and breast. I was lost in the familiarity of the love enveloping me, and a calm surged over me, like a wave I was not ready for. After ten months of marriage, despite some distance, Aric's voice was beginning to join that chorus of sweet, recognizable sounds. It made me remember being a girl, falling asleep to the sound of my father talking to my grandmother. She had loved him as her own, though he was a foreigner, and even more so because my mother had died. Aric was also a foreigner, and I wondered, not for the first time, if he felt the same pangs of loneliness without his family of origin.

I felt my heart softening with the thought. I had spent my entire life—thus far—in love with one person, but that didn't mean I couldn't feel compassion for this man, my husband, gruff as he was. I felt his beard scratch the top of my head and realized I was leaning against him, listening to Ros and grandmother exchange stories from the harbor. We lived on an island off of a bigger island, and to the north were dozens of smaller islands. Some were permanently inhabited; others were only inhabited by animals, just providing a place for a fire, rest, and replenishment from the wilds of the sea. Ros built boats like his father and grandfather before him, and the technology was evolving rapidly from the spread of ideas and designs. Boats came to represent the village society and the warriors themselves, so everyone wanted the largest and strongest. Luckily, our forests provided plenty of lumber for such endeavors and we sailed constantly, gathering stories, goods, and new villagers along the way.

Ros was a different kind of boat maker. He could look at a boat from a distance, as it came into dock, and note all of the details—the sail material, the weight, the shape of the hull, and the exact height of the bow and stern. He had drawings of massive ships that he had been working on since we were eleven. He said they would go farther than anyone had yet imagined.

Ros's memory was also built for stories, especially the bawdy ones told by the sailors of the seas that he met down on the beach. Hearing details of the lives of people from neighboring islands and places even farther away was always exciting, but not for the obvious reasons. The stories of intrigue—stolen boats, angry shamans, wild boar, rough seas, and long nights searching for land—had kept me riveted for the last decade of my life; Ros and I shared the temptation to go and explore for ourselves. But now I was a Druid and a wife, and what intrigued me the most about the stories was how similar these foreigners seemed to us, how much we shared, and how I felt so connected to them through the vastness of the world we inhabited. I had come to imagine them more as family than as strange and exotic.

We sipped our tea until it was gone, and without my even realizing it, our drinks became wine, poured for me and Aric from a leather flagon that he wore, fastened with leather and draped from his shoulder. Grandmother and Ros drank a sweeter, more aged honey wine that she poured from an earthenware vessel older than any of us.

Somewhere in the middle of Ros's story of the battle of Chiefs Muir and Erlan the Great, I began to let myself drift, knowing that the singing would be coming soon, for what else could top this epic tale but a round of songs from Aric and Ros, deep enough into drink that they forgot their own differences and instead seemed to be competing with the village bard?

My favorite tales were the ones about the other stone circles and monuments and our brethren who were connected to us through them. There were a series of stone monuments on all the surrounding islands, constructed at different times but all with similar purpose and connection. I knew, through the Druids, that the major civilizations of this age in which we lived were centered around such monuments. I loved to hear of the intricacies, differences, and similarities. I knew that stones from our islands had been carried hundreds of miles to the south to erect a giant henge for the people there. One stone circle to the south was made of massive stones moved from the western tip of the sea to the center of the island. There were tales that the stones had been moved down river, with salmon and sea otters coming to help, and then across land by tying them to tree rounds that turned in circles, carrying the gigantic stones gracefully over the hills and valleys. I had to remember these questions for Ray the next day, for at dawn, I would head to the stones to begin preparing for the Ceremony of Samhain, the postharvest celebration that ushered in the darkness of winter. Samhain was the midpoint between the fall equinox and the winter solstice. It was the time of year when the trees began to shed their leaves and spiders made intricate webs in the bare branches. The dew on the grass was colder, and the earth smelled sweeter, preparing herself to sleep over the winter months. Hearth fires were kept strong all day and the smokehouse worked endlessly to cure our meat and fish for the long winter. I love this time, and I inhaled those musky, fiery scents of fall. It was also a time when the veil between this world and the next was most thin. Our ancestors came down to visit with us on this ceremony, and I felt their presence as I sank deeper into the satisfaction of warm stories and drink on a cold night.

Grandmother must have lit a pipe. The smells of herbs, hides, wine, and soot overwhelmed me as my eyelids became heavy. So I settled into my pillows, pulled a fur up over my shoulders, took one last sip of wine from the full cup Aric had poured for me, and vanished into Ros's story in a hazy state of mind achieved from the mixture of strong wine, warm fire, spirit tea, pipe smoke, and exhaustion. I felt the grooves in the earthenware cup I held, and as I drifted off, I thought I felt Aric's fingers entwine mine around the grooves. As I closed my eyes, the story was in bright color before me:

Erland had been a great shepherd and wise man on the isles to the north. He spoke to his sheepdogs in their native language, and birds landed on his shoulder and spoke to him of what the world looked like from the air. One day he got into an argument with a golden eagle about who was bigger, man or the eagle. For when the eagle, the highest-flying of any of the island birds, took flight, he saw the world as smaller than any man had, looking over his prey and the tops of trees and mountains alike as little ants.

"You are no bigger than a rabbit from my perspective, Man," the eagle said to him. So Erland set out to prove to the golden eagle that man was the dominant animal of the earth and larger than any bird. He told the golden eagle to take flight, and he climbed to the top of the tallest tree in the grove, a giant pine that towered over the rest. Erland sweated and struggled and feared for his life as he reached the highest, thinnest branches of the tree, and at the top, he waved his arms and made himself as big and proud as he could.

When he came back down, the eagle glided down next to him and said, "Man, you were still as small as the mole-rat to me, looking down from the sky on all of my prey. You are small, inconsequential even. You are not as large as you believe, man."

Erland, knowing more than a bird, refused to believe such nonsense, so he did what any reasonable man might do: he decided he would climb a mountain. The next day and night and the day after that and the night after that, Erland climbed the tallest mountain on the island—the Old Man, the locals called it. When he finally summited, with only his hide bag of water hung around his neck and bits of grasses and herbs to eat on the way up, he waved to the eagle, exhausted and freezing, from the top of the mountain.

The eagle took flight and circled around and around the mountain, over Erland. At one point he seemed almost to touch the sun, and Erland squinted to make out his great form silhouetted against the setting sun, giant wings spread so steady, gliding through the air. It was majestic. Then, a freezing gust of wind knocked the exhausted man over, and there was the eagle, landing gracefully atop Erland's recumbent form.

"I'm sorry," the eagle said solemnly, "even still, these mountains look large, but you, the sheep, the grouse, and the owl are all small in comparison."

Poor Erland was defeated and confused. He looked up at the golden eagle, tears streaming down his muddied face.

I felt Aric settle and let out a loud snore underneath my head, which rested on his chest. I clapped my hand to my mouth in order not to laugh and wake him. Grandmother looked up from the wool stocking she was darning and smiled at me knowingly across the fire.

"Well, what happened then, Ros?" she asked him.

"Did the men from the northern isles have to catch the tide out to sea and leave you without their story's end?" I whispered, giggling.

"No, I'm sorry," Ros replied quickly. "I thought Ailsa's husband might choke to death, but I'll go on."

I widened my eyes at him, trying not to laugh again. Sometimes it was as if he wanted to pick a fight with Aric, a man twice his size. Ros, who barely cleared my own height, seemed to rely on his pugnaciousness and Aric's relative calmness—or in this case, unconsciousness.

The golden eagle leaned over and wiped Erland's eyes with his soft, feathery wing. Then he comforted the man under his wing and said, "But look what you have done at your small size! Man can scale mountains like a goat, he can climb trees like a squirrel, and he can command birds of prey like the wind. If you need something big enough to be seen from the heavens in order to assert your power, then you, and you only, can *build* it, Man. Build something to your majesty and to those who came before you. I will not be able to see you from the sky, but I will be able to see what you have left behind.

"And that's their story for why their stone circles were built, aye?" Grandmother looked across the fire at me, flames reflected in her yellow-green cat eyes. "Now the storytelling passes to you, my beautiful Druid granddaughter. Tell us today, on this cold eve of Samhain, why the stone circle was built on our own island generations ago."

I sat up a little, licked my lips, which were dry from wine consumption, and began the story Ray had told me when I became a Druid, a story I had known in my bones as long as I could remember. Everyone was asleep before I finished. Aric must have brought back strong wine, I thought. There wasn't much time before the Druids would be called at dawn on Samhain to the stone circle, so I covered grandmother with an extra blanket, quenched the fire a bit, and headed off to have a few moments alone at the stones before the others arrived to call the sun.

CHAPTER 7:

THE CLIFFS

Ailsa

I followed in his footsteps as closely as I could, my bare feet sinking into the imprints his leather boots left in the black peat. The tall grass blew dizzily in the sea wind, scratching my ankles as I kilted up my dress to keep up with his quickened pace. The night was black but brightened by stars as we crested the hill toward the cliffs. The sea made herself known with a freezing, salty wind, and goose flesh rippled up my spine and arms. The Druids met at dawn to pray as the sun came up, and he knew that sometimes I would leave my roundhouse a bit early to walk alone and gather my thoughts beforehand. It was an easy way to catch me alone, which he had, just outside my doorway, that morning.

As I exited my house and rounded the corner, I found him waiting for me there in his black seacloak. He bade me follow, so I did, without asking questions, as I had since we were children. This wasn't the first time he had done this, wanting to show me a new boat construction or boats that were coming in with the morning tide; he always preferred we went alone or in secret on such occasions. We had snuck out of our houses many times before dawn, but this was different, sneaking around behind Aric's back, and he knew it.

I should have known we were going to the cliffs, but the urgency of this night was a different beast. The urgency of purpose echoed in his stride and voice, and I felt it in my bones. His sudden apparition had nearly made me jump out of my skin, and my body hadn't quite settled since that moment. I normally felt completely safe walking alone in the darkness, one with the shadowland and the creatures that inhabited it during the night, but tonight all my hair stood on end, like a dog who had caught a wild scent on the air. My stomach was in knots of anticipation.

"Why are you walking so fast?" I finally asked him, wrapping my arms around myself, pulling my green wool cloak tighter around me with the hood up, my thick, dark hair stuffed inside keeping my neck warm. The winds were so bitter along the coast this time of year, people rarely made the trek this far.

"You could have told me we were coming to the cliffs, Ros; I would have brought my fur or a blanket, or something..." My constant chatter was yet another peculiarity of the morning and made Ros stop in his heavy tracks. Ros was younger than me by three and a half months and not much taller, but tonight his body loomed over me with powerful presence, his red-gold shoulder-length hair on fire, his heavy brow creased as he looked down his too-straight nose at me.

"Of course we're going to the cliffs. Where else would we go, Ailsa?" he muttered, barely audible, looking back at me with the moon glowing over his shoulder.

The edges of the cliffs were mostly used for the Druid ceremonies in which we "called the sea," so the people of the village had become superstitious about visiting the cliffs on days that weren't marked by the festival of the wheel of the year. Of course, it didn't help anyone's feeling of safety that there had been occasional accidents at the cliffs, especially with foolish teenagers. And of course, my own father had thrown himself from a nearby spot nearly a decade ago. It was a place where Ros assumed he and I could have some privacy for all these reasons, and as kids we had dared one another to sit on the cliff's edge, dangling our feet off, grasping each other's hands tightly in equal fear and exhilaration when the wind blew.

Just like I collected my thoughts deep in the woods, among the trees, Ros felt calmed by the roar of the ocean and the promise of the caves down below where the boat builders stored their tools and provisions. Since returning from his months abroad, studying boat making on the other islands, he had often come down here by himself to think. He enjoyed the solitude of the coast and ship's caves during the winter months, when boats were being built, patched, and cared for but new ones were not being tested on the rough seas.

Samhain had come and gone, which meant the winter solstice would soon be upon us. My one-year anniversary. This time of year, just before the snow starts, is wet and frigid. The damp cold of the air and ferocity of the wind on the edge of the island send a deep chill that reaches to the bone. Ros had stopped to wait for me, his winter cloak flapping in the wind. He stared out at the sea, and I stood beside him; our knuckles brushed, and my stomach clenched. It was like touching a lightning bolt. We walked the last several meters to the cliff's edge together. I crossed my legs and slowly sat, knowing that it was safer to be lower to the ground for balance when there was this much wind roaring on the cliffs in the winter months.

He stood over me, looking out into the ocean and a sky full of fading stars, slowly dimmed by the rising sun. "It's beautiful," I said, breaking the awkward silence. I never felt the need to chat aimlessly or fill silence, but the discomfiting quality of the night, now turning to morning, continued to rattle me. "There's nothing like the darkest moments before the sunrise. How quiet and still the whole world is, just waiting for the new day," I said, more to myself than him.

"I know what you mean," he responded. "It's incredible that the mighty sun has to sleep every night just as we do. And rise again, just as we do. Even when it is hard to pull oneself out of bed and face the day."

I looked up at him. "On the contrary, you don't look like you've been getting much rest." I smiled up at him, reaching out for his hand, out of both sympathy and desperation to reach out to him and have him open his heart and spill its secrets like he had when we were children. What is it about the touch of a hand that helps us to unfurl our hidden parts?

"You're right, I haven't. I lie awake all night, and when morning comes, I have no desire to rise," he said without looking at me, still standing over me looking out into the ocean, which blended with the sky. Soon light would come to touch everything, and the colors that bled together now would separate and be wholly their own, but as long as the night lasted, they would blur together as one.

He smiled down at me as he laced his fingers with mine, and his piercing sea-green eyes warmed me like the sun for one fleeting moment. And then he unfurled his hidden heart.

"I could jump off this cliff right now. And I would be less miserable than I have been this past year. At this point it's either that or leave home. Those are my choices." He motioned with his chin out to the shore below, where the boats he was working on were racked inside an adjacent cave in various states of disrepair. Among them all, a large and elegant craft stood out because of the enormous sail attached to it. It could carry twenty people. Ros had been working on new sail technology for the last eighteen months, inspired by notes and memories of sails he had seen docked on neighboring islands.

He clenched his jaw, and I saw the light fade out of his face. I should have felt kindness and sadness toward him, but rage bubbled up uncontrollably as if in a cauldron inside of me, as it so often did when it came to our contrasting views, and I pulled my hand away. "You actually think that leaving me, your parents, and your sisters here without you would be *your* sacrifice? You would jump into the sea and become a part of what you *actually* love the most and leave me just like everyone I have ever loved has?" He began to shake his head and continued to clench his jaw. "That's your version of bravery, Ros? To kill yourself in the same manner my father did? or run away? All you would prove is your weakness and self-love, which everyone expects from you, anyway."

"OK, then tell me, what's your version of bravery, Ailsa?" he asked.

"The brave thing," I answered, "would be to stay and bear this with me." I wanted to stand up, but my stomach was in knots and wouldn't allow me. I knew everything was about to change now that we were truly bearing our hearts. Regardless, the wind was too strong, and I knew it wasn't safe, so I rooted myself to the ground.

He stood immobile as a statue for what seemed like an eternity. Something in me told me he would never jump, and I was able to slow my heart rate and take a deep breath, but I couldn't shake the vision of it. Then his fingertips brushed my outstretched hand, and my heart began to race again. "Bear what, Ailsa?" he whispered. I could barely hear him over the ocean and wind, even though we were close. I pulled him down next to me so we were safe and sitting on the ground, back from the cliff's edge, icy wind still blowing. I looked into his ruddy face with my dark, crescent-moon eyes.

"You did this," I said with tears in my eyes. "And you'll bear it out with me since you were afraid to tell everyone that you loved me and wanted to marry me." I was yelling now to be heard over the wind and waves.

"What do you mean 'afraid'?" he asked. He had pulled his knees up to his chest and was looking over at me, shielded from the wind.

"Ros, you found any excuse to be seen with any girl other than me," I said. "You made your intentions clear, and they were not aimed toward me, not ever."

"I *did not know* one could be married to a *Druid*, Ailsa!" Ros screamed. "Isn't that what they tell you when ye join? What you told me before I left? That you're married to the other Druids? Everyone told me it was a lost cause and not to make it worse for you."

I walked backward on my hands, moving away from the edge quickly, like a spider. The wind was too strong now, and I didn't want to yell. I shook my head for clarity, and Ros crawled over to me, staring in disbelief. "No, I…I guess because I'm the last of my bloodline in my household, they always told me I could marry. Ray always said I would marry." My heart was racing now, and I could barely get a sentence out. My frustration with the Druids, my grandmother, the elders, and the politics of the island had been cresting for the past several months, since my marriage to Aric was arranged without my approval, but now it was hitting a peak, as it seemed that contradictory information had been set afloat.

Confused and frustrated, I spoke with my face hidden in my hands. "But you were with so many other girls, Ros." I couldn't look at him. The painful memories of catching him in the woods with other girls or hearing him brag about it to the other boys were rattling around in my head, confusing me more.

"Yes," he answered. "It was a futile attempt to get over the loss of *us*." He was sitting up on his knees in front of me, the stars spread out behind him, framing his face in a celestial halo. He was so beautiful like that, I had to look away.

"Oh." The wind had died down, and I responded quietly now. "I guess I thought you were bored of our childish friendship and just ready for something more."

"More? More *what?*" he yelled with a hysterical smile on his face. I was totally surprised to look back up at him and hear the sound of laughter. He was laughing so hard he rolled over and his ribs seemed to ache with it. It had been so long since I had seen him laugh like that.

"Ye make me feel many things, Ailsa, but bored has never been one of them." I laughed then too. He reached up from the ground and grabbed my face with both of his frozen hands. Being trapped between the two blocks of ice gave me chills, and then he said it. The words that he etched on my soul: "And as for wanting more… there is nothing that could *ever* be more than us." I breathed a sigh of relief as he pulled me gently toward him by my wool cloak, and I bent my forehead to touch his and closed my eyes while his nose pressed into my cheekbone. I shivered, partly from cold but mostly from this touch I had longed for for as long as I could remember.

I shouldn't have done it, but almost reflexively from the cold, I pressed myself against him. Both of us were shivering now, and his laughter turned back into tears.

I slid my fingers into his wild auburn hair, and with my thumbs on his red cheeks, wiped the tears away, then I kissed the trails they had left on his face with eyes open. Because I had to know how it felt, I kissed him, desperately and deeply. His eyes were closed, but he smiled the biggest smile I had ever seen, and then, closing my eyes, I sank into the kiss and let go of all my worries.

Ros relaxed from my loving, confident touch too. I felt the warmth of him pressing into me and the blood rushing through his entire body as we melted into one. The kissing and the rising sun both had a thawing effect and I started to move more fluidly and quickly. I was warm enough to sit up and remove my cloak and pull my dress up around my hips. I wrapped my legs around him and he lay flat still, smiling up at me. We laughed breathlessly for an instant, fingers intertwined. Then he kissed each of my fingertips and I smiled back at him, haloed in pale, orange light from the rising sun. He held me by my hips, steering me as lightly but firmly as a ship. It was simultaneously relaxing and invigorating to be one with him after years of building tension.

Soon he shuddered and reached up to pull me down to his chest, where he stroked my black hair from crown to waist. "You've never done it like this with your Norse warrior, have you?" he asked. Without answering or looking at him, I silenced him with the tips of my fingers.

"The sunrise this morning is the color of your hair." I smiled, and he thought for a moment. I could always feel him thinking.

"And you're as beautiful as the star-filled night was; that's certain. But sometimes I'm afraid ye hold as many secrets, Ailsa." He sighed deeply into the top of my head.

"I do hold many secrets. Just not from you," I replied, looking at him.

He nodded. "Well, then I'm afraid I've just created another one for you to keep. But if we're really going to do this, I mean really be together, then we have to leave," he said seriously.

I nodded down over the cliffs at the cave full of giant boats made from hollowed oak. Making our boat from the oak grove was like bringing the symbols of me and Ros together, bringing the woods to the ocean. Perhaps we were meant to be.

"When do you think you can finish *it* for sure?" I looked over at Ros, and his mouth was still agape. I couldn't help but laugh.

"Do you really mean it? I mean, sure we used to fantasize about going on adventures as kids, but you're a Druid, Ailsa. You can't just leave unless they say you can or send you somewhere else."

I thought about that for a moment. "I know the way up to Orkney; we can go there or beyond that. I know the Druids, and they will welcome us there."

"Come down with me to the boats." Ros extended his hand, palm up, waggling his fingers, enticing me to take his hand, like he had done since we were tiny. "I want to show you everything."

I grabbed his hand and followed him gingerly down the coastline to the only spot on the cliffside that was graded gently enough to descend to the beach. It helped to store the boats down there because Ros knew there was only one way to approach from the land, so he felt they were safe.

"To answer your question," he said as he helped me maneuver over the mossy rocks and boggy holes of our descent, "I should be done with the sail by Imbolc time. It's not safe to face the sea so deep into winter anyway. So around Imbolc I'll finish and begin taking her out." He continued after we jumped the last few feet onto the shore, "I'll have a good feeling from the spring sea of what she can do and what needs fixing. Of course, during my test excursions on the boat, I'll keep an eye out and learn where we can easily go when we leave. We will have to stop off somewhere before Orkney."

"So we could leave by the summer solstice, then?" I asked. Feeling eager for my nineteenth birthday.

"Maybe," he responded. "But I swear by the gods"—he took out his flint boat carving knife and slashed it in a quick motion against his open palm after we ducked under the lintel stone that led into the cave where the boats were stored for protection—"if ye say it's what you truly want, Ailsa, I'll make it happen and take us away from here as fast as I can."

He knelt down in front of me in the tradition of a blood oath in the doorway to the cave, and I kissed his bleeding palm and pressed it to my heart. Water lapped around my feet, and I pulled him up to stand again. I took the knife and cut my own palm, an act of faith and devotion we had first done when we were nine. I pressed my palm to his and kissed his lips sweetly. His bottom lip was full and pink and felt like home between my lips. I didn't want it to end, but the Druids would be expecting me. "Show me what you've made, then," I answered, and we disappeared into the darkness, hiding our love away, deep in the recesses of the cave.

CHAPTER 8:
YULE, THE WINTER SOLSTICE

She was beautiful against the black sky. The lack of moon on this festival meant that the stars shone as brightly as the fire, and the entire night was bright and dazzling, the more so with her at the center of it. Aric felt on fire himself looking at his young wife perform her priestess rites across the fire. They had been wed for over a year now, but he could count on one hand the number of times they had lain together. It was true that his responsibility to travel to neighboring clans and villages often pulled him from their shared marital bed, but if he was honest, he had also been overly cautious.

There were so many reasons to be cautious with Ailsa, and he found himself listing them over and over in his mind, repeating them to himself as a mantra to relax the urge that was pulling on him watching her perform her Druidic rites underneath the stars. Her body was undulating with the sound of the drums, and despite the cold he could see the sweat glisten on her collarbone from the exertion of dancing and, of course, from her proximity to the sacrificial fires where the goat would soon be roasted on a spit and passed around for nourishment. Female goats were revered in the village and kept for their milk. Only male goats were typically eaten, so this female was a huge sacrifice, one that would hopefully pay off in an early spring and abundant summer.

Ailsa had never seen a human sacrifice, Aric thought. She had been born under stars of peace, and that was all she had known in her lifetime. She hadn't witnessed the constant war and fighting that he had grown up around in the north in the decade before her birth. The Druids that Ailsa knew and had grown up with were gentle. They sought answers through wisdom, deepening their worldly knowledge of medicines and infrastructure through trade and travel. As a leader, the head Druid Ray sought to build, create, and connect with their island neighbors, whereas many of his predecessors had believed in taking and destroying. When Aric had come here as a child, he was taken in by Ray during his first days in the settlement, and the ways in which this culture differed from his own were thoroughly explained to him. He and Ray had spent many years earning one another's trust, and part of that divulgence had involved his hearing the elder druids gathered at Ray's house to discuss Ailsa—and the role she had to play in the coming shift away from peace. Aric had heard the talk surrounding her birth since the day he arrived on the island, and he had always been intrigued with her, maybe a little afraid of her, as strange as it was to be afraid of a four-year-old when you're sixteen. But this feeling of love was brand new, something that surprised him.

And thusly, he had come up with his list of reasons to exercise extreme caution with her. First was the obvious: he had been alive over thirty years; he was practically an old man. He didn't think he would marry again after he had lost his first wife to a sickness that had spread through the village in their first year of marriage, and so he had let the years pass him by in the company of his friends and fellow warriors, without thought of retaining his gentleness and the tender touch a woman needs. Ailsa had been just a girl when his wife had died, running around with Rasha and Ros like triplets, Aric thought. He noticed the pang of jealousy that the thought of Ailsa with Ros gave him.

And then the other pain, not as sharp, more distant, yet still there like a hole in his heart. Poor, sweet Iona, Aric thought. It had been nearly twelve years; the same amount of time he had lived with his father and his native Norse culture had passed since his young wife died. Her red hair splayed out around her perfect pale face like the fire that consumed her in her sickness. He remembered her green eyes losing light as he watched her die, helpless. Ray had done everything to save Iona. Losing her, so young and perfect, felt like the pang of losing his mother all over again. He was so young then, and he had vowed never to love a woman again. It had weakened him too much, seeing the woman he loved so fragile, her unearthly beauty intensified by the paleness of her skin and the blue tint at the corners of her once-rosy lips at burial. Aric remembered the chill of Iona's hand as he held it one last time before Ray had wrapped her face in her shroud, a thin flock of wool, and kissed her head. He bade Aric do the same, and reluctantly he had, before carrying his bride off to her funeral pyre.

So there it was. The truth of his caution was a fear of losing another wife, a wife he hadn't thought he would have. Aric had been with many women since Iona's death, both women in the village and women elsewhere on his voyages. He could set himself free with them and let go because he didn't love them, but he was realizing more and more how much he had allowed himself, against his better judgment, to truly love Ailsa, and that truth was his second big reason for exercising caution. He wanted Ailsa to feel comfortable and at peace. More than anything, he wanted Ailsa to choose him, and for that she needed more time. She was like fire, he thought—volatile, powerful, and sacred, but she could burn him. It took care, caution, and intelligence to use and wield fire, and it was the same with his wife. He wouldn't push her for fear of pushing her away.

But the truth gnawed at him: he needed her. And as more time passed, his need grew deeper and stronger, in such a way that he had not felt, even at the age of seventeen, when every feeling is intense, as it had been with his first wife.

Aric was transfixed. His eyes were set on his wife as she moved around the fire with the goats that had been given herbs to put them to sleep before their sacrifice. The drum beat quickened, the voices around him grew louder, and the music became more powerful, everyone drunk with the night and the festival, but she remained still as the sun, planets orbiting around her in chaos, focused on her, as she moved, slowly, gracefully, holding the goat gently, sweetly, like a newborn baby asleep in her arms. She lifted its head up to her chin, and the sleeping goat faced her now. The smoke and herbs must have been getting to him, because Aric thought for a moment he saw her feeding their newborn baby at her breast. But then, a quick movement of her long fingers, and the short, sharp, ritual knife fell to the ground ahead of the spill of blood from the goat's throat. He had seen animals sacrificed before but never in such a way. Everything she did was unmatched in grace. Feeding the goats herbs to relax them during the ceremony was a practice he had seen, but he'd never seen an animal stay asleep, resting so peacefully in the arms of its sacrificer. What was this magic she possessed? He wondered. Ailsa laid the goat at the foot of the altar stone, kissing it, and painted spirals in the stone with her blood-tipped fingers. The ritual would be continued in six weeks' time at Imbolc, when the dried goat jerky would be consumed with milk, a prayer for a quick winter and an abundant spring. Aric said his on prayer for an abundant spring with Ailsa.

He thought about the beauty of his mother, Gunnhild, and of Iona. He couldn't imagine a woman more beautiful than either of them—both small and frail, light and fair, with eyes brighter than the summer sky. But Ailsa's beauty wasn't celestial like theirs; it was elemental. She smelled of herbs and earth. Her long brown hair, in its many braids, curls, and tangles to her waist, looked like tree roots, and her skin was almost bronze from constant sun exposure. Her feet were large and flat like a man's and pounded the earth as she took long, intentional strides. It was as if Ailsa calmed the earth and fire and goats as she commanded them because she was such an essential part of them. He had caught her on more than one occasion talking to the trees as if they spoke back to her.

He looked down at her grass- and peat-smudged feet and ankles, showing under her robes as she reached up in the act of purification. Her fingers were red with goat's blood, and her eyes shone with brown, green, gold, and every earthly color in between. None of the blue of the heavens. Even her wool robe, dyed dark green in the color of the Druids, seemed a part of her body, like she was the rolling hills themselves, and he looked at her long, strong arms, thinking she was akin to some magical tree come to life.

Ailsa had to be purified herself for the ritual, and he hadn't seen her for days while she was with the Druids undergoing the processes. They fasted, smudged themselves, and prayed for hours on end. The time away had stretched his desperation for her, and he resolved there, in the firelight, the pulse of the crowd around him, that he would take a risk to love this strange, beautiful, wise woman.

"What good is caution where love exists?" he asked himself. He liked that. It sounded like something his father had said to him once. He chuckled to himself thinking of how much his father would have loved Ailsa yet how foreign her ways would have been to him. The Druids were gentler than this people; that was for sure. His time with them, specifically Ray, had made him more gentle and more tied to nature. Yet he smiled at the thought that they were just as formidable in their own way. The things Ailsa and Ray knew about the earth, about the future even, were astounding, and Aric wished he could share them with his father, bragging about his wife as any proud husband would want to do.

Then the dancers came from between the stones into the center of the circle, where they wound around the fire and the Druids, spinning like dervishes, and the earthly beauty of his wife dissolved into the night behind the bright lanterns and white robes of the female dancers. Aric looked up into the blackness of the sky and the thousands of twinkling stars. It was vast and beautiful and reminded him of being at sea with his family so many years ago. "Are you up there?" he asked them—Aric, his father, Gunnhild, his mother, his siblings, and Iona—silently, in his heart. "If you can hear me," he continued, surprised at himself, for he had never been one to pray, "help open her heart to me." He closed his eyes tightly, in earnest. "I need to know love again."

CHAPTER 9:

⒞MBOLC

Edie

I held my wine glass up so that it reflected the incandescent light beaming out from the kitchen behind me. The glass was getting cold in my hand, and I shivered, pulling my wool scarf around me. Ahead of me was all darkness, and beyond that, the North Atlantic Ocean. I was close enough to the water that I could smell the saltiness in the air, but my cabin was tucked far enough into the hills that the roof sustained minimal salt and wind damage. It was still strange to think of it as *my* cabin.

There were four neat rooms inside, all with stone exposed instead of plaster-covered walls, which I preferred. The east side of the house held the bedroom, bathroom, and study, while just behind me, the kitchen, dining area, and living room were one great room opposite the others, roughly the same size as the aforementioned three rooms combined. The kitchen had an old Aga stove that Frank loved to cook on, and I shared the house with him, free of charge, except for the full Irish breakfasts he made us every morning to sustain us through a long day of wind-whipped winter walking and amateur archaeology. The rest of the year, he lived on a boat that he had been meaning to fix up, and while it was good enough for his needs, I worried about him this time of year when every morning was frosted over, a remnant of the unimaginably cold night before. I suppose it was a little less frigid on the canals of London than here on the North Atlantic, but something told me he liked to get away from the city as much as I liked having him with me.

We had always shared everything freely, without counting debts owed or expecting recompense. Our sharing went beyond the material, comprising our deepest thoughts, feelings, and most bizarre impulses. We shared with that rare freedom and abandon that isn't bound by propriety, self-consciousness, distrust, or sociopolitical correctness. This type of rare and raw truthfulness can only be shared with a true soulmate or best friend. But there was one thing I had been keeping to myself, from everyone. Even him.

I saw the glowing tip of his cigarette and heard the crunch of his boots on the icy gravel drive before I saw him coming around the corner of the house, wrapped in a massive hand-knit scarf, some old Christmas gift from an ex-boyfriend, I thought.

"I was thinking about the etymology of Imbolc," he said, without preamble.

"Mmhmm, I poured you something to warm you against the chill," I said with a coy grin. He grabbed it from me sprightly and went on, getting more and more talkative the more he imbibed, exciting himself about the conversation. I could see this was revving up the big linguistics nerd in him. "Do tell." I raised my glass in a motion of cheers.

"You say Imbolc is a proto-Celtic festival, so the language of it has to be older than what we have in the form of early Gaelic from fifteen hundred years ago. Even if medieval Gaelic language speakers heard 'Imbolc' in the core sounds of the word, they still would have just designated the meaning to fit their own understanding."

I stared at him blankly. He tried again after a long drag of his cigarette. "OK, I mean, if the culture was assimilating, they wouldn't have given the celebration a new name altogether; they would have stuck as close to the original name as possible to avoid confusion. Like, think of Easter sounding just like the pagan spring festival of Oster. *Capisce?*"

"Right." I agreed, dizzied from jumping from modern English to ancient Gaelic to Italian in one sentence. Frank was like a language acrobat.

He jumped into the air a bit as he excitedly began again, fulfilling that acrobatic image.

"And so the translation would have just shifted through time as the proto-Celtic languages were lost but the traditions and festivals passed through time and culture. Which means, the question is really what words in proto-Celtic languages make *sounds* like *im-bolc* because it's almost certainly not derived from the medieval Gaelic *emmolc*, meaning goat's milk, as is currently believed. Catch my drift?"

I nodded, and he started to pace as he continued. "Well, I think the etymology of some of these festival names is pointing us in a bit of a specific direction. The furthest we can go back linguistically is to the word *emholg,* from the Indo-European root *hmelg,* which relates to purification. So maybe with Imbolc, we're looking at a purification ritual, which would fit with the stone circle sites you've described to me."

"That's true," I agreed. "And the timing within the wheel of the year seems right. Maybe they needed to purify themselves for the

same reason we work out and drink green juice in the New Year."
Frank nodded excitedly and took his first, long sip of the whiskey I
had poured for him. "And of course, February was the holy month
of purification for the Romans, and they actually used goat's milk in
some of the rituals, so it makes sense that it would be muddled together or rather…conflated through time," I pointed out as I grabbed
the untouched, burning, hand-rolled cigarette from his left hand
and took a puff myself.

"I thought Ireland was the only place in Europe never invaded
by the Romans?" Frank asked.

"It is," I responded as I exhaled smoke. "That reminds me, I need
to tell you something I've been thinking about."

Ignoring me, he continued, "But the Romans did go to Scotland.
Of course, they only made it to the lowlands before they were terrified, ran back to England, and built Hadrian's Wall, but there still
would have been contact and an exchange of ideas."

I cleared my throat again and prepared myself for his response
to my next revelation.

"I wanted to tell you…I've been meaning to mention—"

"What? Just say it! Out with it." He stood, facing me, hand on his
hip, and I looked beyond him out into the blackness of the sea and
what was on the other side of it. Waiting. The answer to the book's
completion was waiting for me over the horizon. I just knew it.

"I think Sully and the research he is referencing are wrong."
I paused to let the weight of saying it out loud settle. It felt worse
than I had anticipated.

Frank raised one eyebrow again, this time even higher. "Hmm?"

"I…I think I'm going to have to rewrite a section of his book on
the rituals at the standing stones—I mean, in addition to finishing

the etymology bit we're talking about. I think we need to—I mean *I* need to—" I was clearly struggling with my confidence and articulation and started to wring my hands.

"So what are you asking me to do?" Frank asked impatiently.

"What I'm saying is, I think you're right. I think the etymology of the festivals is derived from Scotland. I think early Scottish and Irish people island-hopped and exchanged ideas that informed the rituals they performed." I pointed to an invisible map in the air of the North Atlantic and Irish Sea, the bodies of water that lay before us. "There was a series of small islands off the coasts of the larger ones. The receding ice of the Holocene, which invited ancient people to settle here eight thousand years ago, would have revealed hundreds of, if not more than a thousand, habitable islands."

Frank drank the rest of his whiskey from the small glass and turned to look out into oblivion with me. The wind sent an icy gust up from the ocean, and he wrapped the giant French scarf around the both of us.

"Most of those islands are here, on the western side of Scotland, just as accessible from Ireland," I said.

Frank made a noise deep in his throat. "Damned ferries," he said.

"Just as accessible with proper boat technology...maybe not quite as accessible given current ferry timetables." I laughed. "The answer is out there; I know it."

"Isn't there a standing theory—I was reading about it—that the creation of farming in the Neolithic didn't render people quite as sedentary or stationary as we thought?" Frank asked.

"Right! I believe that we currently drastically underestimate the extent of movement and boat technology of the people who built the stone circles. I think they were worldly. If they picked up and moved their Welsh blue stones to the south of England for Stonehenge, then why wouldn't their temple complexes be larger, comprising multiple islands with many structures?"

Frank nodded, eyes narrowed for understanding.

"And I think I can prove it…if we go."

"We need more wine!" Frank chimed in as he turned to make his way to the kitchen and the wine rack that Sully and his family had so conveniently left stocked. I laughed, and suddenly my insecurity and fear were allayed.

"So we're taking a trip?" Frank asked as he came back out of the house, equipped with a bottle of Spanish red. He poured his little rocks glass to the rim and refilled my wine glass, which I had been practicing my speech on earlier.

"I'm *asking* if you will go with me and be my research partner," I said and held my glass up to toast him. "I'm also asking if you think I'm crazy to do this. I'm not even thirty, and Sully's the most esteemed Neolithic archaeologist in the world."

"Then I would trust him." Frank spoke certainly as he touched his glass to mine. Now it was my turn to raise my eyebrows. "You should trust him for choosing *you* to finish his work, my dear." He stared back at me, glass raised in the air, the light refracting through it from the house turning the wine to melted rubies in a cup. "Here's to hunting some spirals," he toasted.

"To new adventures," I added.

"Sláinte!" we said simultaneously. And we drank.

CHAPTER 10:

FERRY TIMETABLES

The rich smell of fresh coffee woke me from my latest lucid dreams, accompanied by the pop and hiss of fried eggs and sausages on the griddle. "Yum, coffee!" I called to Frank as I slowly stretched myself up off the pillow nest I had made and swung my legs over the side of the double bed pushed up against a cedar wall, just low enough that its inhabitant was unable to see out of the large picture window a couple feet above. I fumbled in the sheets for my socks after feeling the cold wooden floorboards on my feet. Once socks were secured and the rest of me was wrapped against the freezing morning in the extra quilt, I crossed the small hallway over to the kitchen, ready for something hot.

Frank passed me a handmade earthenware mug without even looking, keeping his eyes on the frying pan. "So glad we stopped at the Euro Spar yesterday. I woke up starving after all that late-night theorizing and researching."

"Mmhmm," I mumbled into my coffee mug as I pulled out one of the three leather stools that sat at the kitchen counter.

"So where did you sleep, the sofa?" I presumed, nodding over at the disheveled quilts and pillows on the old Ikea sofa and the still-closed door to the study, which likely held an unbothered futon and neatly folded linens. "I see you're still totally against bed-sleeping."

"Essentially yes, unless I have a tall, dark, and handsome Welshman to cuddle up with." He winked at me and served up two eggs, two tomatoes, and two sausages for each of us, then joined me on a stool at the counter. I dug into my eggs, watching the bright yellow yolk flow in grateful silence. I cleared my throat as Frank wiped up his eggs with the butt of a piece of brown bread.

"I think I have an idea of how to start the fieldwork I need to do to prove my theory, finish the chapter on standing stone rituals, and rewrite the conclusion of Sully's book."

"You *think* you *might* have an idea?" Frank laughed through his nose, cheeks full of food, and loudly sipped his coffee to coat the rough egg-covered bread on the way down the gullet. "Well, that certainly sounds promising."

I gave him a look as I cut into my tomato with the side of my fork and then refocused on my plate as I salted it to perfection. "OK, so I'm working on my confidence," I quipped. "I have a couple coastal locations that would have been well connected in the Neolithic and possibly into the Bronze Age. They have the middens to prove it."

"Trash?" he asked, gobbling down his eggs greedily. "Of course, the best evidence of trade is the trash."

We couldn't help but peer over the counter into the kitchen recycling bin, which sure enough held an empty bottle of well-known French mustard, the remains of a broken bottle of Spanish red wine, a jelly glass from jolly old England, and of course my guilty pleasure: American Oreos.

"There's already proof that goods and foods were brought from nearby islands, so I'm keen to trace the rock art and positioning of the stone circles and compare them with one another and those on the continent."

Frank sipped his coffee and listened intently, humming and groaning with agreement as I spoke, questioning myself, my theories, and the best location to start with. "You know, you're not doing yourself any favors by questioning everything. I've never seen stuck-up academic types doubt themselves as much as you do."

"I'm just going about the scientific process," I stuttered, brushing off his criticism.

"Ha! Bullshit." He slammed his fork down. The noise from the seagulls and waves outside seemed to stop. "Don't you have a PhD? Aren't you supposed to be a professor or something?"

"I just want to make Sully proud." I looked down into my plate with one sausage and one tomato slice left. A stone had formed in my stomach, and I couldn't finish them.

"Look around you, Edie! Where are we?" I looked up and around the kitchen, then behind us into the living room and out the glass doors into the sea beyond. "He's not the top Neolithic monument archaeologist in the world anymore, Ed."

I gave him a cold, emotionless stare, clearly not ready for what my best friend had to serve up to me alongside my eggs that morning. His voice softened, and he urged me to believe in myself as we embarked on this important research. "He's not *in* the world anymore." He grabbed my hand and smiled. "But *you* are." I nodded, slowly, in agreement, but Frank wasn't done. "It's you now. And you did make him proud. That's why we're sitting in his damn house! Just because you didn't feel love from your own father doesn't mean Sully didn't love you and that you're not worthy and smart and capable. Don't let that man who called himself your dad keep you down anymore." I nodded and sipped my coffee, bitter and cold tasting instead of refreshing like it had been moments before. "You know who you are, Edie, and so did Sully. He's the only person who knew you better than I do."

He paused and stood up, heading toward the back door, messy plates ignored on the kitchen counter. That first morning cigarette was a craving I understood even though I hadn't been a regular smoker in over seven years. Frank was, though, and he saw the knowing response in my eyes and lit me one of his cigarettes without me having to ask.

"The car is gassed up. The map in the dash. Beef jerky, water, and chocolate still in the backpack from our excursions yesterday. I'd say we're just one museum curator's granddaughter short of a real *Da Vinci Code* adventure," Frank joked.

I laughed, breathing smoke out through my nose into the freezing gray spring morning. The fog had lifted just enough so that I could see the edge of the most western Scottish islands jutting out into the sea, and I felt an invigorating tingle in my toes at what lay ahead, even though it was sure to rain the entire time based on what I could tell from the cloud cover. Frank took a long drag of his cigarette and grabbed the corner of the tattered quilt I held around my shoulders, lifting it just enough to cozy up next to me and wrap it tightly around both of us, snuggled up against the morning frost.

"OK, but we're going to need a better coat than this," I said.

We both laughed, and our foggy breaths floated out and over the sea, mingling on the horizon between Ireland and Scotland.

No doubt a serious coat was needed for this excursion. The North Sea ferries, including the one to Lewis, ran between March and October, but it was a risk to step on board in those bookend months, especially on the Irish Sea, which was always unpredictable. "It's calm enough—you'll be fine." Frank waved off my incurable seasickness.

"We still have two months until Beltane. Ancient people didn't sail until then." I could practically hear Frank rolling his eyes. "Don't discount them; they knew these seas better than we do," I protested. "And for the record, me being seasick is most certainly related to my genetic predisposition for vertigo, so there's not much I can do about it."

"Here. Lie down and close your eyes; I'll tell you when we're there." Frank handed me his balled-up The North Face jacket, opened a book, and gave me a reassuring pat on the head. "We'll be there in an hour and forty-five minutes."

As we stepped off the ferry, Frank lit a cigarette, and the slow pull and burn reminded me of the fire ritual we had been discussing in the car on the way up to the ferry departure point. It was a beautiful, winding road, full of the most dramatic vistas one could imagine, and it was all I could do to keep from throwing up on the myriad switchbacks, despite my overall enjoyment of the drive. The trick was being behind the wheel, but that was never something Frank would allow when it came to his precious refurbished 1994 classic Mini Cooper. He was most proud of it, however, because he had managed to squeeze it from an old lady who had had it for twenty-five years at the remarkable price of six hundred quid, which he liked to remind me of regularly. Anyway, it was nice to not have to pay for the rental car, and Frank had brought his Mini over on the ferry from Holyhead, Wales, that past Christmas when I had arrived. It made more sense for him to keep the car here in Northern Ireland since I had a house and he lived on a boat in London's canals.

"I have a house." That sentence still tripped up on my lips and was unbelievable, even though it had been over a year since Sully had told me he was leaving it to me. I had spoken those words out loud without realizing, and Frank gave me a bizarre look, shaking his head and laughing to himself at my random outburst of thoughts as we stood, awaiting the minibus that would arrive any minute to drive us up to the highest point on the island, the location of the stones. "Remember what you said in the car on the way here?" I asked, drifting back to our conversation from earlier.

"If you look at the wheel of the year, the eight pointed star of Celtic holidays and spirituality, now considered a neo-pagan symbol and largely denoting our own significant calendar dates in the Western world, half the festivals make up the X." I made a crossing motion on the dashboard with my hand, envisioning the top left corner of Samhain connecting down into the bottom right hand corner with Beltane and then from the top right corner of Imbolc down to the bottom left-hand corner of Lammas or Lughnasadh. "It's called a cross quarter," I continued, "while the others, the main solstices and equinoxes, form a cross," and on the dash and in my mind, I drew my finger straight down from the due north, Yule, the winter solstice, to due south, midsummer, and from east to west, the spring equinox, Oster, to the fall equinox, Mabon. I thought about how the most famous and prevalent image of a cross over an X might illuminate my point further: The Union Jack. "Everyone knows that the X on the flag of Scotland is meant to represent the crucifixion of Saint Andrew since he is the patron saint of the country, and of course the cross on England's flag is St. George's cross. Maybe it's not a coincidence but rather Christianity superimposed over Celtic paganism, and the Saint Andrew's Cross of Scotland is also the cross quarter part of the wheel of the year because Scottish monuments are aligned with those festivals, and English monuments are aligned with the solstices and equinoxes."

"I see what you mean by Christianity superimposed over paganism, the way Easter adopted the Ostara or Spring Equinox festival," Frank offered. "But what if it's not an act of assimilation or appropriation? I mean, what if they're truly trying to keep a part of the previous culture alive by intertwining the two?" Frank asked. "The creators of the country flags had to appeal to the crusaders with their saintly designs, but maybe they had a double meaning."

"Have you ever been to the lighting of the Tlatchga fires on Halloween in Ireland?" I asked. Frank laughed in response to the rhetorical question, which I knew the answer to. "There's this local man. Near Tara, but I'm not even sure where he's from. Maybe county Tyrone? He's not from Meath, I know that. Anyway, I think he comes south...or—"

"Yeah, yeah, yeah—get to it." Frank's patience with my dilatory way of explaining my revelations was waning. Some people simply didn't have his grasp on the human language, I often reminded him.

"Anyway, he lights it every year, still, this O'Riordan guy, to remember the fire festivals and the people who celebrated them. Do you think that's all it takes for a legacy to survive? One person to remember?"

"So as long as old O'Riordan is doing it, these people and their most important fire festival ritual, at the beginning of the new winter, remain alive?" Frank posited. I held my paper coffee cup with both hands, inhaling its warmth as deeply as possible.

"Well then, would you predict," I began as we pulled up to the station to grab the morning ferry out to the island, one of only two departures that day, "that this damn Irish ferry is leaving thirty minutes early?" I reached over and laid on the horn as Frank rolled down the window, waving his arms uselessly at the tiny boat on its merry way to the neighboring Scottish Isles.

I kicked the dash. "What are we supposed to do for three hours until the next one?"

"Pull up the timetable on your phone," Frank demanded. "We're here. We might as well walk over and see what it says on the board over there; maybe it will explain the early departure."

We strode over, and lo and behold, as Frank read, "Twelve thirty is the summer departure time when there are three crossings at nine, twelve thirty, and four. It's twelve and three in spring and fall. None in winter."

"Damn!" We both said together.

I said, "I'm barely going to have time on the island to get the information I need at the stone circle before sundown."

"Wishing you had some five-thousand-year-old boat technology right about now?" Frank asked.

"You have no idea," I responded. "Modern people are pretty helpless when it comes to stuff like this." I covered my face with both hands in despair.

"I could probably row a Viking long boat faster than the ferry," Frank added helpfully, then with more gusto went on, "Fancy a pint at the pub, then?"

"Yes," I responded with a huge sigh. "I'll pay this time."

"Bangers and mash too?" Frank asked.

"Bangers too," I affirmed, and we hiked off to the neighboring pub. I wasn't sure how much it would help my usual seasickness, but it seemed like a good idea.

Edie. What's that short for?" the bartender asked me in a local lilt as he cleaned glasses methodically. I turned from the conversation I was having with Frank, one in which he was apparently using my name enough for this friendly bartender to overhear.

"Edana," I answered, smiling. He looked stunned.

"What were you expecting—Edith or Edwina?" Frank asked.

The bartender blushed. "No, no. It's just very Irish. And I wasn't expecting *that*," he answered with a wink.

"I thought you were named after the character in *Kindred* because your mom was reading it when she was pregnant with you," Frank said.

"I was. But Edana is also the Irish word for 'fire,' Mr. Linguistics Expert," I answered.

"How appropriate," Frank replied, brandishing his lighter.

The bartender smiled and pointed to a nearby side door that Frank could slip out to have a smoke. "You should come to the Beltane fire we have in Donegal next month," the bartender said. He was probably ten years older than me, with piercing blue eyes and black hair. "Hello…Edana?" I had drifted into thought a moment too long.

"Edie," I replied and smiled back at him. "Um, I don't know about that."

"Well, you won't have to worry about the ferry timetables." He laughed, clearly referencing the conversations he had overheard in which Frank and had I tried to blame one another for who had misread the schedule.

"Will there be hawthorn bushes?" I asked, and he nodded.

"And I suppose I don't have to tell you when it is."

"Midnight on April thirtieth," I replied.

He winked at me in reply, and I was annoyed. Not at the overtly male gesture or apparent eye moisture problem he was developing. I was annoyed with myself for feeling something from it. But if I felt something from it, then the next thing really threw me for a loop. "You sure do know a ton about ancient Irish customs and folklore for a wee American girl."

I stared back at him, wanting to declare my worthiness, my full knowledge, but I held back. I thought about Sully and how he would be curious about such an accusation and not offended. I smiled, imperceptibly, and Frank entered the side door loudly, already in deep conversation with me, spilling the top of his Guinness, an Irish sin, and I was thankfully startled out of my feelings.

"Edie, how the hell are we going to prove that these stone monuments were a collective, interconnected series of monuments in the Neolithic if we have to depend on these damn unreliable ferries?" Michael, the bartender, raised his eyebrows, and to this Frank replied, "Present company excluded" and plopped down beside me.

"He is talking about *f-e-r-r-i-e-s*." I blushed.

"Aye, I know." Michael smiled.

"All I can do is present my theory and the data to support it; that's enough to have it considered, especially alongside the growing evidence of boat technology that allowed movement between the islands."

Michael was pretending not to listen now, but I felt him perk up at my confident reply. Then he was talking up another customer in my peripheral vision. *I suppose it's his job*, I thought.

"And if they were moving between the small Hebrides, why would they not move between the larger islands?" Frank asked, rhetorically. "And if they were taking time to build boats and sail from port to port, then what would keep them from going inland? Who is to say that the stonemasons from Orkney didn't visit the Stenness Circle on Lewis or the smaller circle on the Isle of Arran or even Stonehenge down south?"

"Precisely! They are the cohesion of a culture; these types of precise structures are virtually nonexistent outside of Britain and Brittany, just like the spiral symbols that sometimes adorn them and the passage tombs that came before."

"But aren't the stone circles all different ages? Like, Orkney and Callanish stones are hundreds of years older than Stonehenge in Southern England, and Stonehenge is hundreds of years older than some of the local ones here." Michael the bartender was back at it, but I had to admit I was impressed with his knowledge.

"You're right," I answered, "but I think that actually supports my theory." He raised his eyebrows again and slid another Guinness over to Frank, giving him a wink. "Monument culture dictates that the cultural center shifts through time and generations to new locations. This would explain moving stones from Wales to Salisbury Plain for Stonehenge or moving stones from the Wicklow Mountains for Newgrange, for example. They wanted to keep an aspect of the old monument, but the new one needed to function differently for their new needs and developing culture, so there were nuances to the stone circles, but they didn't completely abandon the older ones. They still held significance."

"Well, if you think this map of the henges will lead to a buried treasure, I'm here to help you, love," Michael said.

"What are you, a pirate?" Frank joked.

"Don't call me love," I added, and Frank covered his mouth in an effort not to laugh.

"I know the stones in the area well," Michael insisted. "Not just the henges, the passage tombs and Iron Age tombs as well."

"Oh," I said, a bit sheepishly.

"You could say I grew up wit' it. And yeah, the locals gravitate toward different monuments depending on which fire festival it is." I didn't know what to say.

Luckily, Frank stuck his hand out for a shake and said, "Then you're our man, Michael!"

"So I'll see yous in Donegal on Beltane, then?" he asked as the loud horn of the ferry blared from outside, and we reflexively grabbed our coats and bags.

"Maybe," I said as I wrapped my scarf around me twice and threw my bag over my shoulder. "Thanks for the tip!" I called.

"A ferry waits for no man," Frank said as he guzzled his remaining Guinness, slammed it down, and ran after me.

CHAPTER 11:

PEARLS AND OYSTERS

Ailsa

I swept the floor of the roundhouse, humming a tune that had been in my head for what seemed like weeks. Grandmother's figure darkened the door. She came in to add peat to the fire and seemed to be busying herself with anything to avoid eye contact. Finally, after what seemed like an eternity, she sat on the furs by the hearth. Wordlessly, she beckoned me to join her. I picked up her comb from the table and sat behind her, silently stroking the long silver and black locks, holding the fragile ends between my pointer and middle fingers. To brush someone's hair is such an intimate act. Grandmother always said it eased the mind, bringing truths to the surface.

I was the first to break the silence, nodding toward the fire that I had stoked. "I've covered the fish in clay to bake for dinner tonight and have quite a few oysters to go along with it. I thought I could make some barley cakes too. I've been soaking the oats."

I gathered Grandmother's hair up, separating it to plait it down from the crown of her head. Before I could begin, grandmother's hand reached around and grabbed my fleshy white fingers between her sun-browned, strong, knobbed ones. "I know" is what the pressure into my palm said. My heart thumped hard in my chest, and I was sure she could hear it.

I smiled, and then returned my hands to the work of plaiting. I looked over Grandmother's shoulder into her lap, where she was tracing symbols on her left palm with her right pointer finger, as she often did in contemplative moments. I finished the braid and wound it around the old woman's head into a spiral shape, which she fastened with the mother-of-pearl combs she had been holding in her pocket. I watched as her stiff hands, fingers swollen at every joint, deftly smoothed her hair and found the exact places where she always fastened her hair with the combs. I had never known her to not wear them, cherish them even, and all of a sudden, I wondered for the first time in my life where she had gotten them. They seemed too exotic to be from this village.

My throat felt thick, and my eyes burned with tears. I seldom cried, but I felt the unusual feeling of fighting tears back that had become too typical these days. I had not kept anything secret from Grandmother since my father passed away, and the need to share the news that Ros not only had finally returned my love but that we had consummated it and made promises to each other bubbled up in me uncontrollably. No one could forgive the betrayal against Aric except Grandmother, not even me. And perhaps that was what I needed the most from her: absolution from someone who loved me unconditionally. Older people always had a way of explaining the emotions of younger people in terms that made them seem fleeting and unimportant. I needed to feel insignificant for a moment after months of being pulled back and forth, between lovers and between my duties as wife and Druid.

As a Druid, I had learned to separate myself from the earthly sways of emotion that normally plagued people my age. I was meant to be aligned with nature and manifest calm in the face of all the problems in the world. In fact, that was also my duty as a Druid, to remain in aligned peace and inspire it in other people, to regulate the nervous system of my people. Here, at Grandmother's hearth, I sought that which I was meant to give: peace and absolution. Sometimes grandmothers are more magical than Druids.

"I see him torture himself daily with cycles of pain and glee," Grandmother said as she looked up, tapping the pads of her fingers together simultaneously.

"Who?" I asked, eyes wide.

"Why, the husband of your heart, my child," she responded as she turned toward me, holding me there by the warming fire. "I know there is only one thing that could bring him so much simultaneous happiness and pain."

I nodded, gathering my thoughts. "How do you see him so well?" I asked.

Grandmother bent forward toward the hearth, peering into the clay cauldron that boiled the day's water. Still mostly full, it hadn't yet reached a rolling boil again after I had let the fire die down through the day's chores.

"I see him because he is like still water, Ailsa. Like the lake to the south, where the birds gather in winter. He casts a perfect reflection of himself in his stillness for anyone to see who pays enough attention. Yours is the heart none of us can truly see."

My eyes brimmed with tears, and as the cauldron began to boil over, I felt myself do the same. I kicked a bit of dust into the fire and wiped my tears.

"Oh, my darling Ailsa." Grandmother took both my hands now. "You can't run away from unhappiness. It will chase you, as it chased your father, so you have to face it down." I shook my head at the impossibility, and she touched her forehead to mine. "I did so when I lost your mother and your grandfather. Though I wanted to run many times."

"Why am I the Druid and not you, Grandmother?"

"Because Jord was my able Druid brother, of course. He deserved it as much as me, but we couldn't both do it."

"But you're so wise, and you've become renowned for your healing. Didn't you want to challenge Jord for the right to your destiny?" I asked.

My grandmother laughed and reached into the fire bare-handed, offering me a bowl of oysters before unwrapping the fish we had baked in the embers. "No," she answered simply. "Because as much I could see myself as a Druid, I didn't love that picture of my destiny as much as I loved Jord. He's my little brother, and I cherish him. I only wish you could have known a love like that."

"I suppose that Ros's sisters are the closest thing I've had to siblings. But when you have a real little brother or sister, I imagine seeing them radiantly happy is almost like having the feeling yourself." My mouth began to water from the smell of the fish, and I unwrapped it, saving my favorite, the oysters, for last.

"Well," Grandmother began, sifting cautiously through her fish as well but searching for words more than bones, "Jord and Ray were born days apart and grew up together. It was known from a very early age, because of some...*happenings* at the stones, that Ray would become the head Druid. It was meant for him, and he has fulfilled that destiny beautifully." I narrowed my eyes at grandmother as she hesitantly spoke, waiting for further explanation. "Jord and Ray were perfect complements to each other from a young age, so Jord became second to Ray when Ray became head Druid, and together they have helped to encourage more peace and acceptance in the village. Before you were born, outsiders like your father were looked down upon. But Ray and Jord have a natural ease and acceptance about them. They see how we are alike more than we are different. And of course, adopting Aric when he washed ashore from his ship deepened Ray's affection for outsiders considerably."

I thought of my tall, worrisome reed of an uncle and the short stump of utter blissfulness that was Ray. They were quite a pair, and it made me smile to think that they had made a difference in their time leading the Druids. "All I can hope for you is that you have a husband who complements you and your vision for a better world." She smiled at me from across the fire, her eyes glistening in the light.

I ignored her assumption that I had such a vision and instead narrowed my eyes and tilted my head at her suspiciously. "Did Grandfather give you those hair combs, Grandmother?" I asked.

Grandmother's mouth was filled with fish. She chewed slowly and responded carefully, "I trust you will figure out who the right man for you is, my dear. But as for me, I absolutely found my happiness with your grandfather and with my herbs." She gestured above her to the strings of dozens of herbs hanging together in over twenty bunches all over her ceiling. Along the wall were grooved pots and querns full of herbs for grinding, and by the doorway, the only source of natural light, were dozens of tiny clay pots and vials filled with herbal tinctures. She was a true medicine woman.

"Being able to wield my medicines and herbs without the heavy burden of wearing the Druid cloth gave me freedom to travel, heal, and earn renown for my talents. I know you don't remember, but before you were born, I often sailed to the mainland or went to many of the neighboring islands to help the sick and learn from distant healers, as well as share some of my medicinal tricks and knowledge. In some places there were herbs and flowers I had never seen here, and it was quite an education." Her eyes grew misty and settled on something far away, beyond the dark room in which we sat.

"Is that where the combs are from?" I asked, already knowing the answer.

"A woman's heart is full of secrets, Ailsa," she said. "And that is how it should be."

I nodded and, looking down into my bowl, began to open up the oysters that were peeking out from their shells with the knife I kept tucked in my pocket.

"For a time, I believed I could find something that would help your mother with bearing children." She waved a dismissive hand in front of her face and clicked her tongue in disapproval. "But that turned out how it was meant to in the end, and there was nothing I could do." She said this more to reassure herself than me, while reaching out to stroke my cheek with her wrinkled hand, gnarled from decades of precision labor.

"To be a Druid is a great responsibility to your people, Ailsa, but I know that is not lost on you. In the end, I am happy, so is your Uncle Jord, and so you will be, too, when you accept and align your purpose." She leaned over and kissed my forehead, smelling of salt water from the oysters and smoke from the fire. I clasped the smooth wooden bowl of oysters, looking down at the six I had opened, tucked neatly into their shells.

"Sometimes you hope for pearls but settle for a fat, juicy oyster, right, Grandmother?" I giggled to myself a bit as Grandmother dumped her empty oyster shells into the boiling pot to clean them for their next use. Sometimes she used them to hold tiny amounts of crushed stamen or fish eyes. She smiled the sly smile that crinkled her cat-eyes and showed the round apples of her cheeks. She could look like laughter without making a sound.

"Well, their effects as an aphrodisiac were well tested in my experiments as a young medicine woman," she said before sipping her tea, and then we both laughed until our sides ached.

Rasha danced barefoot over the pebbles of the river bed and looked more elegant than a waterbird, gliding on the surface. There were places where the great river was deep and strong, where the currents rushed against giant boulders, flowing heavily over falls that could catch young bathers unaware and toss them dangerously. Just as there were powerful swells, there were streams that gave way to small eddies and lees that lapped gently and barely covered your ankles. That's where I found Rasha, Ros's sister. It was by mistake, really. I was out at midday picking herbs, when the sun was hottest and thus the oils were most potent on some medicinals, like grandmother had taught me. The nettles and lemon balm often meandered around the riverbeds, and it was true what father had always said, coming from a seafaring people, that all life draws closer to the water. I saw Rasha before she saw me and couldn't help but feel like a voyeur watching her water-dance in flowing white wool draped over her broad and pointed shoulders. It was not yet Imbolc, and there were still spots where the river was freezing, if not frozen solid. I knew exactly how stinging cold the water felt on her ankles.

Rasha would be seventeen soon, and while she had been dancing in the Druid rituals for four years, this summer solstice would be her first as leader of the dance. It was what she was born to be, clear from her long, lean torso; pointed toes; and long, angular nose and jawbone. Her features were all so pointed, which made her graceful movement even more captivating because of the way it was perfectly punctuated. Ros's mother was a dancer too and had the same broad, angular shoulders Rasha had.

When they weren't busy with the day's chores and farming, they gathered with the other dancers of the village to practice and teach the younger girls the dance of the Druids. Of course, over the years, Ros had snuck up from boat building with his father to watch his mother and sister and had been caught absconding with several different dancers, in various places, including in a boat he was building, and his indiscretion had led to him being banned from dance practice by his mother. I shook my head at the thought of Ros's past impetuousness, lost in a labyrinth of such thoughts at the moment Rasha called to me.

"Many blessings, Sister Ailsa." Rasha smiled and seemed to float over to me, out of the shallows of the cool water. Rasha was the only woman in the village taller than me and was thus taller than her older brother as well. She rested her hand on my shoulder, and it felt as light as air, like her bones were hollow as a bird's. "You look so beautiful today," she said, her thin lips pressed together in the slightest of smiles. "But what were you just thinking of? You look perplexed."

"That's funny, I was just thinking the same thing about you," I replied, laughing uneasily. "The beautiful part, not the perplexing one." She waited a moment for me to answer her question, but of course I did not.

"I remember when your father used to call you 'little dark one,'" Rasha continued. "Such beautiful black hair." She reached out and pulled a feather, light and fluffy as goose down, from my thick braid. "You are him to the life!" she smiled. "Now, what did you come to the river for?" she asked pointedly, though still smiling.

"I suppose I was hoping to—" I cut myself off and opened the pocket tied round my waist and revealed to her the mass of water herbs I'd been collecting. Rasha's long, skinny arm dipped into it like a lightning bolt before I could close it up. She rolled the delicate stem of the tansy flower and carrot seeds between her forefinger and thumb. She smelled it, smiled, and handed it back, saying nothing but speaking loudly enough through her piercing blue eyes, which were so much like her brother's. I cleared my voice and said, "I suppose maybe I wanted to find you," taking the flower back and dropping it into the pile in my large pocket bag.

"Ahh, how's wedded bliss, then?" Rasha joked. "I haven't seen you as much this last year." She raised her eyebrows.

"I think you probably know it's not going so well." My vulnerability jumped out of its hiding place like my herbs, and I looked up, directly into Rasha's river-blue eyes. It had been over a year since my marriage to Aric, and it would certainly be strange to Rasha that I was carrying the seeds that women, at least those knowledgeable enough in the arts of herbal medicine, would carry to protect themselves from pregnancy.

"Mmhmm," Rasha almost hummed, "and what else do I know?" She smiled at me, the friend—the surrogate sister—she had known since birth. "I'll tell you what I know. I know my brother has always left the roundhouse, wandering late at night—since he has been a teenager." She paused for effect and shook the remaining ice-cold river water from her legs, wiping and warming them with her long blue cloak.

"I know it was often to meet girls in the moonlight. It's his nature to be cunning in this way, but you know that better than anyone else, I think." The last comment fell to the pit of my stomach like a stone to the bottom of the river.

"I'm not just another girl to him. We're in love," I said.

Rasha bent down to retrieve her dark-blue wool cloak, wrapping it in one graceful swoop around her tall, razor's edge shoulders. As she secured it at her clavicle with a deft knot, she spoke gently.

"I won't ever tell your secret, Ailsa. But as someone who will soon be involved in ritual ceremonies as well, I'd advise you to be wary of using your Druid meetings as your cover. Perhaps the gods don't want to be mixed up in your earthly caper with my brother." She raised her eyebrows at me, and I stepped toward her to speak quieter. Even the trees listen, sometimes.

"Of everyone in the world, I would think you would be most excited about the prospect of Ros and I finally being happy together, Rasha."

At this, she turned her sharply angled chin at me. "How could he ever be happy like *this*, Ailsa? True love can't be a secret. It can't come second."

"I'm learning great lessons about the nature of true love and the intertwining of courage and vulnerability, and it's not that simple," I answered.

She sighed miserably. "I pray that my brother does not pay for these lessons of yours," she said as she began to follow the light out of the deep wood, where she would pass through the lighter woods and eventually into the clearing where our houses lay, having stood next to each other for generations.

"Rasha, come back!" I called after her. "I won't be blamed for my lies as well as his."

She turned around, and her voice, now risen above a whisper to reach me, had lost all of its sweetness and become almost shrill, like a broad-winged hawk's.

"Ailsa, it's not that I blame you. I just expect more from you than I do from Ros."

"He lied to me for so long," I cried out. "For years, I didn't know his true feelings. Not until I was betrothed to another."

"I know," she said simply, walking back toward me with a sympathetic smile. "But I also know more than a few women who, like me, would feel a tremendous amount of sympathy for Aric." A tiny grin flashed across Rasha's narrow face, and I could tell she meant well as she continued, "Aric lost his first wife at seventeen, and if he loses his second wife to my ignorant, selfish brother, then he will have no one's sympathy more than mine."

We had been so small we barely remembered her, but it had taken him twelve years and many foreign conquests to remarry, this time not for love, I thought, but for honor. I thought about it at night, lying next to him, that maybe that's what he wanted—to be interlocked with someone who would not love him so he didn't have to give that part of himself away again. He needed someone who could solidify his place in this village that he had inhabited as on of the only Norseman. With me, he could go on loving his first wife without interruption or insult to his devotion. Maybe all that was true, or maybe it just made me feel justified in my own actions. This is what we do as humans. We justify our worst actions and impulses because we have to in order to press onward and start each new day.

"Iona," I said with tears in my eyes.

Rasha looked at me, questioning, and sympathetically brushed the hair from my face. Afraid to press further into the delicate territory of my marriage, she changed the subject abruptly, though to something still quite topical. "Ros and I are supposed to meet with twins from the outer islands to negotiate our marriages at the next full moon."

My heart felt like it was in my throat again. Not necessarily because this information was a surprise but because I was finding out from Rasha instead of Ros. "The snow moon," I said.

"Yes, Berk and Onda," Rasha replied. "You may know them from your cousin's village. It's a good match, and they've agreed to sail here to build homes."

"Ros didn't tell me, of course." I scoffed, blowing loudly out of my nostrils like a bull. My hand moved from a frustrated position on my hip to pinch the bridge of my nose in disgust and finally to that place of calming, the back of the hand placed flat on my forehead. "Sometimes I have to remind myself that I'm risking it all for true love, and that ideal is greater than the flawed manifestation of it in the reckless form of your brother." I moved as if to walk away, before Rasha, in a storm of white and gray skirts, swirled around me, blocking my path like a funnel cloud. "I mean, congratulations." I smiled, pitifully.

"He's risking his neck too, Ailsa, and the difference is terrifying to me because, you see, you're actually afraid of losing yours." She drew her bony forefinger along her long, long white goose neck slowly in a symbolic representation of beheading. "But Ros has nothing to lose; he's not afraid of dying for you, so I'm scared of what he might do."

I squeezed Rasha's hand. I knew she was right because of what Ros had said at the cliffs. I looked up at the violet sky, where a faded half-moon was beginning to rise.

She pulled me to her in an embrace. "Maybe it just wasn't meant to be." Rasha was the closest thing I had to a sister growing up, and I knew in my heart she was trying to help, but the concept that Ros's birth had saved my life, that we had been fed and weaned together and grown up as best friends but were not "meant to be," just felt wrong in my gut. She pulled away, holding me by the shoulders, looking down into my eyes.

"My prayer is that this experience will teach you to embrace your femininity, Ailsa. The Druids push you toward androgyny because it feels more comfortable to them for you to embody both sexes, but there is power in your womanhood that needs to be wielded. That's where the power in the dance comes from, and this is the reason that only women can lead it. Our power is sacral, from our wombs, and gives birth to all other power there is." She gestured toward my middle, as if to illustrate.

"I find it nearly impossible to balance my earthly desires as a woman with the spiritual way in which I'm supposed to conduct myself. I fear I'm spinning out of control."

"Nonsense!" Rasha said, eyes wide. "You can be a Druid priest, you can live half your time in a spiritual trance, and you can be in love with the *worst* womanizer on the island, my brother, whom only I could love better than you." She paused for a small intake of air. "*And* you can still be the most powerful woman the village has ever known." She brought her left hand down into a fist and placed it over her lower abdomen. "We contain multitudes. Our impulses are so much more than good or evil. The future is entirely within us." I nodded. I believed the future was within me, but I couldn't see clearly what it held.

Rasha reached deep into her own pocket, which was hanging around the cloud-white wool of her dress, underneath her indigo cloak, and produced what appeared to be a small stone. She placed it lightly in my hand, wrapping her impossibly long fingers around mine to signify the moment, the prayer, and the gift.

"It's a black pearl. It's rare and beautiful like you." She smiled and continued, "The oyster makes the pearl when something wrong, something foreign or dangerous, penetrates its shell. The pearl itself is actually a protective coating, but what's at the core of the outer beauty is the inner disturbance, which made the beautiful thing in the first place."

A tear dropped from the corner of my eye, into the palm of my hand, sealing the gift exchange in sacred water. "Am I the pearl or the disturbance?" I asked.

"You're both," Rasha answered. "If a freshwater oyster can do the hard work to make a pearl out of sand in just a year, what could you do during the wheel of the year, Ailsa?"

In a flurry of skirts and naked feet prancing over slick stones, she was gone.

"Why does everyone seem wiser and more fit to be a Druid than me today?" I laughed out loud and asked the silence of the late-winter wood.

The woods, through which the river ran, were just north of the village. The waters came down from the peaks in the north, cascading in various waterfalls, until they calmed and quieted, broadening through the village on the eastern side. Another river ran into the sea on the western side, but it was brackish and full of fish, surrounded by bogs and tall grasses. This river by the village was powerful and peaceful at once, glittering with hidden gems like my black pearl that peeked through the river rocks underneath. The sounds it made, from the rhythmic tripping of water over rocks to roaring cascades, created a comfortable silence when one entered the woods. It made it easy to drown out conversations like the one Rasha and I had just had. The colors were vivid and calming, cool blue-gray in the shade of the woods with moss-green rocks jutting out in perfect intervals.

I particularly loved this spot of the river that ran just by the oak grove. Here, everything became euphonious, a hushed susurrus of the wind in the leaves of the trees, the noise of the world drowned out by birdsong, chipmunk chatter, and river whispers. I suppose that's why the festival dancing must have originated here; there was a certain musicality so the dancers could practice without Druid drums. It's also why I was drawn to this spot for the herbs that day.

"Since when does Rasha have all the answers?" I said out loud but suddenly had that uncomfortable feeling of being watched. Instantly, my mind grappled with embarrassment and moved to defend itself. *Had someone heard our conversation? Could it get back to Aric?* I was reaching for a response in my mind when I realized the animation of the noise was right in front of me, on the opposite bank of the river, camouflaged by the brown and roan layers of dead leaves blanketing the ground. I held my breath in my chest, watching the heartbreaking wobble of the tiny fawn's spindly legs, which seemed to vanish up into her giant golden-brown eyes.

"Oh, well you're a beauty, aren't ye?" I asked in a soothing voice, automatically reaching out my hand, extending my arm across the river, wading in ankle-deep without lifting my robes, slowly, patiently, desperate to make contact with this most innocent creature. I noticed the white spots standing out from the tan pelt, all her marks of youthfulness.

"You're born too early, like me, wee one. It'll be too cold for ye for two moons still." The fawn continued to stare at me, piercing my heart. It gave only the faintest of head movements to confirm that it studied me too, but she dared not move or walk to reveal her weakness, let alone fall. No, not weakness, I corrected myself. Just *newness. Yes, that's like me too.* New to the Druidic Order, new to marriage, new to it all. Yet this spot was a good place to practice prancing, the gentle leaves breaking her falls and cool, clean water to quench her thirst, and I suddenly saw in her the desire to frolic.

"Where's your mother?" I asked. "She must be working hard to keep you warm since you came before spring." I found myself reassuring her that there were plenty of mosses and winter herbs around the river this time of year. They would be fine as long as they stood clear of the predators and bedded down for the upcoming snow moon. I suppose that's why it was important for the little fawn to practice her prancing.

After several minutes, I realized that I was frozen in place, having waded ankle deep into the river, arm extended, eyes fixed on the fawn who was equally frozen. How long had we stood like this, analyzing one another, lost in one another's dark eyes? I flinched first, huffing as I realized that my ankles and feet were numb from the winter river. Slowly, I stepped back to my side of the riverbank, grasping a rock so I didn't fall over for lack of feeling in my feet. I removed the fur from my cloak and wrapped my feet, patting them dry and rubbing them for warmth. A quick movement in the periphery of my vision caught my attention, and I looked up to see that the fawn had vanished, replaced now by a giant red stag, dark auburn and furry, red eyed with towering antlers, at the peak of their size and about to be shed so they would grow strong and pointed again by mating season in October.

Startled, I backed up on hands and feet like a crab, resting against a hazel tree and flattening myself to look as harmless as possible. I had expected to see a doe, but the appearance of the sire surprised and frightened me a bit. He stared me down until I felt my heart start to race, and then a motion from behind his right shoulder pulled both our attentions away. The fawn pranced off into the distance, lifting herself perfectly into the air like she might take flight. The sight was dazzling, and I couldn't help but laugh at the tiny thing's sudden strength. Together we watched the fawn prancing off through the dark wood, where the hazels and oaks gave way to thicker walls of firs and pines, their evergreen needles still bright, offering shelter in the cold. Then the stag turned back to take one last look at me, to measure up the threat I posed, before he followed his young into the setting sun that shone in shafts of golden light through the thick fir trees in the distance.

I finally let out a deep breath and rose to my feet, which now had feeling restored to them. In fact, my whole body seemed to be buzzing. I wrapped the black fur around the shoulders of my green cloak and buried my cold, pale fingers into it, shivering with the frost and my thoughts. I brought my fingers to my lips, blowing warm air into them and wiggling them around as a thought occurred to me. "Born too early, but she'll be fine because she has a good sire." I lost sight of the stag in the woods and turned north toward the oak grove. "I know you are here with me, Father." I whispered into the swirling wind as it lifted the tail of my cloak and seemed to sweep me off my feet and push me gently toward the oak grove. "Time now for Druid things." I told him. Nature conspires for us all to end up where we belong, I thought as I rubbed the dark pearl in my pocket.

CHAPTER 12:

GUNNHILD

Aric

Eighteen years earlier

The sky was red and swollen, as if it might burst. Every sailor on the ship noticed, but no one mentioned it. It was bad luck to count blessings before they were in hand, and sailors, especially Norse sailors, were always superstitious. Aric stood at the mast, wind blowing through his dark hair. Not all Norseman were blond, especially the ancient ones, who developed seafaring boat technology and visited other lands. Aric's father's people were as dark as the southerners who sailed their ships from the Iberian coasts. Aric had never met an Iberian, but his father had on his sailing adventures to the southern isles. In fact, Aric, his father, and their men were going to settle the northern tip of the green isles called Eireland as his father knew there were already Iberians in the southwest there and that they would be friendly and useful for trade.

As if conjuring him through thought, Aric suddenly felt the presence of his father behind his shoulder. He turned away from the sea and looked up into the large, lined face, dark as leather from years on the open seas and creased with concern. That was the only way he could think of him—plus those formidable scars and a tan that matched his cowhide breastplate. Tonight there was a frown on his father's large mouth. Aric thought he looked like a shunned dog given no supper, and he smiled. His father was called Aric too.

"What are you daydreaming about up here, Aric?" His voice vibrated in a deep baritone; the timbre was so low it hummed, beautifully, in his throat, which didn't have room for the acoustics of such a sound. You could feel his voice before you heard it.

"I was just wishing that we were exploring a new land and discovering something no one had ever laid eyes on before. I want to meet the greatest warriors from other lands and their priests, too."

His father interrupted him with a deep, rolling laugh, like thunder. "I'm not sure places exist like that anymore, Son. I'm not convinced there is a land that hasn't been discovered." They turned, both looking out at the horizon now.

"But there are places *we* haven't seen!" young Aric chimed in.

The older Aric nodded and lifted his hands in animation of vision. "That's true. I've heard that Eireland is the greenest, most lush land you can imagine and that the hills roll on and on for days. The cliffs fall straight into the ocean, and in summer the sun shines and the rain falls and the crops grow insatiably."

"Will you farm once we are settled, Father?"

Aric had never known his father to farm. In all his twelve years of life, his father had been moving and exploring, leading his people to new, more prosperous land. Aric had stayed at home with his mother and sisters, amid a generally safe and happy childhood, but no happiness touched the feeling of the moments when his family was all together, snuggled up for long dinners, stories, and music at the long table of their longhouse.

"Maybe so," Aric's father answered. "But you will farm and build a nice home for yourself with a beautiful woman to wed. And bed." He smiled. His voice sounded less certain and a little wistful, his son thought.

"It's important not only to discover new places and gain land-holdings but to sew ourselves into the land through marriage and children. That way we leave a piece of ourselves everywhere, and we all become kings through the generations."

Young Aric furrowed his brow, creating a deep crease in his forehead to match his father's. "What am I, a woman? I'm to be mar-ried off and traded like chattel to make a good relationship with the local warlords? I don't ever want to be married, Father; I just want to stay with you forever." His father laughed again, this time with less ardor, and tousled his boy's hair playfully.

Young Aric looked up at him through thick, dark lashes and navy-blue eyes, the only echo of his mother. He was hurt, and that looked like anger on the boy who would soon be a man. "You're trying to get rid of me?" It wasn't worth the fight. The older Aric was too tired from weeks on the water and the prepubescent rage heaped on him by his only living child. As he turned to walk back to one of the rower's seats, his son continued to gaze out into the ocean, with no acknowledging farewell. Then he heard the boy's voice barely raised against the wind.

"Mother wanted me to be a warrior king." It was spoken with such pitiful earnestness that Aric's father realized only a twelve-year-old boy could possibly believe such a ridiculous claim.

"Hear me and remember this, boy," his father said, sharply.

Young Aric turned around from the bow, unable to ignore the urgency of his father's voice. The wind whipped at his hair, which fell just over his ears and nearly covered his eyes. He wore his best linen shirt, a leather vest, and his grandfather's obsidian knife around his hip, slung low in a leather belt. The sunset behind him was radiant and full of colors that had no name. The clouds were large and fluffy and looked like giant ships themselves, headed for the horizon. It was devastatingly beautiful, and his father knew it was the way he would always remember his son, so he paused for a moment to take in the exquisite scene. Purple, blue, orange, red, and everything in between.

Aric was large for twelve, like his father had been and his father before him, but his face was a boy's, innocent. His eyebrows touched each other in the center of his perfectly symmetrical face, and his bottom lip quivered. This, paired with the dreamlike scenery, made his father feel like he might cry for the first time since his young, radiant, clever, and kind wife had died five years before.

"Listen, Son," he said more gently, "all she wanted you to do was to *live*. Live through these turbulent times and live life every day with a wife you love as much I love her. That's what she told me when she knew she was dying." A single tear fell from the boy's eye. "And Aric, my son," he continued, "we will see her again if we remain strong and good."

He laid his hands on the boy's shoulders, and they sailed off under the giant clouds, dotted with evening stars and a silver moon. They didn't say a word; they just stood there in this warrior man's embrace that was close enough to the maternal hug that the twelve-year-old desperately needed. The sky eventually faded to deeper purples and indigo. Aric's eyes felt heavy, and he leaned his head against his father's chest, feeling the steady rise and fall and the husky intake of breath and low hum of his voice reaching for some tune. What was it? A lullaby his mother used to sing to him, he thought. He couldn't ever remember his father singing it, but just for a moment, he felt wrapped up in Gunnhild's arms once again.

Then, he was transported to her lap. Her warm, scratchy, wool dress itching his face and the impossibly smooth skin of her neck and face smelling of breast milk and honey, her breath sweet with beer, and her soft, springy, goldenrod hair falling around him like curtains. He leaned into his large father for just a moment more and took a long, deep breath, feeling his strength and smelling the smoke of fires and fish on his clothes, the rough feel of leather and sun-aged skin, the black wiry hairs on his huge forearms, and the soft reverberation of the lullaby in his chest. This is how he would remember him.

Aric lay on the rock, feeling the lap of the water beneath him. The heat of the sun-warmed stone permeated his torn, seawater-soaked clothes, and he focused on the tiny ball of fire he could still feel burning within him, stoked by the warm stone and the feeling of the sun on his back. He wondered how he had managed to pull himself out of the water. He could tell from the roar of crashing waves around him that he had reached shallows near the beach, but he had no strength to move from his rock or even roll over on his side to take in his surroundings. He just stared down at the gray pattern of the rock and noticed how it was silver in the sunlight in places, almost like liquid, it was so smooth and shiny. *Odd*, he thought as he forced himself to swallow, his dry throat working as hard as it could to lubricate itself. Consciousness was fading, and he was afraid, but not for long.

A calmness came over him as he closed his eyes, and he saw his mother's face, young, thin, and pale, too beautiful for this world. Her jaw had been strong and her chin square, but the masculinity of the shape had been softened by the most delicate pair of pink lips, which widened into a broad smile that created deep creases in either side of her face and opened as wide as a songbird's beak to belt out even more beautiful songs. She sounded celestial. She was singing the song his father had been singing to him before the storm came.

His mind rejected that thought, and he quickly focused on his mother again—her long nose, which he used to run his pointer finger down, gently, soothing himself, as she rocked and fed him. Her blue-green eyes were large across her face but narrow and slightly turned down at the ends, like his own. And they were thickly lined with auburn lashes that lightened to blond at the tips and matched her fine and fair brow. Aric started to slip from his thoughts into a numbing peace.

To stake a hold on some sort of conscious thought, he pictured her curly hair, soft as feathers and springy to the touch. He could never quite describe the color. What was it? Not golden, nor yet red. It was something rosy in between that he had never seen since. It was like the sunset, he realized. That's why she had come to him on the ship's bow as he watched the sun go down the night before. It was the color of the golden hour. The vermillion bleeding into the gold of the sun and azure of the sky created colors that had no name.

Aric cried at the loss of her and the pain of failing to live, her last wish, but he was so dehydrated that no tears came. In his mourning she comforted him, and he felt her arms cradle him as if he were a babe again. She told him she was there to protect him. Aric shook his head, feeling like he was hallucinating his mother's presence, but it felt increasingly real. He couldn't tell if it was a part of him speaking from deep within him or if it was really her spirit, come down from Valhalla. She said that love stretched across time and death, and a mother could always pour her love down into her children, no matter what. He nestled into her chest, feeling the ridges of her clavicle and the softness of her pale, supple skin and breast. Being with her again, one last time, felt so good that he decided to let go and go with her, and just then he felt as if he were being lifted by strong, stout arms.

Aric sat by a fire in a huge cave across from a small man. Aric was just twelve but could tell he was much larger even as they sat together, hunched by the fire, both holding their legs, folded into their chests, like distant reflections of one another. The size realization made Aric feel safer because he knew he was stronger if he had to fight. Somehow that didn't seem likely. The man had given him water and nursed him back to consciousness by the fire. Aric was wrapped in the small man's cloak.

Though this man couldn't have been much older than his father, there was a way about him that seemed ancient. He wore nothing but a hide tunic; Aric realized that was probably because he had given him his cloak, a beautiful deep green. He wore furry boots Aric had never seen before and a leather pocket full of what smelled like a variety of healing herbs and tonics. He spoke to Aric in the Norse tongue, and he was clearly learned or well-traveled because he was almost positively not Norse. Aric spoke back to him in the broken language his father had begun to teach him when they were preparing to settle the green isles.

"I am Ray," the little man said, his lips curling into the most charming smile Aric had ever seen. "I am a Druid, and I will take care of you here in the king's cave before we find you another boat in the village." Aric nodded in understanding. "You sing quite beautifully," Ray said to him. "You were singing softly but with such passion as I carried you into the king's cave after you came back to life."

Ray began to gut a fish, and the smell filled Aric's nostrils. *What did this little man mean after I came back to life?* he thought.

"My mother," Aric tried to reply in the Gaelic tongue. "She would sing down in the hall, and it filled the longhouse to the roof tree. They were all in love with her as much as her song. I remember many a night falling asleep to the sound of her voice telling the oldest stories known to men."

"Ahhh, I've actually heard the song you were singing before. In another longhouse, some time ago." Ray smiled like a toad again, and though Aric felt safe and at ease with him, he knew at once that the little man was hiding something behind that smile.

"You speak the Norse tongue well; I can tell you are well-traveled," Aric responded.

"Yes." The little man smiled again.

"Why is it called the king's cave?" Aric asked, craning his neck to look above and around at the vast caverns and their carvings.

"Good question," the little man answered as he covered the salmon with gentle, deft hands and placed it on a smooth stone in the center of the fire. From the fire, he grabbed a torch, and Aric marveled at how the heat didn't seem to burn his hands. "I guess it *will* be called the king's cave. Right now it's just a special, spiritual place where we come to ask for blessings." He held the torch up, and the light on the wall showed hundreds of carvings from floor to ceiling, some meters high. Aric's eyes widened, and he noticed the little man casting a massive shadow on the carving wall. Maybe these Druids he had heard of were magical after all, he thought.

The little man gestured upward at the carvings. Some were animals—birds, horses, and fish—while others seemed to be more like symbols or some sort of writing Aric had never seen. The little man talked for a long time about the art and had funny stories for some of the scenes. Aric half listened while fighting distraction from his own fear and exhaustion. What would he do now, he wondered. An orphan, alone in the world.

"What do you think it all means?" Aric asked, eyes wide, scanning the many pictures and looking for something that reminded him of ones he had seen at home.

"You, my boy, are full of good and interesting questions. I see you come not only with a body fit for fighting but also with an inquisitive spirit."

Aric just stared back at him, a little confused but mostly detached as he was starting to let the magnitude of what had happened rest heavily on his shoulders. He hadn't been able to think of the loss of the ship: the image of his father drifting off to sea when he was fighting the current and grabbing onto the boards from the hull floating by him. Aric had been solely focused on his own survival because of what his father had told him just before the storm set in. Because that was what his mother wanted. The little man saw the pain in the boy's eyes from across the fire and came over to sit next to him and offer him all he had: a little bit of kindness and a lot of fish.

"I think what it all means is that people have been coming to this cave because it's special for a long, long time," Ray began as he removed the fish from the fire and sliced it open with his flint knife.

Aric noticed the blade was held in place by a whale bone handle carved at the end into a spiral form. It was not the most magnificent one he had seen, but it reminded him of one his father had carried that looked like a wolf carved into the antler of an elk.

The salmon was as large as the little man's entire forearm, and he took one cheek and one small filet for himself before gingerly setting the rest on the stone in front of Aric. "And I think it also means that people will keep coming to the cave to pray or chant, hide or hope, for a long time after we're all gone." Ray motioned to himself and the carved and painted walls around them. Aric devoured his salmon flank, careful of the thin bones as he always was at home when he and his father caught salmon in their icy Nordic rivers. He thought for a bit and sucked the fatty juice off each finger.

"Is that what you meant when you said it *will* be called the king's cave?" he asked as he savored the last of the warm, fleshy pink fish. He felt the beady, dark brown frog eyes of the little man piercing down into him. Suddenly, he felt uncomfortable—not afraid but as if he was being sized up or assessed. Then the man spoke in gentle tones, now in the Norse language so Aric understood perfectly.

"Nothing evades you, does it, Aric?" Aric shook his head back and forth, staring up at him. "You're wise," Ray continued, holding up his knife. "And your mind is like the fine point of a blade." The firelight glowed off his flint dagger and sparkled in his eyes. "You have the red aura of a warrior, though, and you are built for fighting. We could use you here, among my people. I am actually their *head* Druid—it's, uh, like a priest."

"My father told me what Druids are," Aric retorted, with all the wisdom that a twelve year old believes he has. The mention of his father closed his throat back up as if he had swallowed another gallon of salt water from the sea. He rested his head on his arms, which he had wrapped around his knees. Ray took a deep breath.

"There are no other survivors. I think you know that," Ray said quietly, placing his hand, strong but with very short, stout fingers, on Aric's arm. He hesitated to go on, seeing that it caused the boy pain, but he also knew, from experience, that the only way to survive was to go on, push forward, and seize a new life rather than bemoan the lost one.

"You would have a great place of honor in the village as one of my household. You would be familiar with the Druid customs, but you would be trained as a warrior and free to travel and explore as your people did, as you were meant to. You wouldn't be a prisoner, Aric; you would have more freedom than you could imagine and whichever wife you choose."

Aric lifted his tear-strewn face from his arms. "I don't want to choose a wife." He made his request so seriously that Ray couldn't laugh at the boyish crack in his voice when he said it.

"Well, we have a few years until then." Ray smiled at the boy and wrapped short arms that couldn't meet around his shoulders. He stood, silently encouraging the boy to do the same. Aric stood, with Ray barely clearing his shoulder. "I will take good care of you, Aric. Tonight is the summer solstice, and it is good luck that you have been reborn today. I have just attended a joyous birth this morning in one of the oldest households of the village."

Ray kissed the top of Aric's hand and led him out of the cave by it. Aric still wondered what he meant by being reborn; he had never heard that term before. And it was *midsomer*. That was when their ship was supposed to land in Eireland, so they must have been quite close. These thoughts vanished as soon as he and Ray stepped into the blinding light just outside the cave on the rocky beach, because Aric was once again taken aback and confounded by something the little had Druid said: "Yes, I see it. You will live happily from now on and be married, in love, just as Gunnhild wanted."

CHAPTER 13:

(LEY (LINES

Edie

"Rage, rage against the dying of the light."

Frank was muttering lines to Dylan Thomas poems as I measured and sketched the rock art in the stone circle on the west coast of the island. Squinting, I covered my eyes and peered over the western horizon to the Irish Sea and the setting sun. "You're right, we're going to miss the last ferry home if we're not careful," I said.

Leaning in a James Dean–esque pose against a menhir, Frank whipped out the pocket watch his dad had given him for his birthday. I sat across the stone circle, finishing my detailed sketch of the circle and the carvings on the center stone.

"There is a great deal of data on the stones themselves, of course. Every circle has information on the sizes, types, and placement of the stones, but their carvings and markings aren't as seriously considered."

"Why?" Frank asked.

"Well, there's no effective way to carbon-date the carvings, so the argument is that we can't prove that the carvings are contemporaneous with the stone circle."

"Mmm, I guess that makes sense."

"Sure it does, but it's also not precisely the point. If we want to understand what the circles were used for or what their significance is to the culture, then it doesn't really matter that the carvings match the building dates."

"Right. But if some really bad folk band on mushrooms, for instance, came and carved these stones up in the early 1960s, then that's hardly an archaeological explanation for the last four thousand years of their existence," Frank pointed out as he fidgeted with his camera, looking through the dozens of photos he had taken over the last few hours.

"Fortunately for us, that's not what it means. Monks recorded some spirals and similar etchings on the stones when they arrived in the ninth century. If we know how pre-Christian society inter-acted with the stones, then that gives us a pretty good inkling as to the cultural significance in prehistoric Britain. You don't have to extrapolate too much to have a solid theory, especially if you find something magically simple like a datable carving tool next to a stone."

"You're telling me that we missed a ferry, caught another one, came out to this island, and hiked up here to find a *datable tool*? I have four dating apps for that on my iPhone currently," Frank said.

"And I'm pretty sure we just met one at the ferry bar," I added.

We broke into delectable laughter before we heard the first clap of thunder.

Frank examined his watch for a moment and then started to pack up all the equipment. Frank doing anything in more than a lackadaisical manner was a sign of the ferry timetable and impend-ing bad weather without me even needing to ask. So I folded my sketch pads in my lap and tucked my pencil neatly behind my ear.

We met in the center of the circle, and I reached into his inner coat pocket for the beloved pocket watch. "I wonder how much of his hair he had to sell to buy this," I smiled, hoping my O. Henry reference had reached the right audience. Frank smiled too but often hesitated to gush about his tight relationship with his dad in front of me.

Without waiting for a reply, I dropped the watch, and with its reasonable heft, it swiftly plummeted in free fall for a millisecond, about ten inches from my palm and several feet above the earth. With the old, tarnished chain securely wrapped between my fingers, I stabilized it. The watch was in tailspin from the sudden force of gravity, but as the spinning slowed, a forceful back-and-forth motion began, making it swing like a pendulum, first one way and then, very dramatically, as I had predicted, switching directions and moving steadily counterclockwise. Frank seemed surprised at that and looked up at me. Most likely he had just been expecting me to examine the watch or perhaps read the inscription his father had chosen for it: *Timor Mortis Conturbat Me.*

I always thought it was a cruel inscription on something meant to be passed on by death, but Frank saw the humor in it, a sensibility I'm sure was as inherited from his father as the watch itself. Slowly, the watch began to make larger counterclockwise circles, and as we grew stiller and the calm before the storm grew quieter, the circles widened.

"Well, this is weird. So I guess now is the time when you confound me with your witchcraft and lead me blindly to your lair as a virgin sacrifice?" Frank asked, swinging the heavy pack up on his shoulders. I stuffed my books in the bag, zipped my coat, put the watch in my pocket, and we began the descent in a quick-step down the mountain trail.

"For real, tell me what just happened," Frank said as he lit a cigarette for our walk down the hillside after reaching into my jacket pocket to take back his watch.

"One theory is that Neolithic tombs and circles are built on ley lines, where there is magnetic pull to the earth's core because of mineral and metal deposits. The phenomenon that causes the magnetic reaction in the metal watch chain is the fluctuating magnetic field of the earth, what gives us the north and south poles and a lot of weather phenomena and reactions."

Frank nodded, and I took a deep breath, struggling to keep up with his pace and explain simultaneously. "Anyway, there are a couple theories Sully had. One is that the magnetic fields of the earth fluctuate, which is obvious, but they may have been much stronger around 2500 to 1500 BC, when monuments such as these were erected. And what's significant about that is that the monuments themselves could have been a reaction to this increased magnetism, which the ancient people of the time naturally felt because they were so connected to the earth. Essentially, they were marking the pull they felt by erecting a monument. We've really lost touch with that ability within ourselves through modernization. Especially as the era of technology has conned us into believing that we're somehow better linked now through social media and online dating." I raised my eyebrows, looking over at Frank. "So often you see people on their phones or devices whenever they're outside in nature, and they don't truly experience or perceive the depth and detail of what surrounds them. We're missing connections with the earth, and thus we're missing both small *and* big messages it has for us."

"We're also missing connections with our transportation."

Frank laughed as I continued with my boring lecture: "And because of that distance, we continue to lose or distrust our intuition, which is that ancient sense tying us to the earth."

I could see Frank nodding in agreement in my periphery, but he was nearly in a jog, racing to catch our boat, which happened to be the last one off the island since we had gotten a late start.

"Think about how we treat the people who use their intuition and connectivity to nature to tell us what's happening to us."

"Like Al Gore?" Frank asked, half joking.

"I was just thinking generally about people who identify as intuitive or psychic, but climate change prophets should definitely be included in that," I responded.

"So...like Rasputin!" Frank exclaimed.

"Frank, one could consider your ability to weave Rasputin and Russian history into any conversation a superpower in itself," I replied, out of breath from jogging and lecturing with a pack on.

"Anyway, not go get too *Ancient Aliens* on you, but there *is* a theory of geometric gridding as a sacred design or sacred geometry of ley lines, but there are also some more pseudoscientific ideas, like the vile vortices, which all seem to have the properties of the Bermuda Triangle. There are, of course, the Nazca Lines in South America and Buckminster Fuller's work, which you remember, I'm sure. Even Plato had ideas about energetic gridding as represented by the five solids."

"Ok, I get it, but what's the point of them? Like, why do they matter other than making my pocket watch do magic party tricks?"

"Well, it's hard to say. I mean, maybe on Armageddon we'll see. They'll all light up or explode or something. There was an amateur archaeologist in the 1920s who pointed out that they're like modern-day monuments and skyscrapers in that they give us a concept of where we are and where we're going, not only in the sense of which cardinal direction but also related to other settlements, like a road map linking them through man-made topographical features. And a couple of bros at the British museum actually took that hypothesis and proved that there are these underground rivers and magnetic currents, using dowsers."

"I knew we were overdue for a visit to the Elgin Marbles!" Frank was now almost at an all-out run, which worried me. What time was it? I followed on his heels. "But how can topography be man-made?"

"Well, if you're standing in Trafalgar Square and someone has to be at Parliament in ten minutes, do you tell them walk southeast or do you tell them to look for Big Ben? It's that sort of concept, but that only works locally. And of course many of the stones are brought in from faraway places, so was that done to recall a homeland or to connect to those places? It's hard to say. But if the monuments are meant to refer to other ones built on the same ley lines, like the sacred geometry theory, then it makes sense that they would also use material from the places to which they refer. Or maybe there is something else to the rock choice, like the magnetism of the metals that run in the colored veins. Or maybe it's both. I think many of the kerbstones and menhirs of Britain's most famous stone circles are from shared sources, particularly the Welsh and Scottish coasts,"

"OK, so they didn't just choose the place to erect the monument; the place chose them. They felt it, and the monument is a physical representation of that feeling. And it's been theorized that there may have been stronger pulls from these magnetic fields at certain times when the monuments were built, which is why so many of the stones contain veins to make bronze alloys. So what do you think the world was like when these magnetic fields were pulling on people like that—how did they explain it without science?"

"That's a great question. Maybe people are polarized—the individual is polarized from the group, ideas are polarizing, and most of all, they felt it, intuitively, physically, through the nerve endings in their feet, in a way we can't anymore," I said.

"So you're saying that the ancients dealt with these times more *constructively* than we do?" Frank laughed at his own pun. He was the only person I knew who could be simultaneously fast and witty.

"Whatever drove them to create the monuments, I definitely believe, above all, that the pull toward the earth is positive. It's what we want to feel, what grounds us, and what gives us important internal cues and information for decision-making. Feeling it is what some people call being *centered* or *in harmony*."

"Maybe we should have a pint or two and try to imagine what it all means," Frank offered.

"We already had a pint or three waiting for the last ferry. Oh shit!" I yelled, rounding the corner to catch up with Frank, who was waving on the gravel slope as our ferry pulled away so slowly its movement was nearly imperceptible. I ran after it, waving my arms. No use. And neither were ferry timetables. They simply did not follow them.

Frank had apparently already seen that we had missed our ferry yet again. By the time I turned around, he was squatted, sitting on the pack in a comfortable resting position after our little jog, counting out the cash we had brought with us.

"Oh my *God*! To be left by something *that* slow?" I exclaimed, attempting to rile him a bit so I had someone to be angry with. "It's like a receding iceberg. I can barely tell it's moving. All we have to do is jump in and swim to catch it."

"Simmer down, honey, I have enough cash for the pub inn if they don't take cards. Anyway, a) we don't have extra clothes so, let's avoid hypothermia and *two*) they won't let us on if we swim for it. You know all those ferrymen are on a power trip. In fact, it makes me hot just thinking about it."

"In that case, I'm thankful they're headed away. Don't tell me how far a walk the 'pub inn' is! I don't want to know. Just walk there, and I'll follow you."

"We just passed it when you were deep in thought, dear." He turned me around by my shoulders. "Let's navigate toward that flat-top hill in the distance. You can barely make out the tippy-top of the thatched roof of the pub and the vacancy sign, some man-made topography for you."

The inn was the standard—a dark pub on the first floor with very subpar yet *warm* food and single and double rooms upstairs. I was correct in that the island was not a popular vacation destination at this moment in seasonal time, but because of a personal family gathering that the innkeeper was having, there was just a single room left. One tiny, twin bed on an ancient wooden frame stood in the corner with a small nightstand next to it. In the opposite corner was a large leather chair, ripped in the seat, with stuffing exposed, next to a full bookshelf. I knew that was where Frank would be spending the night. He was quite chivalric as best friends go. So we carried the pack up, locked the room, washed our faces and hands, and headed down to the pub, where raucous singing could be heard as soon as we descended the stairwell.

"This will easily go on past midnight," I whispered.

"And it's only seven o'clock," Frank bemoaned.

We smiled and nodded at the garrulous company, wishing we shared their mirth. But the impending night of uncomfortable sleep kept us less than joyful as we slid into a corner booth. Frank doffed his beanie and ran his hands through his thick, wavy hair, making it stand on end and thus appropriately display his emotional state.

"OK, what are we having? It's my treat—it's my fault we missed the ferry," I said. "With the number of sheep and cows at pasture out back, I imagine either the mutton or burger might be best. And you'd think the fish would be OK at least, it being an island and all…I'd kill for another Scottish herring." I peered over my menu with a smirk on my face. The joke was quickly received and delightfully rebutted.

"I told you if I saw another herring on a plate, I'd jump off the Arran Cliffs and take you with me," Frank reminded me. The corner of his mouth neatly turned up at the end as he focused on rolling a small cigarette. "I'm ordering us both the burger because if you don't get your own, you'll want mine. Join me?" he questioned as he licked the end of the paper and waggled the neatly rolled cigarette.

"No thanks. I don't want to smell like cigarette smoke and wet wool. I can't imagine anything worse than sleeping in stinky clothes."

"I think thou dost protest too much."

He shrugged and started to walk to the bar as I shouted, "Fries, I mean *chips*, for me too!"

Facing the barkeep, different from the innkeeper—his son, perhaps—Frank merely raised a thumb in reply. He ordered at the bar, blessing me with a pint of local cider before heading out the back door with his own pint.

Solitude was always helpful to my thoughts. Despite knowing me quite well, Frank was still an outsider to the workings of my mind, and as of late, I had found myself deep in a contemplation that was part academic, part intuitive, and the result was leaving me a little more than perplexed about where to head next with my research.

It was funny how I never needed headphones to study or write, I thought; the background susurrus of the jubilant crowd, now fully engaged in a less-than-coherent version of "Eamonn an Chnoic," was the perfect soundtrack to my deliberation.

The tartness of the cider cut through the bitter taste in my mouth, and as the chorus came back around, I zoned out completely, focusing on what tidbits I had that I could link. Funnily enough, it was the herring that pulled my attention most. I knew that the cliffs had significance. How could they not? How could modern tourists park themselves on these fragile shelves, reminders of our frail existence, without thinking about how people used to interact with the landscape? I wondered, in a macabre moment, how many people had actually thrown themselves off of Slieve League or the famous Cliffs of Moher or the ones on Arran, in a moment of despair.

I knew with certainty that these monumental landscapes themselves must have an important relationship with the monumental creations I was uncovering. Standing at the edge of a nine-hundred-foot cliff is life-changing. You feel the deafening power of full control, and then, looking out into the vastness of the Atlantic, you know you're utterly powerless. The Druids never would have let the Paris Environmental Accords fail, I thought. Then, *plonk*, our fresh burgers were dropped on the table like manna from heaven by...Michael?

"What are you doing here?" I asked, surprised.

"I should be asking you that question." He smiled. "I live here, Edana."

I had never been regularly called by my full name. Not by my parents. Not by my grandparents, whom I barely knew. It was only ever uttered in that first day roll call at school each year before I corrected the teacher. I couldn't tell if the way he pronounced it with his Irish lilt irritated me or enchanted me. At this news I looked around at the pub automatically.

"Well, not here in the pub!" He laughed. "I live on the island, just across the way. Do you need a place to crash tonight?"

Frank's head appeared just then, bobbing inside the nearby doorway; he was ready to devour his delicious burger and relax to some authentic Celtic pub music. "Yes!" he confirmed as he approached the table. "We only have one bed upstairs, so one of us needs to stay with you."

I turned a deep red color, which probably made me blend in with the Irish more than stand out, I thought. I wanted to eat my burger and go up to the room alone to sleep, but Sully had always said, with his green canteen full of black coffee, "There's no time like the present!" and I felt like I had something yet to learn from Michael. He slid in next to me with his nearly gone Smithwicks in hand. He was warm, wearing a flannel over a black T-shirt and faded black jeans with workmen's boots. He was clean-shaven and smelled of beer and some sort of aftershave I couldn't name. Had he shaved at the bar before coming here? I thought I remembered stubble from earlier. He rested his arm on the back of the ancient bench seat behind my head, and I leaned back into it a little bit as I sipped my cider.

"Just arrived on me boat," he said into my ear. "Was that you I saw runnin' at the ferry terminal?" I nodded, embarrassed, and he smiled, amused.

The music picked up strength, and we couldn't hear each other for a chat at the table, anyway. We ate and bobbed and swayed along to the rhythm of the bodhran and fiddle. Even sitting, it's impossible not to move your body with the sounds of traditional music.

After a few minutes, Frank looked over at me and asked, with his mouth full, "What's that look, Edie?"

"What?" I asked in a daze of music, food, drink, and Michael's musk.

"Are you going to fall asleep?" he asked.

"No, I'm just happy," I replied.

Michael's chest seemed to expand as he accidentally overheard this exchange. "Yous two can go across the way to my house if you're tired. It's the one with the red door and barking dogs. Door's open. Dogs are friendly. There's one bed and one sofa. It's an old crofter cottage, so just two rooms. I can sleep here at the pub. Won't be the first time." He winked at me and finished, "Or the last."

Then the lead singer's voice came echoing through the microphone, which he spoke too closely into. "This one is for all you young lovers on this weekend of Ostara."

I had almost forgotten the spring equinox was the next day. "It's always some fecking pagan holiday," Frank said across the table.

"Will you go with me up to the stones in the morning before the ferry?" Michael asked so close to my ear it tickled, but it was the only way to be heard above the singing. I nodded, looking into his earnest blue eyes. "I have something I want to show you," he added.

While my mind began spiraling into what secret the stones may have up on the lonely hill, the Irishmen I was sitting with gleefully joined in the singing. I couldn't help but laugh and clap along to the beat as best I could.

> I'm as happy as a king
> When I catch a breath of spring
> And the grass is turning green as winter ends
> And the geese are on the wing
> And the thrushes start to sing
> And I'm headed down the road to see my friends

The next morning I met Michael at sunrise at the stone circle. Frank slept. As I approached, the sun was rising and shining in long shafts between two of the largest stones. *That's no coincidence*, I thought. I reached into my bag for my journal, but something stopped me. Michael was leaning against the kerbstone, paper cup of coffee in hand, staring off into the distance. The sight was so perfect it took my breath away, but I had never let feelings come before work, and I couldn't now, not when I was so close to finishing Sully's book. Anyway, I hadn't had a boyfriend since high school, just over a decade ago, and I had no idea what to say or how to act.

As I approached, he turned toward me, and I saw he had a cup of coffee for me as well. "Thanks for letting us crash at your place, and for the coffee," I said quietly. I pulled my journal out and turned to my most professional tone to ask what he had to show me.

"Coffee first," he said simply.

We sipped in companionable silence, and I pressed my back against the kerbstone. The fingers on my right hand dangled by my side and grazed something on the stone. There was a very precise carving. My eyes popped open. Michael smiled as I knelt down and searched for my tracing paper in my bag.

"I can't believe it's a triskelion!" I exclaimed. The triple spiral motif was something I had only seen at Newgrange.

"Bit of a sundial too, like at Newgrange," he answered, squatting next to me, speaking my thought out loud. He was smiling so big that I noticed the neat space in his front teeth for the first time.

"Thank you," I said, maybe less professionally this time, trying to take my eyes off his mouth. "We were in such a rush yesterday—I can't believe we missed this."

"Weeeell, yer no Indiana Jones, that's for sure," he joked. "It's well hidden, 'round this side and small. Most people miss it," he said. "I have plenty of drawings and etchings back at my house. When you're done, I'll show you, and we can bring Frank some coffee."

He stood up again and picked up my bag for me. I finished the transfer to the tracing paper while he hummed his favorite tune from the night before, an American song, "Galway Girl."

CHAPTER 14:

OSTARA, THE SPRING EQUINOX

Ailsa

The oak grove was just barely touched by frost. The spring equinox was that night—and the full worm moon would soon appear. I loved seeing all the happy earthworms devouring the spring plants and turning, belly up, into the sun in resplendent glory. It was an early sign of better weather. Recently winter had become long, and we needed such a promise. I picked one up, wriggling, and dropped it in my pocket to later bless the soil in our kale yard and barley patch.

I rubbed my eyes because it was early, and everything seemed unclear. The fog was only just lifting over the land and my mind. The trees were budding; everything was an endless new green color—that quiet, perfect moss green before it brightens and darkens, descending in dark green shadows upon the landscape.

I had risen well before the dawn to have time in the oak grove before the other Druids arrived—and hopefully some time alone to talk with Ray. My own weight felt heavy, and I leaned against the trunk of a tree for support, looking down at my bare feet. No sooner had I closed my eyes and rested my head than Jord appeared in his green cloak in front of me. He did not ever walk; he glided, his eyes crescent moons of pleasure and his chin long and angular like the rest of him. I straightened up and squared up to his glare. "I knew you'd be first," I said.

"But it is actually you who is first." He smiled down at me from his great height, and his gray features shimmered in the dawn light that trickled through the young, blossoming trees.

"I'm so tired, Jord." He nodded, coming closer to hear me. "I can't remember a time anymore when I didn't feel this great pull in all directions: the pull of the earth, of the Druids, of my family life."

"Yes," he agreed, his creased eyes focusing on something in the distance. "Your life has been a time of peace for our village, but much is changing. You feel the shifts before most." He placed a hand on my shoulder. This wasn't exactly what I needed to hear.

"I'm supposed to be the centered one, Uncle, the sage, but lately it seems like I'm just siphoning wisdom from those around me because I can't steady myself." I looked up at him, distressed. "I don't sound like much of a leader."

"Well, surely that's a part of growing wise, gathering from other places and choosing what you hold on to and what you let go of," he answered with a questioning head tilt.

"I just want to help people and be respected like Ray is. I want my destiny to feel undeniably right like it did in those days on Orkney."

"It's easy to feel strongly when you're 15, before you've worked out the complexities of everything. Is certainty even what you're truly looking for? Do you think you will find it where you're looking?" He spoke with a gentle smile and narrowed eyes.

Silence fell as the other Druids, like a tide, descended upon the oak grove in their dyed-green wool garments, hands upraised. Their bodies matched, and thus their uncloaked heads were the only distinguishing feature. Most of those heads were shades of dark to light gray, some were white, but mine was the only head black as a raven's.

Jord circled the other nine Druids, touching each head in a blessing, and I remembered the earthworm in my pocket. "This first morning of spring, we summon the ancestors and the earth with an origin story for our meditation. Gather hands now, and Ailsa will lead us in Ray's place this morning, since Ray has been called to a difficult birth."

I wasn't sure I felt like leading the circle this morning, but Jord was clearly trying to make a point in inviting me to lead what should have been his ceremony. No sense in overthinking it. I loved this part; it was a time to truly escape my thoughts by entering chant and oneness through meditation with the other Druids. I shifted my feet in the spring-green grass in order to reach for the hands around me. My toes dug into the loamy forest soil beneath my feet, and I wriggled my toes like worms, seeking deeper comfort and coolness from the friendly earth. *Give me strength*, I asked the earth silently.

I felt a worm friend wriggle between my toes, and I giggled out loud. Jord, whose eyes had been closed tightly, peaked out of one at me and made a funny face. I think his look was supposed to quiet me, but it actually made me laugh even harder. Soon, as a connected force, my laughter had intoxicated everyone, and each of the eight other ancient Druids around the circle was giggling along with me. *This is the way to bring in spring*, I thought to myself. And then aloud I said, "The emergence of spring is the laughter of the earth: the frolicking lambs and kids, the boisterous flight of newborn bluebirds, the scratch of squirrels and chipmunk feet on tree trunks, the giggling trickle of the defrosted brook, and the bright flowers in the lee are proof that the earth laughs too."

"Blessed be," everyone said in response, and I breathed a sigh of relief as Jord squeezed my hand in the tender way uncles do.

I took a deep breath, centered myself once more, and began. "Now we go back, back to the earth before the long winter was done. Our world is covered in snow; the rivers are impenetrable with ice." My voice was full of melody and a cadence halfway between singing and chanting. I felt Jord's long fingers wrap around mine, and on the other side, the clammy hand of Milor, the oldest Druid, grasped mine tightly. The birdsong that had once echoed my words was now drowned out by the humming of my fellow Druids.

"There was a time, not so long ago when we consider the age of the world, when our land was too cold to farm, and man and woman roamed free in the south, with no roots, no village, no stone circle for worship. We were simply another animal in the forest, gathering food for winter, hunting anything smaller or slower. No man dared venture into the frigid North, but as the ice receded, a force began pulling men to the North, stronger even than the promise of fertile lands for planting. You see, the first men who came here were not yet planters, but they felt pulled from their ancient seats, nonetheless.

"And when they met the ice as it receded, then what did they find? An empty land, unpopulated, with no enemies or competition for resources, ripe for planting. But this was a strange new land, and they missed their home. They tried to build a bridge over the ice bridge they had crossed so that when everything finally melted, they could go back to what was known, what was safe. As they felled logs and made a great truss for this bridge, the natural ice bridge melted away, and their hope was lost. They began to use all the timber for boats, but as they built these boats to be able to go home, the ice slowly revealed the richest and greenest rivers, filled with hundreds of fish."

The humming and chanting of the other Druids grew louder and louder. It was like being in the center of a beehive, and all my senses were awakened from numbness and fog.

"A strange magic happened, and as the snow began to melt on the mountaintops and the ocean was warm enough to swim and fish in, the forest grew, and so did its bounty. The seeds it provided were folded into the land and sprung up, higher and higher, year by year. The very intuition that had pulled the people north told them to cast away their bridges and boats—this was their home!"

The beat of the bodhran grew loud against the sounds of humming, and the Druids fell into a deep meditation. I continued; the words sprang up from the ground into my heart as the story unfolded. "Just as the earth pulled us to this land, so it pulled the stones to their place on the moor. And the stones they carried would be seen as a new kind of structure to demarcate a new kind of world, one in which we belong to the land and it belongs to us. We sing the songs of the fathers and sons who carved and erected the stones. And we sing to their mothers and daughters who cultivated the land, giving us barley, kale, and fruit trees. Their ashes are sprinkled on the sacred ground to symbolize its abundance and purity. It is not the stone monument that is sacred to us; it is the ground that it marks, where we were called and where life was sacrificed to bring forth more life. Don't forget this important detail when we gather for each festival at the stones. These stones were consecrated by their blood."

"Blessed be!" they answered me in turns.

Normally we'd end there, but I had a new idea I wanted to try out, so I squeezed Jord's hand and sent a pulse through the group and added a new blessing. "Just as we had been called and chased the ice away and made space to plant and build, other people felt the call north, slow as ice at first and then quick as a fox. They did not wreck and plunder. They intermarried and became one with our own culture, sewing their history, their ancestors, and their own ways into ours. They erected stone circles like ours in their own sacred places, and so monuments sprang up like young trees on the landscape, and we became brothers, sharing festivals and feasts. At our stones we will forever mark the solstices and equinoxes—and with our brethren, we will travel to celebrate the cross-quarter days."

As I called out these names, they were repeated in unison: "Imbolc, Beltane, Lughnasadh, Samhain."

At this I was somewhat pulled out of my trance, my eyes popped open, and my heart simultaneously ripped open to the face of my father, tall and dark, with black hair, big white teeth, and a smile like a wolf's.

It was my mother's family who had given me direct lineage to Druid life, but it was my father, from a northern isle, who had colored my world green and blue and led me into forests and glens when I was a child and did so now in my dreams, even still. How does someone smile through it all and then throw himself off a cliff? Did he think I was better off without him? Did he actually eschew the responsibility of raising a Druid on his own? Suddenly, after all these years, I ached to know what had consumed him so. What if he had acted on impulse and instantly regretted it? Midair even, before the shock of impact killed him? What if the primordial scream I heard in my sleep had been him calling out. *"I'm sorry, Ailsa,"* it seemed to say.

Then Ray was in my mind, clear as day, though I could still only feel Jord and Milor beside me. "Magical as your mother's family is, as much as you are the echo of the bone of your Druid ancestors, you are your father's child, Ailsa. He wanted to protect you from his magic. He came to me, afraid the village would think your Druid abilities were not from nature if they were trained by him—he was a dowser. What you possess are gifts from both your parents."

And then the cadence of the Druids' chant brought me back to the story I was telling with my lips, even though my mind had been engaged with Ray. I could barely speak, but I managed to finish my meditation with the Druids. "And so now the earth pulls us back to one another, and we are called to the westerly isles, to the North, and to the mainland, to the magic of other ancestors, my husband's ancestors, and their...their...cir-circles."

"Ailsa, are you OK?" Milor whispered in my right ear. That's the last thing I remember before my mind went white.

"I dream of my daughters' daughters and the sons they will have, the roles they will play in the spiral of the universe." I traced the carved spiral on the largest stone in the stone circle with my lily white fingertip in my mind.

"Ailsa, are you OK?" Ray asked, looking down at me, patting my cheek.

"I was just going to ask you the same thing," I said, looking up into his wrinkled, happy face for the first time in a while—I was a head taller than him, after all, and usually looking down.

We talked for a bit in silence, using our telepathic gifts, until Ray prodded Jord to leave the oak grove with the other Druids so we could speak freely. He knew I was upset. I sat up and picked the small brown leaves from the ground out of my hair while he shooed everyone away and walked back over to me, squatting so we were face-to-face.

"You put me in green robes and called me one of you," I said without looking at Ray or giving him any of the deference he deserved as my superior. Ray didn't stand on ceremony, though. Not with me. "I want to cut this part of me out, like a festering wound. This matrilineal Druid nonsense is not me, Ray! I'm the least-fit person!" I yelled, hands reaching up to the sky in frustration, supplication, or both.

I cut my eyes at Ray when I heard him exhale, expecting, perhaps even wanting, an equal reaction, but he just tilted his head slightly, and the wind blew the fringe on his forehead up. "Well, on this matter, your opinion is not the final one, I'm afraid, my dear."

Rage welled up in me now, and I flailed my arms, unnerving the squirrels and chipmunks and other forest creatures who had been peacefully gorging themselves on the new spring grass nearby.

"*You* appeared to me and told me I'm a dowser like my father— what does that even mean? I'm so confused. How can I be both a dowser and Druid?"

Ray extended his hand to me. "If you're feeling better, let's walk up to the stone circle, shall we?" I reluctantly accepted his help to stand. I knew walking would help clear my head. "A dowser is just someone who feels the magnetic energy of the earth. Sometimes it's useful—you find important things easily, like water or gemstones and other treasures of the earth." Ray's eyes sparkled with some secret he was telling me. "It can also be very painful; the intensity of the feeling can be…overwhelming, like it was for your father." I stared ahead as we walked out of the woods and across the moor to the stone circle, our hair dancing wildly in the wind. All the feelings my father must have felt at the cliff's edge bubbled up in me. "Using your dowsing abilities can help you harness the energy so it doesn't feel as overwhelming as it did for your father. I've received a message that it's time for you to use these abilities with the stones."

I felt the world spin with this new information. "So not all Druids feel the energy I feel from the earth."

"No, Ailsa, you're special, because your father—"

Suddenly, I was furious. "Wait, you're helping *me,* so why didn't you help him?"

"He wasn't a Druid, Ailsa, and he didn't want help. He didn't *need* help. He knew more about it than me. In fact, I wish he were here to help you with it. I just received the information today that your dowsing would lead us to new magic in the stones."

"Why didn't *he* help me?" I wondered aloud.

"Aric is from a patrilineal society. So is your father. Things pass from father to son in such places. It didn't occur to your father that you could be anything but a Druid, your mother's line, in our matrilineal society, but you are both dowser and Druid, and it's happened for a reason. I've been told."

"Who told you this?" I moaned, putting my hands to my forehead and willing my brain to accept the news.

Ray offered a canteen of water and a stick of goat jerky that I grudgingly took, realizing how hungry I was.

"There are patrilineal civilizations to the south. They have pulled a substance from their stones, and a messenger has come to share it with me. I've been told telepathically, but he will arrive with proof within the wheel of this year, Ailsa. In the future, matrilineal cultures such as ours will become fewer and fewer. They assimilate into the patrilineal because of the nature of the masculine possessing the feminine. These cultures are forceful and can be mean and brutish, so the gentle, mothering, compassionate nature of the matrilineal society gives way to them."

We walked slower now as we crested the hill and the stones appeared in the distance. I digested the conversation and the goat jerky with more ease as we kept walking. One should always go for a walk after tough meals or conversations.

"Then why would we want to possess the magic in the stones, if it leads to such a cultural shift?" I asked, innocently, desperate to preserve the peace I knew.

"We are living in the time of the mother-centric world, Ailsa, and it will be over one day, sooner than you think. This magic in the stones, it can create weapons and structures and tools that we will have to have to continue to exist." I chewed on my jerky, calmer now. Food had a way of making bad news more bearable. "We will have to change in order to survive. Women will lose power in this new world, and it's important that you establish your great power, make it known to the world, and have children who can pass on your wisdom and gifts."

I touched the great stone at the front of the circle, full of sprawled carvings. I'm not sure what I expected, but nothing happened. I pressed my forehead to it, begging for an answer. "What if our children are like Aric?" I asked. "What if they want to conquer and raid, or explore and sail away?"

Ray walked over to the stone I leaned against. "They won't be, Ailsa. When Aric came to live with us, he gave all that up. He vowed at your wedding that the children would carry your family name, as your father did for your mother. They have bowed to the matrilineal society, and they will be some of the last men to do so on these islands."

His words brought me back to the crushing thoughts of my father. I had always believed he felt alone because he missed his homeland, but it was even more lonely for him than I had realized. "I wish I could talk to my father about these feelings, the pulls of the dowser, the magnitude of it." I ran my hand over the blue-green veins of the stone. They looked so much like my own veins that I thought the stone might come to life. *Tell me what you are*, I willed it, silently, but Ray's voice broke my concentration.

"You can, my dear! Nothing is lost forever," he responded, squeezing my shoulder. "Like burnt wood disappearing into smoke, your words travel up to the heavens in a different form." I closed my eyes and said a silent prayer to my father for strength and understanding. "Everything you do brings honor to him. He sees you from the beyond, even now," Ray said as I finished my prayer. I opened one eye at a time and saw him staring back at me. "It is the dichotomy in you that must give birth to the future of this land, Ailsa. You're destined to be head Druid because of who you are, both your mother's half and your father's. Who says we have to be just one thing, anyway? Every part of you is true, and there is no point in denying it, or else you deny the possibility of the future.

Welcome in every part of you," Ray finished, furrowing his brow at me knowingly.

If every part of me is true, if there is no part to be denied or cut out, then why can't I love them both? I thought. Ray turned to leave, brushing off his long green cloak, which dragged the ground behind him. "You just have to balance it with honor," he said, reading my mind again.

"I know. You're right. They will kill each other eventually if I continue it this way."

Ray looked down at the ground in front of him, lost for words. Then he looked up at me and asked. He had to. Aric had been like a son to him. "You've seen a vision, then?"

I paused and thought for a moment before responding, "No, truly, I haven't; I would tell you. But I feel it in my gut. Maybe it's a dowser's knowing and not a Druid's vision if I parse it out." I laughed, but not my real laugh, an awkward laugh at the ridiculousness of the truth. "One of them will die if this continues, Ray. I have to end it."

Ray shook his head as if to clarify his confusion by physical force. "But Ros knows you share your bed with your husband. So you truly think Aric would *kill* Ros if the nature of your relationship became known to him?" he asked. "I don't believe him capable of that."

"No, there's something else," I responded, leaning on a nearby stone for support. "Ros doesn't know that I am coming to love Aric as well. In fact, I don't think I realized that until now either. I honestly think that knowledge would kill Ros or would make him kill… someone else."

Something urgent rose up in me as I spoke these words out loud. Ray noticed. "Go home to your husband, child. I will explore this vision of Ros in violence in my meditations."

"I thought he was still gone trading. How do you know he's home?" I squinted at him, wondering just how much he used his psychic powers to check in on Aric.

Ray laughed. "I may see the future sometimes, but in this case, I was coming from your home when I found you had fainted. I was speaking with Aric, who had just returned, when I had a feeling you needed me in the oak grove," he said softly.

I smiled at the mundane explanation, which was just what I needed in this moment in which I had become overwhelmed by the earth's magic. "Let me walk with you to make sure you get home safely?" Ray asked with a hopeful brow, knowing well that my tendency was to refuse help. "Yes, of course." I answered, mystified by Ray's goodness and his uncanny ability to appear wherever he was needed. "Just give me a moment to myself?" I asked. He nodded.

Before returning home, I walked to the edge of the cliffs behind the stone circle. I carried the wild carrot seeds in the pocket tied around my waist still, along with other medicinals and practical items: a comb, mint leaves and lemon balm, a flint knife wrapped in leather, an opalescent feather Father gave me the day before he died, a small wooden spoon for shared meals, and the tiny black pearl recently acquired from Ros's sister. I reached in and felt each tiny preciousness in between my fingertips. "Time to fly on the wind and make wild carrots," I said as I pulled out my seed pouch and tossed it over the edge.

And with that, I turned on my heel and ran as fast as my feet would carry me toward the roundhouse I shared with Aric, forgetting Ray waiting for me at the wood's edge. Now that I had trusted Ray with everything and he had told me the truth about my dowsing power, I felt free. Barefoot in my flight, I skipped and frolicked down the hills toward the valley of the mountains to the north, where the village dwellings were, my heart suddenly having grown wings.

CHAPTER 15:

THE MOON IS WAXING

I lifted the hide as narrowly as I could to squeeze into the house without letting too much of the harsh late-afternoon sunlight in. Covered in dew and leaves from the woods and a sharp, musky, sheep smell from the moor where the stones stood, I stripped myself of my wool cloak immediately and made my way over to the hearth to wash, tiptoeing quietly to not disturb Aric, who was a light sleeper, as warriors should be. I was short of breath with excitement, imagining the feel of the warm water and soft cloth on my cold, tight skin. I went straight for the hearth, positioned to the right of the door, and knelt down in front of it bare naked, not at all noticing Aric propped on a pile of hides, sitting up in just his leather tunic, hidden in in the shadows adjacent to the light being cast by the fire.

His deep voice startled me, sending goose bumps down my bare flesh, nearly tipping me into the fire with fright. Luckily, I caught myself on the edge of the stone hearth. Unluckily, I burned my hand and let out an undignified yelp. Aric's deep rumble of laughter thundered from his chest as he reached out for my injured hand.

"I'm so sorry to have scared you, my love. I was in such a trance, I'm not even sure of what I said."

"Oh no, it's my fault." My voice sounded so high and weak next to his, strange to me. "I was trying to wash after sunrise at the stones because I didn't want to ruin the bed with my sheep smell and make you think you had gone to bed with a fat ewe."

His eyes creased into bright triangles of amusement, but instead of matching my smile or laughing at the joke, Aric remained serious, which was unsettling. "Sorry, I was trying to be funny." I blushed. I felt his eyes on me and looked down at my knees, slightly open where I knelt, the curve of my thighs rising into the secret corners of my hips, from which a strong, straight-back torso, flat stomach, and muscular back rose. I was still cold and covered in goose flesh, but my body always responded to Aric's presence, as it was now, cold or not. Even when my mind and heart were elsewhere, my body responded to my husband in a strong, undeniable way, and he knew it. But today my mind and heart were here with him.

"You're funny," he said without smiling and reached out, lifting my chin so that I could look straight into his eyes, dark and deep, in the low light. "I'm just distracted by how beautiful you are next to the firelight, and the way it casts light and shadows on the curves of your body makes it hard for me to breathe, let alone laugh." His grip moved from my chin to neck, and I smiled into his face. What I had been afraid was suspicion in his tone was actually lust, perhaps even love at this point. He gripped my neck, like the tender stalk of a mushroom, so fragile in his massive hand. He could break it with a flick of his wrist, but the deep trust I had in him to protect me rather than hurt me, coupled with the adrenaline of fear that he could easily break any part of me, sent a deep burning desire into my heart that I had honestly never felt before.

"You've been gone a while this time," I mentioned, trying to cast off his desire as loneliness or distance-increasing fondness.

He nodded and sipped the tea he had made himself with my herbs. "I was. And I thought of you constantly, imagining your face and arms and legs."

"And here I am," I said.

"Yes, there you are, exactly as I remembered you." I raised my eyebrows at him in a bit of disbelief. "You are so different looking. Unlike anyone else."

"Are you getting to the compliment?" I asked, washing my underarms, ankles, and feet while he watched.

"People don't really speak of your beauty," he said, and I couldn't help but laugh. "But you are the most interesting and the most perfectly formed and the most natural and earthly, and that's what makes you the most beautiful woman I have ever seen. You look like you grew out of that oak grove you love so much."

I waited a moment and then finally had the courage to stare back into his ice-blue gaze. "Should I say thank you?" I asked.

"I think I should," Aric answered, laughing heartily. He leaned forward. "It's like lying with a wood nymph, Ailsa. You're completely of this world and not of this world at the same time."

I forced my long, pale fingers between his muscular tanned ones, and he squeezed a little too hard. "I want you to be mine, but I fear I can never fully possess you that way, Ailsa."

I moved his right hand, easily the size of two of mine, to my mouth and slowly, and deliberately, kissed each finger, licking the tips with my tongue, unsure of what possessed me. I honestly felt drunk on the power.

He closed his eyes and moaned helplessly, which made quite the impression coming from such a humongous man. I climbed up onto his lap atop the hides on which he sat in the shadows by the fire and slowly lowered myself onto him, then back up and off again completely, then down once more to join his desire. He sat up straight in his chair, his bright eyes burning, and moved along with me as I rocked my hips in the hypnotic and endless circle motion that entranced us at the stones and was doing so here, in the dark of our own privacy at home. I leaned back, and my long black hair pooled on the floor. He gently gathered my hair up, twisting it on top of my head with one hand while he held my lower back with the other and stood up to his full height as he held me. I moved through midair now, supported only by Aric's hands at the base of my back and his bulky thighs, squatted slightly to support my weight. He kissed me passionately and laid me down on the soft blanket of pelts in front of the fire, spreading my hair out all around me.

"I won't let you do me in so easily," he smiled, looking truly happy. Was every warrior's heart so supple in a woman's hands? "Now, let me show you my talents, as you've shown me yours." He kissed me delicately on the mouth and moved lower over my chin and my mushroom stalk neck and downward, biting each ridge of my ribs on the left side of my body, which faced away from the fire, exposed to cold. My skin rippled with goose bumps and pleasure all over as he continued. I screamed and laughed with an overwhelming joy, and my spirit seemed to leave my body and float above us. Minutes later I woke from my trance, still by the fire with my husband, both of us in convulsions of pleasure, tangled in a living paradise with one another.

I was startled out of this ecstasy minutes later by Aric's voice, now distant from across the roundhouse. *He must have gotten up, and because I was exhausted, I hardly noticed*, I thought. Then I looked over and saw his glorious form bent over the table, looking for the ripest piece of fruit in the earthenware bowl. I liked this view. His massive thighs were tanned and gave way to the most beautiful curve of white, muscular buttocks. His dark hair, gilded with streaks of auburn from endless hours in the sunlight, reached halfway down his back, having come out of his plait. He bit into something and, with his mouth still full of fruit and juice dripping down his chin, spoke again from across the roundhouse. "Come to the doorway. The full moon is magnificent. It looks enormous over the horizon." He walked to the door and leaned against the doorjamb, pointing upward.

"Wh-what?" I stammered, suddenly coming back fully to my senses as if struck by lightning. I rose immediately from the piles of hides and furs—there were surely benefits to having a great hunter as a husband—and ran over to our doorway naked, covered in beads of sweat that dripped down from my neck, below my breasts, and in between my thighs. Aric was lifting the hide that hung from the stone lintel, and the golden light of a full moon made my damp body sparkle like stones in the riverbeds. He wrapped his arms around my waist, and I felt the coolness of his fruit juice–soaked fingers on my hips.

"I'm sure you've seen a full moon or two, but indeed it is glorious, and it's all the more glorious looking on it with you."

I was speechless. I had come to my husband's bed without taking my wild carrot seeds, knowing the moon had been waxing all week until it reached its peak tonight, when I did, which meant I would be as ripe as the fruit Aric had just devoured. I said nothing but laid my head on his shoulder and touched my womb in hesitant manifestation of what was possible now. It had always been *possible*, but now it was quite likely. We are most fertile when the earth is, after all, under a full moon. "Plant a seed when it has the most light in day and night." My father used to say. "It's beautiful," I finally whispered.

Some time later, in the laconic repose that only lovers can inhabit, with rapturously languid limbs covered in furs, light streaming in through the cracks of the doorway, and the sounds of the day well underway outside for many of the village folk, I opened up my heart, just a crack, like where the sunlight came streaming through the corner of the hide. Within I saw that my husband had come to know the hidden recesses of me, even as I hid them, and what I had confided in Ray was true. I loved him. Not as a wife loves a husband out of duty; I loved him for him, simply.

"I've spent my whole life wishing away who I was born to be," I whispered, running a finger down the solid line and length of Aric's arm, which was curled around me. I brushed the hair from his eyes and willed myself to keep his gaze. It is hard to look anyone in the face when you're admitting something so vulnerable. Aric said nothing, but I felt him nod and make an understanding hum in the back of his throat. It was funny: I had seen him do this exact thing before and thought he hadn't been listening, but now I knew he was not just listening; he was processing deeply and intuitively in his own way. I kissed his brow in silent thanks for this and continued, "It's madness how much we try to push away who we truly are just because we are…"

I searched for the words, but Aric finished them. "Afraid of our own power?" He had elucidated my own thoughts exactly. His eyes were shiny, and his beard was damp from sweat and kisses, but his face was serious. "It's terrifying to think that we won't live up to it all—the expectations, the duty. I've felt the same way lately. It's a paradox, really."

"What's the paradox, exactly?" I asked.

"The paradox of thinking that we could ever fail at what we're born for. It's impossible." He said it so simply, yet I felt like I might cry at how much this touched my soul.

"If you're afraid of being the head Druid, I don't think you need to worry about it too much, Ailsa. Ray seems to be in good-enough health. I think he'll stick around for a while to help you learn all you need to." He kissed and traced the edge of my long, sharp shoulder blade with his fingertip.

I nodded and pulled away a bit. "I didn't ever want to run away from the duty of being head Druid," I explained as the realization came to me. "I just wanted to run from the difficulties of being myself: the consuming grief, the personal fears, all the flaws that make me feel like I'm not good enough."

Aric reached over, placing his large hand over my wrist and hand. "Don't turn away from yourself, Ailsa. You can't be anybody else. Trust me, I've tried."

And with that, he rolled over and went to sleep, but I was wide awake.

CHAPTER 16:

MIDDENS

Later that day I finished grinding down all of the food waste inside—bones, small shells, rinds, pits, and cartilages—that could not be put to another purpose. I carried the waste in a large, hollowed-out tree root to the middens pile, east of the village, near the coast. I was shocked to look up and see it was getting on toward midday. We had slept longer than I had thought. I'd have to hurry in order to gather the day's herbs before the springtime sun burned the essential oils off.

The sun felt warm on my shoulders, and I noticed the thickening and darkening of the spring foliage and birdsong. I couldn't help but have a skip in my step, even doing something as mundane as visiting the middens dump. As I reached the pile, I felt a familiar shiver up my spine; I sensed someone was approaching. I lost my breath completely, so when I was abruptly spun around to find myself face-to-face with Ros, I was luckily too short of breath from sheer surprise to give him a tongue-lashing for sneaking up on me. But it wouldn't have mattered. He knocked the tree root bowl from my hand, pulled me to him so tightly I couldn't move, and kissed me, even as I pulled away. He was in one of his moods – as hot with anger as he was with lust. I wriggled like an eel from his grasp and slapped him to awaken him from his trance of madness. He seethed and boiled in front of me like a hot cauldron, eyes filled with steam. I closed my mouth, which had been open like a codfish's during most of this encounter, deciding not to scold Ros in his clearly maniacal state, and instead bent to pick up my bowl and its spilled contents.

"Why are you doing this?" he said in an exhale of breath, deflating himself a bit.

"You really can't be so careless, Ros. You risk someone seeing us. Aric or anyone could be around here." His pain-filled expression didn't change. "Why are you lurking by the middens anyway? Did you and the dogs miss your breakfast this morning?"

I stood, leaving my bowl safe on the ground this time, laughed, and gestured to the dogs sniffing the middens' edges for accidentally discarded mollusks or oysters. I was attempting to get an old friend to smile with an old joke; instead he seized my wrists and whispered, spitting through clenched teeth, "Why do you say I'm lurking? What have you been doing this morning?"

Ros was unable to see over me, and I was strong, very strong, but the force of his personality and his passion were enough to overpower my will to get away.

"Have you been around our roundhouse, Ros? If so, that's dangerous too, and you've clearly reaped your own punishment by overhearing us, so I won't say anything else about it." I glared at him, letting all my aggression out in one long look.

"You love him, don't you?" Ros asked. "I can tell by the flush in your cheeks and the look on your face. It's not just your wifely duty anymore, is it?"

"Of course I love him in some way; we've been married over a year. I can't just remain indifferent or cold."

"Do you love him as much as you love me?" Ros asked, like a child, desperately seeking approval, loosening his grip on my wrists.

More than I love you, at this very moment, I thought, but I couldn't say that out loud. I was surprised I even thought something so cruel about my dear friend, and so I simply said, "Of course I don't love him as much as I love you, but you can't lurk around our house; you can't kiss me in public. You can't lose your head to jealousy."

"Ailsa, you can trust that as surely as I stand before you, when I have the right opportunity, I will kill him."

I didn't change my expression when he said this because I didn't feel fear or surprise. My instinct had been right that Ros was losing control, and I had to do something, but there was no way that Ros could best Aric in any fight. If he could, then he would have challenged him when our betrothal was announced. The memories of the overwhelming sadness of that morning came flooding back, and something hardened in my heart, looking back at him, knowing that he hadn't protested the betrothal. He hadn't spoken up about his feelings until our wedding night, in fact. I set my jaw and clenched my teeth.

"Who do you think you are to talk about me lying with my husband, Ros? You are free to do so with whomever you choose, just as you did with *many* girls before I was married." I walked to the middens to dump the bowl.

If Ros had seethed with jealousy before, now he raged with much more than anger—it was that deep sadness of being misunderstood by the person you love most. He followed me and held me by the waist this time. "Free? How could I possibly ever be *free*? I've been beholden—no, indentured—to you since the day I was born."

"You got around pretty well for someone with that kind of burden," I spat back at him, fighting to release myself from his iron grip. "Stop holding on to me," I said loudly through clenched teeth, realizing that I couldn't yell because someone might hear. The dogs heard the rumble in my voice, though, and began to growl themselves, sensing an alpha struggle.

"You said it yourself," Ros continued. "You don't exist without me. And I can't exist without you." Tears filled his eyes, which had never been so bright.

I softened; his grip softened in response. I let out a deep breath. "Why did this only occur to you *after* I was married, Ros?"

"Ailsa, what was I supposed to do? From the moment you were called a Druid and wore the green robes, I told myself then that my dream of us sailing off together was unimaginable. I couldn't step between you and who you were born to be, so I silenced my heart. And yes, sometimes I found comfort or reassurance with other girls." I raised my eyebrows at him. "Don't look down on me, Ailsa. Being a Druid doesn't make you perfect. The decision of the Druids to support your marriage to Aric was a political one; they were using you to further their own aspirations. You're as much a chattel as the daughters born to kings and lairds on the mainland."

"You speak about my *family* when you tell lies about the Druids, Ros. Don't do it again." I was starting to care less about the volume of my voice. If people found me and Ros fighting by the middens, rather than locked in a lovers' embrace, they wouldn't think twice about it. We had argued insatiably since we began to speak.

Ros smirked. "And here I thought I was your family."

I couldn't help but be affected by what he had said, and I felt the sudden need to speak to Ray about it. I decided I had to find him.

"What about the twins from the island with the Lughnasadh stones?" I asked. "Are you and Rasha going to marry them?"

Ros stared back into my eyes, searching for something. "Yes, we're supposed to at the harvest celebration. At the Lughnasadh ceremony, which you'll be leading." I nodded, unable to hold his gaze. His hopeful thoughts filled the silence. "But I thought we would sail south instead. Everyone from our island will be there for the ceremony, and it will give us a chance to get away." I took a deep breath and started to walk away. "Please, Ailsa!" Ros called to me, but I broke into a run down the beach toward the stone circle, where I knew Ray would be.

Ros escaped to his cave on the beach, where he was working on his new crab claw sail. The technology mimicked the shape of a crab's pincer, with long, curved spars, and allowed for the sail to engage the wind, not only from the rear to push the boat but from multiple angles so that the boat could gain speed without rowing oars no matter what direction the wind came from. He had seen a couple rudimentary sails like this during his island-hopping expeditions, and a couple other boat makers on neighboring islands had shown him basic drawings. He had spent much of the last year focusing on perfecting the sail. This was his eighteenth iteration to achieve the perfect shape and perfect curve of the spars. He felt lucky that he had so many sisters who were talented seamstresses, providing him with different textiles and helping him to sew and resew the sails in different parts.

The experimentation was the only thing that took his mind off Ailsa, distracting him as he worked with his hands. Still, she was ultimately his muse. He was fashioning a sail that was faster than any other on the island so that they could get away without fear of being followed or having to go in the direction of the best wind, so they would truly have the freedom to go wherever they chose. He felt her slipping from his fingers and knew he needed to offer her this luxury in order to entice her away. He would take this sail out soon, and surely by the nineteenth or twentieth iteration, they could run away together.

As Ros set to work, he couldn't get out of his mind how things had felt different with her that morning. *What has changed?* he thought. He and Ailsa had been friends their entire lives, but her heart had secret shadows, and she was able to hide feelings from him in a way that he couldn't hide from her. She had told him that she wanted him, that she had loved him all their lives, but her actions were different this afternoon. Ros's mind raced as his body deftly went through the motions of preparing ropes, hull, stern, and sail. The calluses on his hands burned from steering the large boat, and his biceps screamed as he pushed on the gunwale to move the boat from the cave to the rising tidewater outside. He jumped in, felt the sea breeze on his hot, sweaty face, and breathed in a sigh of relief.

I'm just going to keep working on the boat and hope she doesn't change her mind, he thought. "Nothing can stop true love," he said out loud to the open sea. "Not the gods and not the damn Druids either." He pulled the rigs, tied the halyards, and with a loud *pop*, the sail opened and pulled him deeper into the blue bliss stretched out before him. He beamed with pride, smiling into the late afternoon sun, with the winds of freedom, and change blowing through his auburn hair.

CHAPTER 17:

ℬELTANE

Edie

It was April 30th, and the first raindrop of the day fell from my eyelashes onto my cheek as Frank moved out of my peripheral vision, rapidly snapping pictures of the latest stones we were visiting. They were on the western coast of Ireland, in a little town in Donegal, atop a hill with views of the surrounding landscape as far as the Atlantic Ocean. They were called the Beltany stones because they were used for the Beltane fires: sixty-four standing stones that surrounded what may have been an ancient neolithic tomb location. The setting was perfect for a megalithic tomb, I thought, overlooking the landscape the way it did. Whoever was buried here had long been turned to dust, and the stones that might have housed the tomb were scattered across farmsteads now and had been walls or fences for hundreds of years.

"Do you ever feel like someone's watching you when you come to these places?" Frank asked between snaps.

"You mean like one of my disapproving former archaeology professors?" I asked with a smile. He didn't look up at me but stared off beyond the standing stones into the horizon.

"No. It just—it gives me a chill down my nape. It's like we're here with the ghosts of everyone who was once here to worship or perform rituals, and there's no sense of time. I mean, look around us." He spun, his hands out, gesturing. "There's no sign of modern life anywhere, if you don't crest the hill to see the cars parked below."

I looked around us and up at the clouds gathering. "There will be signs of modern life tomorrow when people have left a bunch of beer cans and remnants of half-burned objects after the Beltane fires," I surmised.

"Why all the pyromania on Beltane?" Frank asked.

"You mean besides the etymology?" I replied.

He squinted his eyes, thinking for a moment. "*Bel- Taine'* — Oh, I see—'bright fire,'" he said slowly and in a Gaelic accent.

"Well, Cormac's ninth century glossary spells it *B-e-l-l-t-a-i-n-e*, so it may also refer to the radiance of May because Aine was the ancient Celtic goddess of radiance."

"So what kind of stuff will Michael and the locals get into at the bonfire tonight?" Frank asked. "This is the research I'm really here for," he added.

I smiled bashfully. "Traditionally, there are two great fires, and all the village cattle and kine are passed between them for protection. You also make sure that your home hearth is put out before the Beltane fires, and you return home at night with the communal fire to relight the home hearth."

"I'm going to have to chain-smoke the whole drive home if we want to get our hearth lit by this fire," Frank said, and I giggled.

"The archaeological record is not definite about this being the kerbstone remains of a passage tomb or a stone circle, so I'm going to compare my measurements and alignments against the other stone circles that are used for the equinoxes and solstices to get a better idea."

Frank sat against one of the stones and began to peel an orange. "These people sure were good with math and geometry for having no written language," he said.

"I suppose that's why I find it all so enchanting," I said.

"Indeed!" Frank had that light-bulb look again. *"Enchant,"* he said, "means both to make magic and to sing out. That's exactly what they did here and exactly what this place is for: enchanting!"

I scribbled that into my notebook so I wouldn't forget it in my draft of the final chapters later.

Unable to shake the feeling, Frank continued, "No wonder they say the fairies are out and about more on Beltane and Samhain. Today just feels especially eerie, like we could just as easily be the people who were enchanting at these stones or the cave people from Lascaux."

I sighed, pretending to be irritated. "Yes, I think some old ladies still leave gifts out for the fairies on Beltane and Samhain. But you do know they didn't *live* in the Lascaux caves—they just hid their art there—right?"

"Disapproving professors, you say? I thought you were the prize pupil?" Frank asked, returning to the former subject to avoid another lecture on cave art.

"Mmmm, I was Sully's favorite. Not anyone else's—that's for sure," I replied.

Frank smiled and set his camera down. "So you have some controversial theories?" he asked.

"You could say that," I replied coyly, rechecking my measurements one last time for precision.

"Why would you want to hide it? Isn't the point of art to share it?"

"Hide what—oh, the cave art?" I looked up from the numbers I'd been scrawling with a ballpoint pen that had started to run as the rain picked up. I closed the legal pad and stuffed it under my jacket and pulled up my hood. *Good old dependable Irish weather*, I thought. "If it's part of a sacred ritual, you probably don't want it out in the open. Part of the ritual may have, in fact, been processing to the back of the cave toward the art, sort of like what you see in the passage tombs in Britain. It's almost like they were trying to replicate the caves from mainland Europe and create man-made caves here to preserve the ritual of processing through the darkness. This spot would have been the perfect place for one, which is why I'm thinking these are kerbstones and not a stone circle." I paused. "It's time to get out of here. The rain is picking up."

I looked up and over the ridge behind us at the dark grey skies rolling in from the Atlantic Ocean. The islands of the North and Irish Seas were unpredictable when it came to weather, but the Wild Atlantic Way in the west was another beast altogether. Even seasoned outdoor adventurers like us had trouble knowing exactly when it would start and how long it would last. At least we could count on the internet weather predictions to be dependably wrong.

We made the trek back to Frank's blue Mini Cooper, which stood out nicely like a bluebird egg against the smoke-colored sky and perennially spring-green grass. As we walked toward the car park, I couldn't help but think of what Frank had said about the feeling around the stones at this time of year and the pervasive eeriness that the change of seasons brought forth at standing stones and generally, in any cultural landscape. Precisely what was the power that we were witnessing? The vibration of intensity that one felt in such places, which folklore attributes to the fairies. Was that magnetic resonance? Or were the ghosts of our ancestors more present as the veil thinned? I laughed at myself and shook my head. Clearly my superstitious friend was getting to me.

We jumped in the car, lucky not to be forced to depend on ferry timetables this time. We had a bit of a drive across the northern coast, but I was hoping the timing would work out nicely, considering we still had hours before sunset.

"Speaking of man-made caves, don't you have a free ticket for the winter solstice festivities at Newgrange this year?" Frank asked.

"I do," I chirped. "And what's more, I have a plus-one." I looked over at him out of the corner of my eye to gauge his excitement.

"I know a cute Irish bartender who just so happens to be an ancient history buff; I think you should ask him," he teased.

"Oh, come on. It won't be that boring for you! Come with me, please," I insisted.

"I don't think it will be boring at all," he protested. "What are the odds that the sun shines brightly enough to illuminate a thirty-foot-long passage tomb on an early December morning in Ireland?"

I smirked. "You'll have to check the line in Vegas; I'm not sure, but those stones we just saw have the same alignment, and they're usually well-lit by 9:04 a.m. when Newgrange is supposed to align."

"I'm not getting up that early," Frank said, deadpan.

I rolled my eyes. "I'm starting to find some links between all the local circles we've been checking out. Everything is within a 300-mile radius, and the stones align. The 300 is significant because that's the average mileage that hunter-gatherers would travel within a lifetime. So it seems that as they transitioned from that lifestyle to the village farming lifestyle we know today, that 300-mile distance might have been a holdover."

I was thinking about how some people must have traveled farther than that and how their culture would have known them as adventurers and explorers, necessary to the fabric of civilization, since they were the ones most likely to spread and trade resources and ideas. "Orkney, for example, was a religious center of the Neolithic in Britain. Several ideas seem to have originated there, like grooved pottery and the neolithic temple complex."

"But it's so freakin' far away." Frank added.

"Exactly. But it's only 300 miles away from the Outer Hebrides. They probably went there." I looked behind me in the rearview at the stones we had just left and the landscape they were stamped on. They were just yards from the sea cliffs, in a wide-sweeping open valley, like so many of the standing stones we had visited: the ones of Orkney and the Hebrides. Unlike the caves of Lascaux, they would have been easy to find and would have made a statement to any unexpected visitors. A chill ran down my spine, and the hairs prickled on my "nape," as Frank had called it. Maybe it was just the chill of the icy wind coming in through the window, or maybe Frank was right—we were in a thin place at a thin time.

Frank sat in the driver's seat, overhearing me whisper the last part to myself. "Is that what your book says? That it's a thin time?" He gestured to the book on ley lines I had sitting on my lap.

"No, not that book, but I do remember reading somewhere that All Hallows' Eve falls on the day of the year when souls feel closest to Earth because there's something about the light that makes us feel the veil between this world and the next is lifted a bit," I answered.

"Sounds like Poe to me," Frank said.

I smiled and agreed. "Beltane, as we said, is the same type of festival as Samhain—the midpoint between the solstice and the equinox. We're onto something," I told him. "I can feel it—the precipice of knowing."

"Quite literally the precipice," Frank said, looking down at the jagged cliffs that dropped into the sea below us as we drove west.

I was glad we had left when we did. The Mini Cooper chugged around the tight mountain bend, and the windshield wipers danced frantically in the heavy April rain. Frank pulled over at the first pub we saw.

"So other than visitation of souls that have already transitioned, what can happen in a thin time?" he asked as he turned off the car, the swish of the wipers stopped, and the rain pounded down on the windshield.

"The energetic vibrations become clearer. I think some people actually feel the shift in the earth, and I think our connection to people, whether they're ancient, passed on, or right in front of us, is clarified and strengthened. Like you said, it happens on Samhain too, which is why Halloween is all about communion with the dead and spirits. But it can happen any time, really, as energies shift or important moments occur. Have you ever seen a baby stare right past you, intent on something not there, knowingly smiling into oblivion? Or do you ever have déjà vu and know with every fiber of your being that you've lived or dreamt the moment you're experiencing before? Sometimes when I'm doing field work over a ley line or in a spiritual place, I feel...a certain presence. I can't explain it, but I think you're supposed to feel what you felt at the stones, that knowing and feeling of coexistence with the people from before... and the people to come after."

I reached out and turned up the Celtic flautist on the radio to form a trinity of ultrarelaxing sounds: the rain, the sound of cars on the road behind us, and the thin whine of the wooden flute.

"I like the sound of that. The fire tonight is going to clarify some connections, I believe," Frank said mischievously. He turned his whole body in the tiny seat to look at me—or to read my reaction perhaps.

I took a deep breath, focused my gaze forward, and, squinting into the cascading water, silently agreed to the unfolding scheme. "Maybe, but what are the chances that the rain stops and Michael actually turns up?" I asked.

"Pretty good, I think," Frank responded, gleefully.

Just then, a rap at the passenger-side window, which I was leaning against, startled me out of my skin. I think I screamed a little. Frank jumped out of the car and ran over to Michael, embracing him. They ran into the pub together, and I gathered my books and notepads into my pack. I pulled the mirror down from the visor, applied some Carmex to my lips, smoothed my wet eyebrows into submission, and tightened my long, dark ponytail. I was practical. My clothes were, my face was, and so was I.

"Time to live a little, in the name of research," a small voice said inside of me. So I pulled my Wellies back on and ran inside.

"You must be seriously blind if you don't go for this guy, Edie. He is gorgeous," Frank whispered to me as we watched him procure our pints and pub grub from a female bartender he clearly knew. He walked over, expertly balancing the triune pints before setting them down on the table, and I greeted him with a handshake and a small smile of apology. Frank covered his face with his hands at my awkwardness.

"Sorry about the rain. I hope it's not canceled." My introvert heart lurched at the possibility of not having to go to my first fire festival in years, but that suggestion solicited a hearty laugh from our host for the evening festivities.

"No need to apologize for the Irish weather, love. You'll likely find it will only encourage our Beltane celebrators." Except he said it in the truly Gaelic way: "Be-all-tee-nay." "They're not deterred by much, especially weather." He smiled and held his hands up to the sky, where distant thunder could be heard offshore.

"We went to the site and saw that the woodpiles ready to burn were covered, so that's good at least," Frank said.

Michael took my hand in his and brushed my fingertips, smiling with mystery behind his eyes, "I knew ye's been playing in the dirt."

I pulled my hand away, despite the butterflies I felt in my chest. "You must be some barfly," I insisted. "We've hardly seen you anywhere else but the pubs dotting the northern countryside."

"You could say that." He nodded as our food was delivered.

We ate, saying little other than remarking on what to expect from the evening's festivities, waiting for the rain to let up. It did finally. And I dragged the last of my mushy peas through some tartar sauce. Michael's description of the festivities had made it seem less magical than Frank and I were dreaming it would be and more practical, like a mundane village activity. I was feeling a little crestfallen as we followed him up the hill to the muddy parking area by the stones, and then I saw it. The warm light of a huge fire and hundreds of torches began to take shape in the distance as my eyes adjusted to the dark. We jumped out of the car and started the ascent like moths to a porch light. A flutter of excitement bubbled up in my chest, and Frank clasped his hand around mine as we approached. Michael waved to some locals and procured our very own torch—a real one, not a flashlight.

Frank pulled me to him and whispered, "It's *Be-al-tee-nay*," the way Michael had said it. "Connections are clarified and strengthened, like you said." He winked at me and held his cigarette between his lips to light it. Before he could ignite his Zippo in the weak drizzle that the rain had eased into, Michael reached over with a lit match.

"Yes, they are, in this world and beyond, loves!" he added with a grin. I felt my cheeks burn; he handed me the torch and grabbed my free hand. "Now, let's dance!"

CHAPTER 18:

MAPS

Ailsa

The leaves were young on the oak trees. I could see the fresh color bursting from the treetops in the oak grove down the river. From where I stood on our cultivation allotment, the tallest, and thus oldest, oaks had recently become visible over the top of the ash grove that had been pollarded during the past winter solstice, one year after my wedding, leaving the view clear and inspiring. I tilted my head in sympathy for the ash grove, however, for having its beauty stripped from it, cut down to little more than stumps. I'd seen this happen to the forest trees for my whole life, but I had come to know intimately what that dramatic pruning felt like for myself over this winter. Still, pollarding was a necessary refining process. It gave us wood for our boats, fires, and structures and kept the trees alive so they could grow up around us and provide for us again years down the road. We kept things alive as much as we could, and sometimes that meant severe pruning.

A year had come and gone since our wedding, and the sage women of the village had come to me bearing raspberry leaves and the foremilk of recently calved cows. As our one-year anniversary had passed us by with no conception, my lack of pregnancy had become a concern to others but a blessing for me. My grandmother looked at me with soft, knowing eyes as the other women explained how frequently to make the tea at the waxing of the moon and when to share the foremilk with Aric. They were very delicate about the fact I had not produced an offspring, and I suppose I appreciated that under the circumstances, but I felt like I was running out of time in postponing the inevitable. Druid rites weren't strictly passed through bloodlines since Druids often didn't marry, but as one of the oldest families in my village, our Druid line was direct, and I was the end of it. It was simple. It was my duty, my destiny. All of Ros's recent pleas for us to run away had elucidated that fact for me as I needed to understand the full picture of that which I was running away from.

Up until the last few weeks, I had been vigilantly collecting stinging nettle and tansy root for tea, in addition to taking wild carrot seeds to protect myself from pregnancy. So far it had worked, but without a pregnancy, people would only grow more suspicious of our marriage, and the last thing I needed was more eyes on me these days. I had lost count of the number of nights I had met Ros at the coast or the cliffs over the course of the last few moons, but I hadn't seen him at all since he had confronted me at the middens after Aric's latest return from his travels, not even in passing at the smokehouse or root cellar, and so I stopped taking the preventative seeds and teas. During this time I didn't even seek the company of my grandmother outside of the daily cooking and cleaning I helped her with. Even then, I busied myself so much with the quern, mending, laundry, and grinding that there wasn't time for idle chat.

Resettlement was happening on the mainland, and that meant Aric took frequent trips with the other village warriors, staking our stronghold and scouting for potential threats or trade partners. From what I gathered from him when he returned, just before Beltane, there were far more of the latter than the former. Aric was excited about the opportunities for trade and had brought back several special totems for me, shiny things of beauty for my hair and wrists that I had never seen the likes of. He seemed distracted by these adventures and not overly worried about our lack of conception, which was such a relief. He himself carried a new whale bone mace head, larger than both my hand put together, and carved to perfection. I tried not to imagine it bursting Ros's skull open.

Over our last meal together, he had, however, told me a story that Ray had once told him about the last female Druid, who, forty years prior, when Ray was a boy, had been unable to conceive despite her favorable marriage to an explorer from a faraway village. Ray said it had to do with differing blood types. He smiled at me and brushed the hair back out of my face when he told me, as if to assure me it was all fine. I couldn't summon the courage to tell him that I had secretly hoped that would be our story too, but it appeared that was not going to be so.

The season changed around me and inside of me. That vibrant, new spring green that was visible as I worked our allotments to raise the barley and kale grew into the verdant landscape that sends children, rabbits, foals, and yearlings tripping through the rolling green hills and rushing creeks fresh with runoff from the melted snow of the mountaintops. Young doves peeked out at me from ramshackle nests as I gathered herbs and tended the vulnerable barley plants that would yield our harvest in half a year. Six moons. Thinking of that passage of time, the cycle of the year, brought my mind to a more personal reflection of my own change.

As I foraged one morning, excited with the recent rain and new mushrooms available, a jay landed on my shoulder. I gently placed an acorn in his beak. "Go plant this for me," I whispered to him. "And grow me an oak that will live for a thousand years." He did. The woodland always listens.

Spring was such a miraculous season in our landscape. I knew that what was happening within me was the perfect reflection of the rebirth and rejuvenation of spring that surrounded me. My long, twig-like fingers pulled aside my green cloak and touched my still-flat belly with a sign of tranquility. It was a visceral acknowledgment of the life that I knew stirred within me, like the Druid's blessing over the hearts of our people.

And so I gave this new, bright-green life within me my own sort of blessing and felt her strong heartbeat respond to my touch and pulse from inside of me. I silenced my own heart's desires and heard her speak from within me.

It was Beltane when I knew without a doubt. We had sailed to the Beltany stones for our ceremony, where the setting sun fell between the two great menhirs, and other villages joined us to relight the fires of our home hearths. When I touched the largest stone at the fire festival that night, I felt her flutter inside my womb. I did what all newly expectant mothers do when I felt it: leaving one hand on the menhir, I caressed my womb with the other, as if to say, "Hello there to you too."

Then I became self-conscious. Had anyone seen me? My eyes darted around as the ceremony continued, wondering who shared my secret now. Everyone was staring at the fire, Ray, or the dancers as they approached for the Beltane dance, which was probably the most beautiful and ethereal dance of them all. I sighed with relief that no one was watching me, despite the feeling I had, and then I saw Ros, who was standing some way off from the stones with his sister and the twins they were betrothed to, out of the corner of my eye. He had been positioned perfectly for watching me. I smiled as our eyes met for an instant, for the first time in a while, and then the drums carried me away to my duty.

I sucked on a wild raspberry while sitting cross-legged in the late-spring grass, looking south over the rolling green hills of our home some days later. We were on the tallest munro, one of seven little mountain peaks that dissolved into the hills we looked on below. We had walked for hours, talking sometimes, sometimes walking in silence, hand in hand. Aric had found a nice boulder to lean up against at dusk, so we sat a while, and I promised him I could lead us off the mountain by the light of stars alone. The day had grown warm, and we sat on my large green Druid cloak, he in his wool kilt and linen shirt, me in nothing but my linen dress, which had begun to cling to my widening hips. I liked that Aric wore the corded skirt or wool kilt of the northern men, like my father. Men of our village often wore breeches or longer vestments like the Druids, and I appreciated seeing his muscular legs stretched out before me. He bent over me, taking another sweet, ripe, red fruit from my hand with his mouth, gently. He had exuded a new peace all spring, and it drew me to him like the forest animals leaving the shelter of their trees for our village fires and feasts, hungry for a dropped morsel or a moment's warmth.

When Aric thought deeply about something, he couldn't help but move anxiously about. I had considered putting a broom in his hand more than once when he paced around the house on the eve of some great exploration. The thought made me smile as I pressed the cool horn opening of my leather flagon to my lips and enjoyed another sip of grandmother's strong birch sap wine. I felt lightheaded and giddy with happiness. There was simplicity in this moment, but I was about to ruin it, unknowingly.

"How did you end up here, in a place so far from your real home?" I asked into the fading daylight. "I've heard stories about what happened to your father's ship, but I've never heard it from you. Weren't you settling or exploring the westerly isles?"

I turned around so I was looking at him, but something about his glare made me return my eyes back to the hills and horizon. There wasn't anger behind his eyes but an intensity like I had never seen before. "I'm just piecing together things Ray has told me over the years. I'm sorry if it's upsetting." And then there was another long pause as I reached for his hand and stroked the worn and cracked knuckles.

"This is my home," Aric responded, smiling just a little and using one finger to turn my chin back toward his face. "Ray saved my life, not just that day on the shore but many times after that. When Iona died. When he suggested my marriage to you. He said I came back to life that day he found me, and since I was born again that day, it is sometimes painful to think of my old life. It feels—" He paused, raised his eyebrows, and made a guttural noise that could have passed for a laugh with someone else, but I thought it sounded a bit more like disgust. "It feels so distant from my life now, and yet it is so close to my heart. Is that possible?"

"Of course it is," I answered, feeding him another raspberry. "So you died and came back too? Just like a Druid priest." I wondered what that meant. Maybe Aric had too.

"It was terrifying." It was barely a whisper, but the words came as such a shock that I heard them ringing loud and clear, echoing over the hills in front of us. It was nearly summer, and the night was just like a midsummer evening: a bright sunset in purple, blue, orange, and red, a carpet of grass and flowers perfect for lounging, midges everywhere despite the light breeze. I swatted at a few flying around my face and realized how stunned I actually was at this admission of his. I tried to picture Aric terrified, even the younger, widowed Aric I could remember from my childhood. He never seemed afraid of anything. He came home telling stories of small battles or skirmishes on the road, cattle raids, blood sacrifices, and much stranger and more frightening things from abroad. He seemed amazed and intrigued but never scared. I was so stunned by his display of emotion that I realized I hadn't replied or comforted him in any way in the minutes that had passed as the sun sank faster and faster below the horizon. After too long of a silence, all I could think to blurt out was "Tell me, Aric."

My posture changed to a more alert squatting position, and I hugged my knees, peering into his face, which was still looking ahead at the colorful horizon, beautiful legs stretched out before him down the hill. "It was like the earth opened, Ailsa. It wasn't a storm like people have said."

"What do you mean?" I asked gently.

"It was a beautiful evening. Almost exactly like tonight," he said, looking at me for the first time in a while. "It was like the earth opened in the water, and there was a great pull to the center that overcame the ship's direction. I could actually hear the strength of the water crunching the ship, as if chewing it up to devour it. I still hear the sound of the timber cracking now. I have never seen men as genuinely terrified as the men on board were, and these were people, Ailsa, who had been in battle, watched their friends, children, and women die. These men had seen rough lands and unimaginably bad men and lived to tell the tale. Until that night."

"A maelstrom," I whispered. I couldn't help but let my mind wander to what Ray had said about the changes that the earth was experiencing at our meeting on the equinox. He had described it in just this way; the strong pull that I felt to the center of the earth was similar to what those who had built the stone circles had felt generations before. They had been called by the earth to erect the structures over a thousand years ago, and there was a similar summoning of our generation—but to what, exactly, he was not sure. Instinctively, I felt that it also had to do with the stones. This was a very long story that the earth was telling.

"I suppose that's what it was," Aric said. "Ray said he had heard tales of such things happening south of here, and he believed the shifts happening in the earth were responsible, perhaps that they triggered one another, even."

I rested my hand delicately on Aric's chest. "But how could you possibly have survived such a thing? As such a young boy among older men, among warriors who had seen battle yet didn't survive themselves."

Aric struggled to answer, his throat too full of emotion to swallow. "It was mostly because of them, actually. They saved me and did everything to get me off the ship as soon as they realized it was going down. My father's men used the cannon launcher to throw me and the raft as far toward the land as possible." He laughed at the clear ridiculousness of sharing that memory out loud, but the laughter caught in his chest, thickened by grief. "I remember the feeling of sailing into the darkness, hopeless. I remember thinking, *This is what death must be like.*"

"So then you just washed up on the western shore of the island?" I already had a vivid image in my mind of Ray climbing down to the caves below and finding, to his surprise, a boy washed up on the beach like a jellyfish.

"I'm not sure how long I drifted or waited before Ray found me out on the rocks, clinging for dear life," Aric confessed, "but I know what day it was when I arrived. And actually..." he continued, ignoring my dumbfounded look. He laughed heartily this time, and just the sound of his resilient happiness calmed me in a way I wasn't expecting. It was like hearing my father's laugh, and I realized in that moment how much I carried with me the fear of the men I loved sinking too far into their sadness to be saved.

"Ray was there, looking down on me when I finally opened my eyes, which had swollen shut from all the salt water. At first sight of him, I wasn't sure if he was God and I had reached some sort of rocky afterlife or if he was the sorcerer who had sent the whirlpool." I laughed at the thought of Ray as some sort of miniature god at this stature, surely disappointing to a twelve-year-old boy. "I just remember him wrapping me in his cloak and plying me with fish and ale in the cave until I finally had the strength to walk up the cliffside."

"I just don't understand," I practically yelled. "Why isn't this story a ballad we sing at every fire, festival, and wedding? It's incredible." I shook my head in disbelief. "Everyone in the world should celebrate this story of your survival, at least our little village should."

Aric smiled. "Sometimes I don't believe it myself. The likelihood of surviving something like that."

"Aric—" I began but didn't know how to finish. My eyes filled with tears, and I waved my hand in front of my face again, pretending like I was swatting midges instead of trying to prevent the tears from falling. "I don't know what to say, or how to make sense of anything you just told me, except death won't be like being catapulted into nothing. I do know that fore sure."

"I trust you," he responded, enveloping me within his huge arms, pulling me down to the grass to look up at the purple sky with him. "I trust whatever you tell me." he added.

I sighed. "Did you say you remember exactly what day it was?" I asked into his neck stubble, curling up like a shrimp by his side and pulling my long Druid's cloak to cover both of us.

"It was the summer solstice nineteen years ago, Ailsa. The day you were born. Ray told only the other Druids about what happened to me, and it was overshadowed by the great loss of your mother a few days later—I've heard the tales of her rare talent and beauty. Ray said it was also the birth of the next head Druid, like the maelstrom was a harbinger of your existence." The words hung in the air, suspended by the twinkling stars that began to come out, one by one, as the sky darkened. "Ray said I was as good as dead when he found me, but somehow he was able to push the water from my chest, and I came back to life."

I felt a tear run down my cheek. I wiped the tear away and looked up at my husband, this mystical Norse creature the gods had delivered to me just before they took my mother from me. The closeness I had felt to him over the last few months was not just me running toward a duty and away from Ros. It was a real closeness, another example of the ordained life I led.

"I thought when I was a child that it was just because you were born on *midsomer* that you were thought to be so special by the Druids, but now I know you are magical in your own right, and the Druids saw it immediately, even through their grief for your mother." He broke his seriousness and smiled mischievously. "You are the most enchanting thing I have ever encountered." He tenderly kissed the nape of my neck and my shoulders, so gently it almost felt like the midges again, and I nearly swatted him away.

"Aric?" I stopped him from his warm, wet kisses, his mouth totally enveloping mine in passion, by placing my first two fingers over his lips and staring, vulnerably, into his eyes. "How many women were you with before me?"

Aric paused and lifted himself up a little. The stars had really come out now behind his back, and he was framed by them, so perfect in his form that he was like a constellation himself. I thought back to the first time I had lain with Aric and how I did not love him then but had rather performed out of duty. It was hard to think about that now. I felt so differently, just a little over a year later. Sometimes it seemed so much longer ago. I was lost in the deep indigo color of his eyes, with those gold flecks at the center. Looking into them was like looking up at the night sky, and the two sights started to blend together.

"Don't ask me that," Aric finally responded, looking down at me. "Ask me how many I truly loved before you." I turned away, unable to meet his intense gaze. "Ask me." He brushed my cheek with the back of his fingers. When I looked at him, there was no way to deny his request. He stared at me, willing the question. "I've never loved in this way before, Ailsa."

"Don't say that," I said, pushing his mass off of me onto the ground.

"It's true." His voice cracked. "I don't care if you believe me. Or even if you judge me."

I stared back at him, turning away from the edge of the northern peaks looking over the hills below. The wind picked up, blowing my green cloak away, and I stood up to chase it. I ran a bit downhill, grabbed it from the breeze, picked the loose strands of hair out of my mouth and wrapped my cloak around my shoulders.

"It's, it's—different." He stuttered, struggling for the words to explain. We stood a distance apart now. "It's the difference between being a boy and being a man. It's remembering my parents and knowing what their love was like. Truly, it's having the fortune of loving Iona *and* loving you—and knowing the difference." I narrowed my eyes at him, not understanding the declaration since it had been widely known that he had mourned the loss of his precious, young wife for many years, and it had been assumed that there was great love between them.

As if reading my mind, he looked into my face and walked toward me in a few huge strides. "Ailsa, I loved Iona in every way I could then, but I pray to the gods that I could have shown her the love that I am able to give to you. The type of love my father felt for my mother. Maybe my love for Iona would have grown into this, but it didn't get the chance. I wasn't even wed to her as long as we've been wed." That realization broke my heart for him and for young, sweet Iona.

Something between Aric and me had changed recently, I knew. And now I was starting to understand what the catalyst of the shift was. I was learning from him. He had experiences in life and love that I did not, and as I opened myself up to knowing him in a deeper way, I had also started to grow myself. I valued his perspective and experience. I no longer looked down from my position as Druid on his position as an explorer. I hadn't said anything to him about this realization, and he searched my face for some clue to what I was feeling.

"I'm afraid of how overwhelming it feels at times—the fear of losing you," he said quietly, vulnerably.

I ran toward him, and embraced him, my green cloak flying up around us. "I didn't think you felt fear." I smiled up at him as I spoke, and I wanted his broad mouth to grin down at me, but he maintained a fierce look, staring into my soul.

"Maybe Druids are braver than warriors," he said, a grin rising over his lips. "I've escaped near-death a few times, Ailsa, but I know what I truly fear, and I don't mind admitting it."

I hugged him tightly, wanting him to feel held. "Fear doesn't prevent death or loss; it only prevents living," I said, pushing his long hair behind his ears.

"I see Ray's gotten to you with that one too," he said, laughing. He kissed me then, for a long time, until I grabbed his hand and asked him to walk down the mountain and go to bed with me.

The walk down was leisurely. We held hands and said little as we navigated moss-covered rocks, sleeping goats, and steep footholds. Luckily, there were no trees or tree roots to hinder our descent, and the dampness had been burned off the grass by the warm day.

As I led Aric down toward the hillside trail that took us back to the village, I thought about the maelstrom on the summer solstice nineteen years ago and what that meant. One of the stones had cracked the day I was born, and this was taken as one of the many signs that I would be the next head Druid. The stones erected for the circles had been chosen by our ancestors for a reason, and that reason lay in the hue that the stones took on in sunlight. From farther away, they were a blue color, while on closer inspection, it was apparent the stones were in fact gray; they just had tiny purple veins, like a human's blood, that shone in the sunlight and contributed to the blue look of them.

I decided I would inspect the crack in the stone and ask Ray about the purple veins before the summer solstice that marked nineteen years since the crack, since Aric's arrival. If the gods had sent Aric to me that day, we were surely destined to play an important role in what was to come. By the time we were on the path back to the village, our pace had doubled. An urgency was driving us both, and I could feel it pulsating between our palms.

I wondered for a moment if he had mentioned his fear because he suspected my current condition. I had just missed my latest moon cycle the week before, and it was possible he could have noticed since I normally had extra laundry to do and often ate his portion of our day's meat to replace the blood I lost during my cycle. I looked at him out of the corner of my eye, questioning, and he looked back at me as lustful as a stag in Autumn as we turned toward our roundhouse. Whatever he might have suspected, it clearly was not what was on his mind at that moment.

Yes, the issue of the stones' veins was something that needed to be observed both up close and far away in every sense. I would speak to Ray about it directly, but it would have to wait until tomorrow.

"Grandmother?" I peeked into her roundhouse the next day with the sweetest voice I could muster. She was stiff in the mornings at her age and swept hunched over her broomstick. I stepped over the dust pile in front of the doorway and walked toward the hearth to warm myself. It was a cool morning for midsummer, and the lightest of frosts had formed on the small vegetable patch outside my bedroom window.

"Ailsa, it has been days since I saw you last. What has kept you away, child?"

"I've just been busy preparing for the upcoming solstice ceremony."

"Ahhh, I see," she said without looking up from her broom, though I saw the crinkles form in her eyes as she smiled down at the floor. I wondered for the first time if her eyesight was going.

"Speaking of midsummer, I have question about my birthday," I said, squatting by the fire.

"Ahh, I see," she said again, this time looking up at me, using her broom as a walking stick to come closer to where I sat by the hearth.

"Why didn't you ever tell me that was the day that Aric arrived? Washed up on shore from his ship?" I asked. And she dropped the broom.

I motioned for her to sit with me. She slowly added some herbs from her pocket to the water on the fire to prepare a tea for us, then carefully lowered herself down to sit next to me. "Aric told you this?" she asked, stirring the pot. I nodded. "I didn't realize Aric knew that was the day he arrived. How incredible, what the human spirit retains! He slept for days after his arrival and then was in and out of consciousness for weeks, sometimes forgetting where he was when he awoke." She handed me a round mug from the table next to the fire. I tapped my fingers on the earthenware mug as it seemed she was still avoiding my question.

Grandmother said nothing but knelt by the hearth, collecting warm water from the cauldron for her tea bowl, into which she dropped several more herbs, one of which smelled strongly of peppermint. She sat down cross-legged by the fire, blowing on the water to cool it, and invited me to snuggle up close to her with a simple gesture of patting on the hides. So I did, breathing in her herbaceous smell while I prepared my own tea.

After a period of sipping teas and pleasantries, I said in a new voice that didn't quite sound like my own what I couldn't explain in my own head, even after days of thinking about it. "At the solstice ceremony where I became a Druid, Ray told the village that my tie to the earth was deeper because of openings and shifts below and what was occurring in the earth when I was born. And Ray told me recently that I am a dowser like Father was, that I can sense what is happening energetically and even where gemstones, water, or other resources might be."

"You *are* very good at finding herbs," Grandmother joked as she motioned to all the ground herb leaves by the hearth and the dozens still intact hanging above us.

I smiled and sipped my tea, continuing, "When Aric told me about how the ship he was on sank on the day I was born, it sounded like that shift was happening and may have caused the great mael-strom. I'm not saying my birth caused this shift, but maybe the shift caused me to be born that day, bringing on mother's labor pains?"

"Yes, just as you were meant to be," I heard my grandmother whisper into her tea.

"Grandmother—" I began, seriously, but she cut me off.

"Ailsa, we have maps of the land and sea to show us the way to new places and new routes to sail on. Those maps change and develop with time as we travel more and learn more about the sur-rounding seas and terrain." I nodded and sipped my tea. "There are places we still haven't been, so the maps are incomplete—and that's why we also have maps within our hearts that lead us to our destinies. These maps of our hearts also change as we explore, go on adventures, and learn more about ourselves, but there are some roads that remain unchanged, that were there long before we even started navigating."

"Why do I feel like there's something you're not telling me?" I asked quietly.

She looked at me with defiance in her face. "I don't know why Jord and Ray have kept this from you for so long." My heart started beating rapidly. "You and Aric have been betrothed since the day you were born, my darling."

I sipped my herbal tea and nodded, partially in shock and, in a way, knowing that had been the truth all along. It had to be. "Did they kill Iona?" I asked.

"Oh no, dear!" I breathed a sigh of relief. "They just knew she was sickly and wouldn't survive into your adulthood. Aric had struggled to fit in with some of the other children since arriving, and Ray wanted him to have his heart's desire." I didn't say anything, so

Grandmother continued. "I asked them to tell you on your trip to the stones at Orkney since Aric was with you and since they had been in Ros's ear for so long at that point."

I felt my teeth clenching as I looked up and into her eyes. "You mean Ros has been telling the truth? They told him I couldn't marry and that he had to give me up, like he's been saying since my wedding night?" Grandmother patted my hand and made the humming noise in her throat that she used to make when I needed coddling as a child. "We were fourteen," I said more to myself than her. "Why didn't they tell me?" I asked, knowing she didn't have the answer.

"Maybe they wanted to see if you could love Aric organically and not feel bound by some predestined fate or prophecy," she answered as she smoothed my hair. "Ray says your child is coming to lead the village to a new time."

I couldn't help but laugh. Part of me wanted to stomp off to the stones, where I knew Ray was lurking this close to the solstice. Another part of me wanted to run as fast as I could to find Ros and leave with him, as he had begged. He had been honest with me about the Druids dissuading him from marrying me. Maybe he was the only one who had ever been truly honest with me. My heart ached for him, and I felt myself questioning everything. Suddenly, the courage he had shown to go against the Druids' secret messages to him overshadowed the anger I had about him timing his declaration of love to my wedding night.

"I think a wise woman learns she cannot outrun her fate," Grandmother said, as if reading my mind. My eyes widened at her, reflecting the fire across from us in their green, brown, and gold flecks, and in that moment, when we held one another's gaze, something passed between us.

"It's catching up to me," I said, simultaneously questioning and answering myself.

"The map of your heart is changing, Ailsa. And nothing changes a heart more than a child." She smiled, and I pulled away from her, not ready to share this secret that still belonged only to me. Perhaps only to me, I thought, remembering Ros's look at the Beltane fire briefly.

"I should know," she continued despite my physical and emotional distance. "I thought I knew grief when I lost my mother and my father to disease." She shook her head, peering into my soul where I held such a similar pain. "But then I lost my child when your mother died so shortly after you were born, and I realized…I knew *nothing* about grief." Her voice cracked as she said "nothing" through clenched teeth.

I reached back for her hand and held it in mine. Once my hand had been tiny in hers, and she had been able to wrap her fingers around it to envelop it completely. Now, her slim, bent fingers looked like a child's hand in mine.

"The map of my broken heart has made new paths, islands, and valleys that I never wanted to know," she said, looking from the fire to me.

I held her hand to my heart. "I am still learning the map of my heart, Grandmother, but I do know that you are my true north. I am thankful for you."

CHAPTER 19:

The Summer Solstice

Ray knelt by the huge boulder and felt the dew drops dampen his knees through his green robe. The sun was rising over the hills toward the mainland, but over the sea to the west, it was still dark. He had walked the beach before dawn, picking up violet pebbles and rolling them between his fingers as he thought. It was a place he could be alone with his thoughts and full of clarity. Even walking with just one companion made his thoughts hazy, the feelings and thoughts of the person he was with always intruding too loudly, like noisy neighbors, into his own consciousness. He even needed space from Jord once in a while, though he had taught his intuition to quiet more around his best friend and lifelong companion.

So much intuition was a blessing and a curse, his mother always said. When Ray was young and read his parents' thoughts, they had called him a seer and sent him away to this island of the Druids. Then came the realization that he had seen colors or auras around certain people from the time he was a baby. He honestly had grown to think that was how everyone saw other people, but the Druids helped him clarify his gifts. Before coming here, he had wondered how long he would be alone in this world, and the thought of that scared young boy made him think of Aric and how he had seen himself in the boy who washed up on shore that day. Ray had been of a similar age when he had come to inhabit this island.

Naturally, the Druid elders wanted Ray to perform his talents as soon as he arrived. From a tender age, he was asked to do everything from predicting crop failures to approving marriages, baby names, and war tactics. The responsibility left him feeling burdened and confused on his good days, utterly overwhelmed and lost at other times. Such was the solitary life of being head Druid now too. And then he smiled, thinking about Jord, his best friend since arriving on the island nearly a lifetime ago. And half of the time he had spent on the island, he had also had Aric as his family.

"I guess it's not so lonely," Ray said out loud, his breath vapor mingling with the morning fog. "We lost souls find one another here." He found a gentle slope that his short legs could climb, and he began the long ascent up the coastal cliffs to the standing stones. His hair was fading into gray on top, but the stringy brown strands reached his shoulders and whipped him in the face as the seaward winds picked up. He pulled his hood up, which he normally avoided since everyone said he looked like a frog when he was covered from head to toe in all green.

Ray's morning walks were for the dual purpose of clearing his head and setting his intentions for the day's prayer. He did this in the ancient way that had been practiced for hundreds of years, finding that the feel of the flint tool in his hand connected him to the ancestral spirit in the stone. He knelt now by the guardian stone of the great stone circle, which was perched on a hill that overlooked the pebbled beach below. It wasn't within the circle; it was outside of it. It wasn't the largest, and it wasn't even sandstone, which was the softest for carving, but it was *his* stone. It called his name. He knew what it felt like to be the stout guardian of taller, more grace-ful stones in the circle.

He set to his carving, which pulled the secrets from the stone. The walk on the beach prior had helped to quiet him for the ritual carving, so now with his soul at peace, he closed his eyes, reaching for the stone and willing the spirits to guide him through the life spiral that he would carve. The labyrinth spiral that was tradition-ally carved and created was a therapeutic process but also a calming sight in and of itself for any passersby or for the hundreds of people who would be gathered at the stone circle for the summer solstice that night. Ray imagined his busy mind, his negative and hurtful thoughts, his fears and overwhelm following the spiral pathway out of the chaotic center of his mind to the freedom outside of the whirling maelstrom.

Just as his responsibility as head Druid bore chains that dragged and tied him down like the spinning center, so too the power gave him a wild freedom. Laying hands on people to heal them, feeling the pulsing of their life and aura under his fingertips, was empow-ering and humbling all at once. Remembering the balance of the spiral kept Ray centered in it all. And so just as he would follow the spiral out to freedom, he could follow it back inside to the safety and huddle of his mind's deepest crevices, where he could focus in a deeper way. Out he went and back inward, tracing and retracing his new spiral. The blue-green veins in the stone held a secret that he had been trying to get at for years.

Sometimes, if he looked up and found himself, after a long walk, at his rock without a tool, he could just follow one of the spirals that had already been carved with a fingertip. He had done this many times before and had occasionally channeled the carver of the original spiral. That person's thoughts flooded his mind with such suddenness that sometimes he couldn't help but laugh, taken aback by the juxtapositions that they had unleashed from his mind—or manifested into it.

It was during one such occasion, on the summer solstice many years ago, that Ray had been on the northern coast of the island, rockier and colder and much less pleasant for walks.

Something had called him out there to the wild northern mountains, though, and so he had found a suitable stone, too difficult to carve into with the sharpened stone he had with him, and settled into a happy crevice that was covered in seven spirals and begun tracing and trancing, taming his mind to be singular and quiet, focused on his morning's work. The waves crashed madly on the shore beneath him, and the wind howled, a portent for bad weather in the northern isles, perhaps. The sound of storms off the coast quickly became as steady as a pulse. It was white noise for Ray's morning meditation, which he settled into deeply and peacefully.

His mind's eye became blue and spiraled like the labyrinth before him, but what he thought he began to see at the center of it jolted him out of his trance. He found the sound of his own heartbeat too loud for his own ears—or was that the angry sea below? Afraid that he had lost touch with information he needed, he fought his way back to the spiral pathway meditation his mind had started on. Again, he saw what he feared he had seen before. There were bodies, flung from the jagged western cliffs into the crashing waves below, sucked into the center of the spiral.

Disturbed by this vision but drawn to understanding it, Ray walked to the cliff's edge. Toes hanging over, he outstretched his arms, closed his eyes, and breathed in deeply, trusting completely that a stiff wind wouldn't blow him off. Might such courage reveal the riddle of this vision and help him to understand? That was when he saw the boat.

It was in the Norse style, long, sturdy, and curved at bow and stern, with room for several men to stand fore or aft and dozens of seats for rowers. At first he was shocked because he had sensed that the meeting between his people and those to the north with such ship technology would occur in generations to come, not during his lifetime. He wondered at this surprising visitation, and as fast as it had appeared, it was gone. Opening his eyes wider, he saw only horizon, no ship.

As Ray squinted, looking for the ship in the distance, he realized that his sight was an omen. He felt the shifts in the earth beneath him and knew something magical was happening indeed. Ray began walking west down the beach, following the sounds of the storms out at sea, being pulled by the magnetic shifts happening deep in the earth's core. There was an outcrop of rocks that were on the western coast of the island that had just come into view, and he was slowly making his way around to them, picking up pace as the crashing waves became more violent. This outcrop housed a deep cave that could provide shelter and safety. This cave was also covered in carvings from the previous inhabitants of the island—the ones who came when the ice receded. Ray had been brought to the cave repeatedly by the previous head Druid, Murlen, for meditation, teaching on the ancient carvings, and moss samples, so he knew a safe way to approach without being seen and felt confident in his hideout.

Just as he reached the cave, he heard the weakest whimper. It sounded like a lamb abandoned by its mother, the barest, bleakest bleating for help.

The boy had appeared to catch himself on a large rock, creating ripples all around him. Ray untwisted the rope that secured his garments and waved to the boy, wading out to within feet of him but throwing his belt out to prevent getting caught in the same riptide. The boy was larger than him but young and weakened from thirst and exertion. His face was ghastly pale, which alarmed Ray enough to situate the boy on a dry, stable rock before moving him to the cave. Ray drew his leather flask from the pocket inside the breast of his shirt and offered it to the boy.

"Are you hurt?" Ray asked, slowly, touching the boy's head and then chest to mime the words as best he could.

Then the boy responded with a clear Norse accent, "Mother?"

"I have to get you to the cave to get you dry and warm quickly." Ray did his best to drape the boy's arms over his shoulders. He used the boy's weight to propel him forward, out of the shallows of the angry water and toward the shelter of the cave.

"Where is my father?" the boy asked, eyes rolling back in his head.

Ray was strong for his small stature, but the boy was immense, and his dead weight pulled Ray to the ground in front of the cave. He needed help breathing, so Ray began to massage his heart behind his breastbone and shared his own breath with the boy's by blowing into his mouth. After several minutes, the boy coughed up the sea and looked at Ray with impossibly red and sad eyes.

"You are alive again. Thank the gods." Ray's voice sounded surprised and foreign, even to him.

"I need to talk to you." A familiar voice broke Ray from his trance. In fact, it was the same voice that seemed to always be interrupting him as of late.

Ailsa

"Hail and welcome, Ailsa." Ray bowed to me in his exaggerated way as I approached the stones.

"I need to talk to you," I said simply, without malice.

Ray gestured with his right hand to the kerbstone on the north side of the stone circle. We sat, overlooking the sea below. "You're up early on your birthday," he remarked.

"I've been walking all night," I quipped. "It's nice to sit down."

"What is it, child?" he asked, concerned.

I fumbled with the strings that hung from my cloak. "Why didn't you tell me your plan?" I asked like a hurt child.

Ray placed his hand on mine, still unsure. "It wasn't my plan, Ailsa. I had no power over it. He was sent to us on the day you were born! It was the gods."

"Then why be deceitful with Ros? If it was in the hands of the gods, then why did you need to meddle with our feelings?"

He sighed. "I guess I tried to steer Ros away to protect you."

"Protect me?" I questioned. "I lost my father, and then you made me think the person I loved the most didn't want me! Because you scared him."

"We didn't scare him, Ailsa. He scared himself."

"That doesn't even make sense," I protested, exhausted.

"He's a scared person, Ailsa. He's not for you. He has much to learn still about self-control and courage."

I wanted to yell; I wanted to scream like a child and stomp off. But my anger was seething and quiet and righteous, so I simply looked at him and said with restrained passion, "That's not for you to decide, Ray." He started to say something to defend himself and the role of the Druids, but I felt Jord's tall, calming presence behind us, and the rest of the Druids appeared out of the mist on the cliff top, ready to lead the village in calling the sun up on the solstice. He had been wrong, and he knew it. Whether it was his affection for Aric, his concern for me as an orphan, or a general disdain of Ros, he had let his personal feelings affect his role as head Druid. *That's not something I'll ever let myself do*, I thought.

We stood and met the rest of the Druids in the circle. Jord struck his flint against the kerbstone and lit the first torch that would become a great fire. One by one, we passed the fire between us, lighting all twelve torches. Jord was to Ray's right; I was to his left. He started to say the words to open the ceremony we had as Druids before the rest of the village arrived, but he paused, looking over at me with tears in his eyes. Jord looked over at us, out of the corners of his yellow cat eyes.

"I'm sorry, Ailsa," Ray said. Jord smiled at Ray sympathetically and looked over at me.

"It's too late. The village is here," I said.

And Ray quickly led the chant as the first group of celebrants crested the hill in the dark of predawn.

Edie

"How do I look?" Frank asked, sliding on aviators and gesturing to his vibrant tie-dye T-shirt and Birkenstocks.

"You look...appropriate," I responded, taking time to search for the right word.

"I look sweet, sure, but look at you!" He paused amid our hike from the car park toward the most famous of all Scottish standing stones on the Outer Hebrides. "I can't believe you went all out with the Druid's cloak and intricately braided hair." He picked up a braid that had a bronze ring interwoven into its plaits. "It's very... appropriate," he finished, winking at me.

"Someone has to remind the New Age folks that this goes back a bit further than their philosophical debates." I checked the weather on my phone for the fourteenth time that day and trudged on. "The way they bicker about opinions on everything makes it seem as if they have some substantial evidence of the truth, which, archaeologically speaking, is very unlikely," I added.

Frank laughed at me. "Are you going to drop the knowledge on them that Stonehenge is likely a winter solstice festival spot and not a summer one?" he asked as he gestured up at the summer sun and around at the bright green summer hills around the Isle of Lewis.

"Let's just try to make friends this time, shall we?" I suggested.

Frank laughed even more heartily than he normally did at my dry humor as we approached the horde of celebrants pitching tents, dancing, mingling, and starting drum circles. It was the day before the summer solstice, and that night would be an epic celebration into the wee morning, followed by the once-in-a-lifetime experience of watching the sun rise above the heel stone and spread its rays over Callanish, my favorite stone henge.

My heart rate crept up, as much from excitement as from my slight agoraphobia. I spared a thought for Sully and how much fun he would have had here. He had this beautiful way of incorporating the human storytelling culture and folklore that surrounded archaeology into the actual science and study. My other professors had balked at modern interpretations of archaeological landscapes and made fun of popular shows that "bastardized" the science by commercializing the art and monuments and the people (or aliens) who had made them. But Sully had this great appreciation for all people and the way their interactions with the monuments and history were actually a part of it, being woven into the complete story even now.

"These monuments are still alive in the culture, and the story of human interaction with them is still being told," he used to say. "Of course we want to get at who constructed them and why, but we don't get closer to that answer by dismissing what the stones have come to mean over the last several thousand years and how they have remained relevant in the culture this long." I was pulled out of this benevolent, idyllic thought cloud by an *actual* cloud of thick smoke being blown in my face.

"Oh, this stuff is excellent." Frank crinkled his nose at the enormous, bearded man who stood in front of me, complete with peace pipe and free samples of his "expertly engineered ganja," as was printed on the bags.

I waved my hand in front of my face, batting away the sentimental thoughts of Sully as much as the pungent smoke. There was no room for sentimentality if I was going to conduct research, and I had better remind myself of that if this was going to be the success I wanted it to be for the specific chapter I was working on in Sully's book. Why was Callanish built later than the other henges I was studying? Why would the circles be so concentrated in a radius of a few hundred miles in the north with one giant one, Stonehenge, so far south?

I checked that the voice recorder on my phone was working, made sure I had my compass and GPS to mark the stone locations perfectly in my journal, and went off through the crowd in Frank's wake, following his trail of fleeting friendships, hoping it led to something worthwhile at the end.

"So you're sayin' there's a whole stoon just missin' from the henge?" The kilted Scottish brogue across the campfire from me was intriguing, or should I say, had been intriguing, before its owner had plied himself liberally with Glenfiddich in "honorrrr" of the solstice. The rolled r's were undoubtedly the best part.

"I don't see how that would make it any different" came one of the more opinionated male voices to my right.

"Well, you're right. It wouldn't really have made a difference for tonight, the summer solstice, but that's irrelevant. You see, the largest stone was paired with that one there."

I pointed over the tops of their heads to the one remaining trilithon, a stone structure consisting of two posts and a lintel. The sky was brilliantly colored, just past sunset, and the gloaming left purple shadows on the stones and everyone's faces. The North Star and Vega, a star in the Lyra constellation, twinkled in the sky already, and the new fires coming alight all around us added to the magic of the atmosphere.

"There was another trilithon there, next to the other tall stones, and if you were here on the winter solstice, then you would see that the rising sun would have come just in between the stones, perfectly. And if the night before was clear, Orion would have twinkled overhead. You have to imagine the whole structure in its entirety in order to contemplate when and what it was used for. On the morning of the winter solstice, the light would have come directly between the largest pillars and illuminated the altar stone, resting on its side, likely holding some sort of sacrifice or the remains of some of the great people of the village who had died that year."

"So you're saying that the winter solstice was more significant than the summer solstice at the time?" came the Scottish brogue again.

"Not necessarily," I said. "But I am saying that Stonehenge, the most famous and widely known stone circle, was used for the winter solstice in particular, but it was also likely part of a larger temple complex, meaning there were other structures used for different festivals and times of year. We know that because they're all over the British Isles but have different orientations and were built at different times."

"Aye, there's Avebury right down the road from Stonehenge; that's even older," piped up a voice from across the hazy circle.

I wafted the smoke away from my face and smiled at the deep voice across from me. "Yes, Avebury is one of the oldest complexes and offers some good examples of how the people of the time would have lived and interacted among the stones. Stenness in Orkney gives us a similar sense of habitation among the stones, as well as an extensive temple complex. It's really not the stones themselves that create the intrigue. At least for me, it's the people who dwelt among them and the mystery of how they lived and who they were since they didn't leave behind any writing other than a few stone picture carvings, some of which we assume to be contemporary with the structures. Others, of course, like the runic symbols carved on these Callanish stones of Lewis, show us the millennia of interaction that have occurred within the stones since the original builders, and that arguably adds to the truth of their whole story as well."

Frank lounged across the fire from me, laughing at my impromptu lecture and the interested, if slightly stoned, class around me. We danced as the sun went down, joined drum circles, shared trail mix and beer with strangers, and made friends around the largest bonfire at the end of the evening, where they had expertly had pizza delivered from the only restaurant nearby.

After my lecture devolved into the typical discussions of wizards, aliens, and archaeological scandals, I went over to share my cloak with a chilly Frank and show him my journal. "You command a lot of attention in that thing, you know." He complimented my Druid's cloak and picked up a long, auburn braid that dangled in my face.

"I have good news on the research front," I said, jumping to the point with excitement. I really didn't mind that Frank was a little high as I was telling him. It would make his reaction more animated, I thought. I opened up my journal to the center, where my diagram covered both pages; leaves of tracing paper were attached. I showed him the original circle I'd drawn, the Stones of Stenness, followed by Orkney, Stonehenge, and now Callanish, which fit into the circle perfectly when they were aligned with the cardinal directions.

"Wow," he said, moving the tracing papers up and down, watching the stones fall into place.

"I know. This last chapter in Sully's book is going to be ground-breaking. I think I have proof that the separate stone circles weren't for separate cultures; they were for one culture of people who moved around, perhaps as a holdover from their hunter-gatherer culture, or perhaps they traveled for big festivals, like we are. This would also explain why they moved stones so far, so that they could share or repurpose special menhirs."

"It's all happening!" Frank said, clapping his hands loud enough that our temporary friends looked over at us, and I laughed.

The night was perfect. We pitched our tent alongside some new friends and crawled in under my giant sleeping bag for a few hours of rest before the dawn. Some people stayed awake all night, but their distant chatter and laughter was a balm to our tired spirits.

"This reminds me of being a child and drifting off to sleep on the sofa while my parents had friends or family over, chatting and telling stories. It's comforting."

"Ahh, she speaks of her family," Frank said gently.

"There are some memories," I said, "that are so hazy and so far back, they're not tainted by anything. So I guess that's a blessing." We lay in silence for a few moments.

"Edie?" Frank began, checking to see if I was still awake. I was, and I rolled over to look at him. "I will go to Newgrange with you in six months, if you want, but I think it's time for you to make a new friend. I want to be there for you, I do. But since Sully died, you've retreated again, and I'm all you have. It's not enough, Edie. I'd be selfish not to tell you so. It seems that Michael really does care about you and share your interests, so why not strike up a friendship at least, even if it's not more?"

I sighed deeply into the orange nylon abyss above my head. I sort of wished we were lying out under the stars, but I knew I'd probably be happy not to be covered in a heavy dew in the morning. "OK, you're right. I'll ask him at Lughnasadh in six weeks."

"Good." Frank brushed my forehead in a benedictive motion. "You'll have fun." He smiled.

"Just as friends," I said.

"OK, so not *that* much fun," Frank joked. And we giggled until we fell asleep.

CHAPTER 20:

THE ALDER TREES

Ailsa

Eight years earlier

❝ᴛhose two trees over there on the hill. They grew up together, my great-grandfather said." Ros nodded over toward the bare winter alder trees, standing side by side on the hill to the north, looking like skeletons holding hands in the gray, twilit evening. We sat in the grass, pulling thick blades to blow between our fingers, buying time, escaping evening chores. Father had sent his dog with us, as he often did when we left in the late afternoons, and the dog's head rested on my outstretched feet, eyebrows raised in constant questioning of when dinner might be.

"Do you think their roots are intertwined?" he asked.

The moon rose like a pearl over the distant hills and peaks. I looked back and forth, from north to south, over the landscape. There was no forest nearby, no grove. The hills rose into mountains to the north, the cliffs dropped off into the wild sea to the south, and between that was only the open ground where the stone circle had been built by our great-grandfathers.

"Well, they're *black* alders. They are often lone trees, not part of a forest." I paused to scan the rich blue sky, quickly fading into indigo and black at the edges. If we weren't back soon, father would worry, and so would Ros's parents.

"How can you recognize every tree so well in the winter? Without the leaves?" Ros smiled as he asked, adding, "Sometimes you know more than the adults. Well, at least about trees." We laughed.

"No, it's just that it's *my* tree."

"I thought that old oak in the Druids' grove with a hole from the lightning strike was *your* tree. How many trees do you have?" Ros laughed again; his infectious, bubbling laughter always made me laugh too. "They can't all be yours, Ailsa. You have to pick one." I looked at the freckles covering his nose, memorizing them like I did the stars in the night sky.

"I like alder trees because they grow better alone, and I think I would too. They are beautiful in fall, when you were born, Ros. I know a lot about them, and about most trees, since Druids are supposed to."

"Most girls like hawthorn trees because of the flowers," Ros pointed out and I ignored him. "But maybe these roots are intertwined, or they could even have one root ball and be essentially the same tree, just growing separately to look like two. Like us," Ros said as he laced his fingers between mine, imitating the roots of the trees. My father's wolf dog raised his head off my feet, eyeing Ros, but he knew him too well to make a fuss. "Sometimes I think I'd grow better away from everyone else too. But I'd want ye with me." He smiled at me, and I smiled back at him.

"Where would you want to go?" I asked. "If we could escape anywhere in the world?" I leaned back on my elbows.

I had never truly thought about leaving the island permanently. Sure, people traveled for trade and ceremonies, but it was mostly men who did that. It wasn't that the thought wasn't enticing. I often wondered what it would be like to travel the open sea or even just venture across the small sea that had brought my father from the north mainland. It sounded strange and different, like faraway lands should. But father said it was also much like this place and that the people were not so different. Father came from a place with green rolling hills as far as the eye could see, where the animals were fat with grazing. It sounded like a dream land, but then I looked around at the steep black cliffs, dotted with black and gray goats that were almost indistinguishable from the craggy promontories they sheltered in. I loved them almost as much as the dramatic cliffs, especially the ones on the western side of the island where you could stand for hours and listen to the roar of the ocean below, wind whipping your hair, wondering what or who could be out there on the other side.

Still, there was no place I could imagine more magical than the Druids' oak grove. Any ground that wasn't covered by moss was so thick with fallen leaves that shoes were never necessary. In fact, you could be much quieter and go unnoticed without, which was one of the reasons Druids wore green cloaks, dyed to match the thickest part of the woods. We were invisible, a part of the forest. Some of the moss was so dark green it was almost brown, and some was bright with yellow like the sun. The trees were many and varied, all coming together with their distinct properties to create a fluid harmony. Some were tall and evergreen. It felt cool to stand in their shade, and they never shed their leaves, only their seedlings in varied cone shapes. They smelled the best to me and had the most textured trunks—some were red, others dark or hairy. Some of them seemed to go on forever, right up to the clouds, but they were impossible to climb because the branches didn't start near the bottom; they were only at the tops of the skinny trunks, so instead we would just stand at the bottom, looking up in awe. Then there were the trunks that were ten feet wide. Six of us children could stand around them, reaching to interlock our hands; these trunks were knotty and gnarly and often had beautiful mosses growing up the sides or even mushrooms and varied animals and critters living inside. There were trees that seemed to sprout from the ground with three trunks, limbs extended wildly everywhere, like a circle of dancing women. There were fragile young trees, just saplings, trying to exist in the shade of giants. Just like I was. Yes, I wanted to travel and see distant lands, I thought. But I would always have to come back to my forest. The land was clearly a part of who I was, the same way my brown hair or big hands were.

"I'd go anywhere with ye, Ails," Ros answered, rolling over on his stomach, propped up on his elbows, looking over at me. "Let's take the southern sea; it's warm. We can swim and live on the beach somewhere where the sun shines all the time."

I giggled, longing for the warmth of the summer sun on my skin. "We'll be adventurers then, you promise?" I asked.

Ros took his flint dirk from his pocket and made a neat prick on his palm. "I swear," he said, extending his palm out to me with the sharp flint knife balanced between his two longest fingers. I took it, delicately. My father's dog made a guttural noise. I poked my palm until I felt the sting that signaled blood, and then when I felt a warm drop of it on my wrist, I brought Ros's hand to my lips and kissed his wound before we sealed our promise in blood, palm to palm.

We said nothing after that and just began the long walk home, which relieved Father's dog. We had walked back entirely in silence, something only best friends could do with ease. We had both been thinking. And we had both made decisions. Ros kissed my cheek at the door of my roundhouse and walked to his house without a word. Those were our first kisses. That was the first time I told myself I would leave this island one day.

Present day

It was fully dark now, and the clouds had covered the moon, allowing only pinhole glimpses of its brilliant light. Ros's fingers tickled my palm, lightly feeling to grasp my hand; we interlocked our fingers as we had done since childhood. The bits of moonlight led us through the tall grass on the western coast, but we could've found our way in complete darkness. We had been there so many times. The village was closer to the eastern part of the island, thus our venturing west for privacy. We walked on, a few more steps to the edge of the cliff. I sat down first, far enough back, as always, that I knew the edge would not give and I couldn't lose balance. He sat close to me and asked the question that had been inevitable since the beginning.

"I'm sorry, Ros." Those words lingered between us as thick as the late summer air. My throat felt thick too, suddenly, and I forced myself to swallow. I pulled my fur shawl and green cloak tighter against my goose flesh skin. It was the end of summer, and the night breeze off the ocean bore a deeper chill than I was used to. But even in the coolness of the night, I was unsure that the goose bumps that rippled over my body were solely from the wind blowing down the front of the dress, not mostly from the feeling of panic I had at the possibility, the likelihood, of letting go of Ros.

"If we left and made a life somewhere else, then we wouldn't be hiding. We would just be living somewhere else, like people do all the time. Your father, Ray, Aric, your aunt. People move. There would be no shame," he said.

"No shame in abandoning my husband?" I asked. He snorted loudly in disgust at that. "And what about Grandmother?" I asked him. She had been a grandmother to him as well. "Everyone we love is dead, and she has no one to take care of her but me."

"She has Ray and Jord," Ros protested quickly, as if that was the excuse he had been expecting. "If you're staying, it's for Aric, isn't it?"

Several moments of silence passed like dead weight. My heart was beating faster and faster at the tone of this dismal conversation, and I knew exactly where it was going. Maybe it was because I knew Ros so well, or maybe I had just already lived this conversation in my mind over the weeks I had practiced it.

I had known that I had to let him go since we were young. Our roots were intertwined, but we were two separate trees. The letting go had already happened long ago on some alternate plane of existence, and the knowledge I had of what was coming, when Ros had no idea what was coming, was making me feel dizzy and breathless. Maybe I didn't have the strength to do it.

"It's so dark when the clouds are out like this at night." He spoke softly now.

"It is. It's beautiful. And it's so nice to be walking in the dark with someone you trust so much. Someone to follow to the edge of the earth, guided only by their hand and a sliver of silver moonlight." I rubbed his hands, which felt frozen, between mine to warm them. He stopped me, took my right hand, and moved it up his thin forearm, over the sinewy, knotted muscles of his biceps, then up onto his shoulders, which just barely glinted in the moonlight. Even in this darkness, his blue eyes still shone and met mine as I curled both hands into his salty, straight hair and kissed him long and deep. Our mouths fit together perfectly. His breath tasted like mine. Kissing him felt as natural as breathing. And it had been so long. It had been so long since I felt I could breathe. My heart rate slowed to relaxation as we intertwined there on the ground. It was gentle, easy, and safe, and being connected with him in this way calmed me in a way nothing else could.

As if reading my mind, he pulled away and took my face in his hands, sweetly, like a father might. "Ails?" he searched my face, his oceanic eyes in shock, and then his hands fell from my face to my ever-so-slightly protrudent belly. The safety and calm I felt in our embrace dove off the cliff in that instant and crashed into the jagged rocks below. I tried to say something, but my mouth wouldn't form words, so Ros continued, "Is it—am I?" but he broke off, unable to complete the question. Unable or unwilling. "No. It doesn't matter, Ails. If it is my child in your heart, then it will be the child of my heart as well, and it truly won't matter."

My heart soared at this, and for a moment I actually thought of leaving in that boat with Ros. In a flash, I imagined our whole departure, during the next quarter moon, enough light to secure us down to Ros's boats and enough time for me to store up food and water while Ros finished the crab sail that could get us speedily away, fast enough to not be caught up by the rowboats that would come to look for us. And then I thought of being without a midwife for the birth, and I thought of dying shortly after, like my mother did, and of my grandmother left alone, and what Aric might do to himself or anyone else. And I thought if I resented Ros now for making me lie and run away, and hide, then how might I resent him for banishing me from my home? I didn't say this, though. I placed my hands on my barely swollen belly.

"I do know it's a girl," I answered, hoping that secret would be something intimate enough we could share in the moment, since I couldn't grant him fatherhood.

He just smiled a huge, knowing grin and touched his forehead gently to mine. "How do you know for sure?" he asked, and then his huge smile dissolved into giddy laughter. "I don't know why I'm asking you that. I must have asked you that a thousand times in our lives together since we were kids. I should just learn to accept your knowing by now. And be thankful for your wisdom." He curled my hair around my ear and kissed the pink tip of it, cold in the wind. "You *must* also know, wise Druid, that I will love you both forever, no matter what."

My throat tightened, and my eyes spilled over with emotion. These days I couldn't help being overcome by it. I looked into Ros's questioning face, his brow furrowed, and though we were close—best friends for our entire lives—I realized then that there was something deep inside him, a piece that I couldn't quite grasp or understand. There was a part of him I could never possess, as much as he loved me. I reached into my pocket for the black pearl Rasha had given me earlier that year. I had decided that if we ever parted ways, I wanted him to have it to remind him of me and to protect him on his travels.

"You make love sound like it's so simple," I said, holding his stare.

"It is, but the situation is not," he insisted, wrapping my arms around his neck and tickling me by nuzzling the curve of my inner elbow before tracing his lips up to my cold, pink ears and whispering, "Never let me go." We swayed and danced like that for a long time, to the music of the earth; the whistling wind and crashing waves.

I kissed him as hard and purposefully as I ever had. And in our passionate embrace, the pearl was lost.

A few days later, I had been sitting among the trees, making my offerings, and collecting herbs for almost the entire morning. I had risen before dawn, and the sun was now high in the sky, though I hadn't noticed through the thick summer foliage that kept the summer sun shaded from me.

"Found you, finally." Ros smiled in his beguiling way, walking toward me, then pulled me close to him.

"You couldn't have been looking for me very long, then. I don't exactly have that many places I wander off to," I responded, pushing him off me gently, out of discretion, and giving him a warning look. The oak grove was shaded and deep within the woods, but it was by no means private like the evening cliffs, especially to the Druids, who spent much of their free time away from the village among the trees. Indeed, this is where the name Druid was derived from, and one often ran into one or two of them, having a stroll or a chant or meditation beneath the canopy of wise oaks, ashes, and alders.

"In fact," he continued, slanting his catlike blue eyes at me in his flirtatious way, "I wouldn't mind you wandering off to our spot this evening."

My heart fluttered at the thought of some of the secret meetings we had had. There was something about being vulnerable in the broad and black night, lying open and naked to the stars with the person you felt most like yourself with. I had lain in his arms those nights wishing that the night would never end and the sun would never come up.

"Ailsa, come back to the earth. You're in the clouds, and I need you to listen to every detail of the plan. It came to me, like a dream, like things come to you—is it intuition? What do you and Ray call it?"

I shook my head like a dog shaking the water off and refocused on Ros's hopeful face. "Yes, sort of. A dream is a different type of intuition from a vision, and then there are gut or impulse instincts that enable you to make fast decisions, which is automatic intuition."

"I have the plan for us to leave, and I think your Druid instinct will be that it will be perfect and go smoothly," he went on, waving away my vision explanation with his hands.

"Is that why you're acting so giddy?" I asked.

"Well, yes, that and the crab claw sail is ready."

"Oh?" I asked, faced so suddenly with a reality I was not ready for.

"It's so fast, Ails. You're going to love it. I can't wait to take you out."

"Ros, we need to talk—" He placed his finger over his lips in a hushing sign and squeezed my hand.

"Can I please finish first? After weeks of thinking about slipping out when the fewest people were around, I realized that we should do the opposite." I raised my eyebrows at him. "A gathering at the stones! When the village is in ceremony at the neighboring isles!"

"For Lughnasadh?" I asked.

Ros's excitement mounted as he continued, "Listen, it's perfect. As a Druid, you would have your hood up during the ceremony anyway. With all the matching green robes, your absence wouldn't even be recorded."

"Of course the Druids would notice, though," I pointed out.

"That's why you'll meet with them initially, but then you'll sneak out and give your cloak to my sister Reina. She'll stand in for you."

"Ros, that's so dangerous! She could be punished for impersonating a Druid or participating in a shamanic event under age. I wouldn't want Reina to risk that for me."

"It sounds like there's not much you are willing to risk. I'm trying to bring the moon and stars down from the sky for you, Ailsa. But rather than think of me, you're more concerned with Aric, Grandmother, and Reina. I'm not saying we shouldn't care for them. But I am asking, or wondering—don't we care for each other the most?"

A leaf fell from the tree just then. It careened its way down, rolling off Ros's shoulder and landing on my foot. Lughnasadh was upon us. We were halfway between the summer solstice, the longest day of the year, and Mabon, the autumnal equinox. I felt like the leaf—letting go of what I was rooted to and careening down into the unknown. And yet the question was never whether or not I loved Ros enough to take the risk. That answer was easy. At the same time, he spoke of intuition, and my intuition kept my feet rooted to this island's ground like the oak tree I loved so much. I stood under its shade now. Feeling more protected than I had in the vulnerable moment on the cliffs a few nights before.

I smiled. "No one knows me or understands me like you do, and effortlessly at that." I looked up into the canopy of the trees, searching for an answer. "I hate having to articulate my deepest emotions and thoughts. Some things should just exist without being defined weakly by language." I motioned to the trees and beautiful forest around us. "Like them."

"Ailsa, listen to me," he began, but I cut him off.

"The more I think about it, the more I feel that marriage or time spent on Earth together isn't the only thing that is representative of the love between people. Our love is more permanent than our ephemeral lives, and I don't think we need to defy everyone else we love in order to be together just to prove the worth of that love. It exists and will continue to exist. And even more than that, I'm afraid that we will grow old and resentful. Life and time will erode this passion, and if we've isolated ourselves, then we'll have no one to blame but one another."

"Oh, now they're really in your head, aren't they? You're speaking in riddles like the head Druid you so badly want to be." He inched closer to me, which pressed me up against the trunk of my oak.

"We both know that's not what I want," I responded firmly.

"Do we?" he asked angrily.

I felt his breath, warm with the fish he had caught and eaten for breakfast. On the nights I didn't meet him, he stayed up all night fishing out at sea. He sought me out on those mornings after most often, days after nights when we had not seen one another. And he always smelled like the sea then, with dried salt water in his hair and on his hands and arms. He grabbed my shoulders with those callused, salty fingers and dug them in. "If you live so much in your mind, you're a prisoner of your thoughts and this place as well. Be free with me."

Reflexively, I wanted to push him off of me, but instead my body leaned back against the tree, inviting his warm, fishy breath to spread over my chest and neck as he spoke. "Our home is not a prison to me. But if it is to you, you should go, Ros."

"Anywhere I can't be free with you is a prison to me!" he yelled at the top of his lungs, hitting the oak tree behind my head with his fist.

"You asked me to choose, Ros, and I have."

He glared at me with the fire behind his eyes that I had seen so many times in the last year, slowly engulfing him. "You're choosing *him* and the lying Druids?" he choked out in disbelief.

"No. I'm choosing myself," I said quietly. "It's not about you or Aric or even the child. Ray told me once that life reveals who we are; each layer of experience is peeled back like a gooseberry to reveal the golden fruit inside. I don't feel trapped here because I belong here, but you belong somewhere else, or at the very least, you have discovered that travel and the open sea are calling you, and there is no reason you have to ignore that. You can pursue your truest self just as I am."

"You're just making the easy choice."

"No, Ros!" I rarely raised my voice, but I wanted to be clear with him, once and for all. "It's who I am. But who are *you*?"

He snorted air through his nostrils, shaking his head in disbelief and backing away from me now. "What if the Druids are wrong? What if we only get one life, Ailsa, and we've spent it apart and you've spent your life dancing and chanting about an afterlife and gods that don't exist?"

I took his palm and pressed it to mine, where we had made the blood promise to one another when we were eleven. "I promise you they're not wrong. I have peace knowing there is eternity, and our souls will be together there, forever. I've come to realize over the last few months that is enough for me." Then I took his palm and kissed it just as I had years before.

He left his palm on my mouth, firmly covering it and stopping me from speaking further. "*Stop.* Please, Ailsa. Just think about the plan. Consider it. I even thought about how to prevent your grandmother from worrying, which I knew would be a concern to you. I have someone I trust who can tell her we're safe, and the babe too."

He took his hand away, bent down to the ground for a moment, rose to one knee, then slowly, gently rested his head on the small protrusion between my hips and kissed my belly. I squeezed his hand in mine as hard as I could. "Think of the sunshine in the south," he said, smiling, as he stood up to face me.

"It's not easy for me to say no, Ros. But it's enough for me to love you from afar, whether you and Rasha marry the twins and move to their northern island or you sail south alone."

"Shhh." He quieted me. "Think with your heart for once, Ails. I'll see you at the Lughnasadh fires." He placed a small wood violet behind my ear, looking at the rosy tips of my too-large ears, lovingly kissing the spot where my dark hairline met my pale forehead before he turned to depart. As he walked away, I heard him say to himself, though loud enough for me to hear, "That would never be enough for me."

CHAPTER 21

LUGHNASADH

Edie

"So what was so special about the stone?"

It was August when Frank and I drove another long and winding Irish sea road, and by eight thirty, the sky was a deep Prussian blue, just preparing for the stars to come out, with all sorts of purple and gold light dying off in the west.

We had spent the summer solstice in Scotland with all the other spiritual vagabonds that show up to Callanish and then driven down to London. Frank was a freelance writer and didn't need to be anywhere in particular, but he had some meetings in London in July, so I went back and forth between the archives at the British Museum and Oxford for my research. I also got a chance to visit some old high school friends in Saint Albans and travel with them down to Avesbury and Stonehenge, sharing my theories.

Now it was August, and everyone was on vacation. It had been unusually hot as of late, and everyone was more than ready for that passage of vacation that led away from the dog days of summer and into the light breeze of September, with its reliable sixty-degree forecast and the comfortably familiar, monotonous grind of the incessant wasting of our workdays. I missed my northern isles and the breeze off the North Atlantic Ocean and the Irish Sea. And now, on the eve of Lughnasadh, we were arriving back at my house, Sully's house, in Ireland, where we would stay until Frank went back after the fall equinox, at which point I'd be there alone to finish the book.

But first, before arriving home, we arrived at the Larne Ferry Station to take the ferry directly across the Irish Sea to a notable Lughnasadh celebration. As we had learned, ferry crossings and timetables in the North Atlantic and Hebrides were of a complicated nature. It often amused me to think of the hubris of modern people regarding how far we had come with infrastructure when it probably had been easier to get from island to island four thousand years ago when everyone had their own boat and knew the tides and currents intimately. Then I laughed at myself, quibbling in my mind that it had likely been even easier five thousand years before that when an ice bridge connected the whole of Britain, not to mention that Britain had been attached to the whole of Europe then too. One large continent with no separation. Given the recent turn of events in the EU, that might come as a surprise to some. I dared not point this out since I was afraid my archaeologist humor was getting tiresome for Frank.

Neither of us was used to spending this much time with one another, so we recognized that we were slightly more sarcastic and bitter than usual—the slow grate of the nerves that comes with blissful time with your best friend.

The sky would be black in no time—the long summer nights were quickly coming to an end—so it was I who drove, as the one far more comfortable with the gentle curve of the back roads that led up the hills to my home. I had learned where to anticipate the curves as if navigating a lover's body. That, coupled with the hypnotic rhythm of the bumpy road below and the low throwback pop music on the radio had me close to a trancelike state.

"Hello? Are you awake?" Frank snapped two fingers in front of my face. "Please don't fall asleep on these jackknife roads."

"Sorry. Yes, what was your question again?"

"What's so special about the stones? Why do they bring them in from far away? Why one rock over another?"

"Well, it's an interesting question, to be sure. Of course, they were using stone for so long before metal existed: to hunt and to carve out boats to travel in, in their homes to grind barley and wheat, and, well, in their monuments, of course. So a stone becomes a precious thing and something to be chosen wisely. It was a tool chosen for its strength, and different stones have different important properties. Like a flat stone for building a home, or slate for drawing and carving, or the malleability of flint for sharp knives and arrows. Then, they noticed the color of stone too. That's what eventually led to the end of the Stone Age, actually. They loved the stone so much, and noticed such nuance in it, that they began to wonder what might happen if they brought together the two most powerful things they knew existed: stone and fire."

"And then, *bam*, metal!" Frank illuminated.

"So when they threw some of the green stones in the fire, they got copper, and the blacker stones by the sea produced tin. It changed everything. I actually hated having to choose between studying the Stone Age and the Bronze Age in college because, like most things, the change from a hunter-gatherer society to farming, for instance, would have been gradual. I suppose that as soon as you discovered that substance, you would attempt to make better tools and weapons, but then the time it took to learn the alchemy, perfect the craft, and spread and explain the information must have been a process over decades, and you know how hesitant people are to accept anything new."

A loud snore erupted from the slumped figure beside me. Loud enough for me to know that it was a remark on my rambling and not a sign that my passenger had dozed off by 9:00 p.m.

The drive up from Dublin had taken longer than anticipated; it always does. So it was nearly 10:00 p.m. when I pulled into Doherty's, the coastal village pub again. We only had a few minutes to quench our thirst before the last ferry.

We walked inside, ordered the garlic chips and Guinness from the menu without hesitation, and plopped down on a comfy leather couch by the fire, the roar of wind on the ocean faintly audible just outside the window.

"Glad we're going to be together this year for my birthday," Frank said as I carried the Guinnesses over to our table.

"Me too," I said.

"Mainly I just want to hear about the crisis of mind that occurred for you when *you* turned twenty-nine a few months ago. I need advice for the vicious midlife spiral I'm about to have."

"Mmm, well I am the ultimate source for advice on spirals." I winked at him, and he laughed at my cheesy joke. "But I think we have fifteen more years until midlife," I suggested.

At this, he fondled one of the few silver hairs that haloed my head in long curls around my face, fallen out over time from the long brown and auburn braid down my back that was practically a uniform. I had always had beautiful, long, thick, wavy hair. It was fun to show off, but when I was working, as I had been for the whole year thus far, it was always pulled back. The only makeup I wore was practical Carmex lip balm and mascara since my brown lashes turned blond at the ends and needed to be defined to be seen at all. My steel-toed boots, Carhartt trousers, and Patagonia all-weather zip-ups in an array of colors completed the ensemble. It was not feminine by any means, but I was confident in it in a way I never had been in my youth. I felt beautiful, not like the girls in the magazines but a deeper kind of beauty that shone from my eyes now when I spoke about the people, places, and history that I loved. I had become an expert in my field before thirty and was self-reliant, with a little help from Sully. I loved what I did, and it showed. I guess that's what makes someone truly attractive. It's less about face symmetry and more about soul symmetry—"a pleasing proportion of parts of a thing."

The bar was nearly empty. And that was saying a lot for a tiny village bar on the coast like this. These towns saw few tourists and were populated by some of the only humans in the world that still spoke Gaelic, people who had never seen an iPhone like the one Frank was chatting on and who probably had plenty of their own speculations and answers about the ancient land and monuments I was here to investigate. They didn't see me as someone providing answers to their questions about their own history. It didn't matter how long I had lived there; I would always be an American and an outsider.

There was an old man sitting at the bar who had a mass of wavy gray hair and small, twinkling eyes to match. He was the kind of older man whom you could tell had been handsome in his youth, and he carried himself that way, still flirtatious and proud, broad shoulders upright as he finished off his pint. He set down the glass, wiped his stubbled chin with the back of his hand, and ordered another Smithwick's as a "Smiddick's." I smiled at him and then turned to the bartender. "Hey, any idea when Michael will be working?" I asked in as casual a tone as I could muster.

"He takes most of August off," he responded as he filled the old man's pint glass, eyeing me up and down, clearly curious about what I had to do with his workmate. I smiled and thanked him for the information.

"So ye've an interest in Michael?" The old man at the bar smiled, revealing stained teeth.

"He's a friend, yes. I met him for the Beltane fires three months ago. You know him?" I asked, more out of friendly conversation than curiosity.

"Oh aye, I've known Michael since he was a lad. Don't make them like that Michael anymore. He's an auld one, he is." He said the last part in a hushed whisper and glanced over at the current bartender.

I bit my lip to keep from smiling so big. "Is that right?" I asked. "He was the perfect gentleman at the Beltane festival."

"Oh, aye, that's no surprise, but that's not what makes him special. He's off today for Lughnasadh preparation."

I nodded, understanding more deeply now what I had sensed in Michael, that he was a true Celt and still celebrated the old festivals of the wheel of the year.

"Do you know what that means?" he questioned me, taking a sip of his beer with one eyebrow raised.

"I do." I nodded and left some space in the conversation, unsure of how to respond.

Then Frank piped up from the leather couch. "She's an archae-ologist."

The old man's face creased with a frown and furrowed brow. "Of course Michael would go and meet himself an archaeologist," he muttered under his breath, but loud enough for me to hear. I blushed a little and quickly changed the subject.

"Where is he spending his time off this month? Do you know?" I asked in a friendly way, trying not to sound too interested.

"Weeeell, he is back at home on his farm—did you know his family has a farm?"

"I think he mentioned that, along with something about a 7th century Viking ship's remains," I answered. The man rolled his eyes, and I felt the need to reassure him. "Don't worry, that's two thousand years out of my wheelhouse."

"Sounds to me like he was trying to impress ye." The old man shook his head and continued, "Yes, he's on his farm, reaping the barley, making beer, celebrating and relaxing with his family. They have bonfires on the weekends and invite the local country folk who can't afford to travel during August like everyone else does."

"That's so nice." I smiled. And it really was. "I'm Edana," I said, offering my hand, and his eyes twinkled in apparent recognition.

"I'm Mickey," he said, shaking my hand and lingering a bit. Then Mickey pulled a five-pound note from his pocket, set it on the bar, nodded to the bartender, and stood to go. "Nice to meet you," he added with that twinkle in his eye. As he walked to the door, I felt an impulse come over me that hadn't in a long time.

"Will you—" I began, but Mickey cut me off as he opened the ancient oak door.

"I'll tell him you asked after him." He nodded, put his cap on, and was gone.

I carried my pint glass into the adjacent room, where four high-top tables surrounded a snooker table. I took a long sip of the dark, creamy liquid and realized that I had already finished half of it. *Slow down*, I thought to myself, looking down at all my cracked knuckles and black peat–filled fingernails. I was daydreaming about a manicure when I overheard Frank's snooker opponents mention a permit for a bonfire happening later in the month. The taller one, thin with greasy black hair, bent over his cue, pulling back long and straight. He hit the red ball hard into the side pocket but with enough topspin that the white ball bounced back across the table and behind a wall of his own balls, effectively snookering the other player.

"Bloody hell," his shorter, curly-haired opponent complained. "All I want to know is whether the cheap bugger is providing the ale or not." He paced and bent down to table height to assess his position.

"Aye, there'll be ale and Dermot there with his guitar, Declan on the bodhran, and the whole village down to celebrate Mabon," the taller man answered.

"Aye, it's bad luck to let the wine run dry on the first day of fall. There'll be plenty. It's nigh on eleven; let's get back up to Campbeltown," the shorter man said as he hung up his cue and then walked over to the table that his half-empty beer sat upon.

Pretending not to be enthralled with their conversation, I quickly glanced over Frank's head, out the window, toward the lacy stone walls that traced a maze over the landscape until it fell flat off a cliff into the ocean.

"Got the snooker table all to yourself now," the short man called over to us.

"Did I hear you say you live in Campbeltown?" I asked as the shorter man eyed me and the taller one looked over at Frank. Campbeltown was just a few miles across a small channel from the stone circle we wanted to visit on Machrie Moor on the Isle of Arran. A direct crossing would be much easier than taking the ferry to Ayr from Larne and yet another to Arran. Frank had disappeared to the bar for the moment. "You know, we're trying to get there for the fall equinox. Do you know the stone circle there?"

"Are you one of those Mabon fire dancers?" the tall, skinny one, Colin, asked.

"No, I'm an archaeologist doing research," I responded.

"I heard they make human sacrifices on the solstices," he responded in a whisper.

This warranted a deep chuckle and embarrassed snort from Charlie. "Don't be ridiculous, *clotheid*, they haven't done that for thousands of years."

"And not even then, really." I smiled coyly, adding my opinion sotto voce.

"Yes, we go down to Ailsa's Craig on the beach for the Mabon fires. It's just down the steep hill from the stone circle that overlooks the sea," Colin responded. He had the kindest soft brown eyes, round as a kitten's.

Frank brought them over two pints of what they were drinking "Yer boyfriend is rather generous," the shorter man, Charlie, noted.

"Oh, no. Just my best friend." I smiled sheepishly, looking over at the taller man, who lit up with this news about Frank being single, as I had suspected he would. Maybe we'd have an easy ride to the autumnal equinox festival after all. I was done waiting on the ferries.

"Lovely, then!" the tall man said, clapping his hands together, bowing chivalrously and introducing himself to Frank as Colin, a lorry driver.

I couldn't tell if Frank genuinely liked him or if it was just brilliant acting in the name of buttering him up to get some information on their boat. Whatever his intentions, it worked. In just about fifteen minutes, the bar was closing, and we offered to drive them to their boat docking a few miles away. We learned it took about an hour to get to Campbeltown from where we were by boat and that Machrie Moor was just twenty minutes beyond that docking, over on the neighboring island. It would take two hours in total instead of ten hours and ferry timetables.

As we said goodbye at the dock, Frank chimed in, clapping his hands together, already picking up one of Colin's more endearing mannerisms. "We will meet you here on September twenty-second for the Mabon fires. Edie here will bring her drum, I'll bring the peyote, and we will dance and commune with the ancestors; it will be grand."

"Can't wait!" Colin chimed in before Charlie could comment. Charlie smiled a lipless smile and waved us off.

"Hey, Charlie, what's peyote?" I heard Colin ask as they walked away before we turned the engine back on.

"That was even more smooth than usual," I said to Frank as we drove away. "I appreciate you using your charm in the name of my research."

"I actually think I like the guy. Maybe that's the craziest part," he responded.

"The good news is that Mabon and Samhain are our last two festivals to research, and now you've made it much easier for us to access the stones that are normally the most difficult to get to. A large ferry can't get around Ailsa's craig, but a small fishing boat can." I said. "But the bad news is…"

And then we said in unison, "We missed the damn ferry again."

Ailsa

Aric stumbled over to me, drunk off ale, perhaps, or maybe just from the general reverie of the evening. He planted a sopping wet kiss on my neck, where his mouth lingered. He laughed, the sweet smell of smoked meat and herbs lingering on his breath.

"You're certainly enjoying yourself, Aric," Ros's sister Rasha spoke up. I gave her a look suggesting she not provoke him, but all women had trouble not engaging with Aric at close proximity. His dark hair gave way to a darker beard, kept long in the fashion of his people. Just that alone was enough to ensure he was exotically appealing, not to mention his washing up on the seashore, speaking a mysterious separate language, and being widowed by the age of eighteen.

As a girl, I had never quite understood why Aric was so appealing, but I was starting to understand. Something had changed over the last six months, and I was no longer cringing at his touch or his wet, sloppy kisses. In fact, I realized, watching him bow to Rasha and strut back to his friends, I had come to depend on his grace and the feeling of ease I had whenever I was around him. I watched him introduce himself to both strangers and friends of this northern isle with such ease and kindness, jovial and welcoming. My heart stayed in my chest, not in my throat, as it was so often with Ros. And there was my husband, bright and shining across the fire, I thought to myself. *My husband.* I felt a little kick in the belly at that. Or was it butterflies at the thought of my husband? Four moons had passed since my pregnancy began, and I was starting to feel movement in the womb.

"I heard you're calling the dancers at midnight," Rasha said as we both watched Aric.

"My first time," I said to her and smiled.

"Does Ros know?" she asked, innocently.

Could he have told her about our plan to escape tonight? I suppose if he had told anyone, it would be his sister. "I don't think he does," I answered, truthfully.

"It's just such a beautiful song, I know he'd want to hear you do it. In case it's the last time." I stared at her. *Did she know his plan?* "I don't think he has any intention of attending his own wedding. I guess I'll have to marry both twins." Rasha laughed.

I hugged her briefly. "I'm sorry, Rasha." I wanted to tell her so much more. "But that's not a bad idea." I joked instead, giving her a playful nudge on the shoulder. I wanted to enlist her help with telling him that I wasn't leaving with him tonight either, but I couldn't ask that of her. And I was braver than that. She kissed my cheek and ran off to join her mother, sister, and the other dancers. I waved over to them and then went to sit quietly next to Ray at the edge of the circle, hoping this might exempt me from further conversation.

My head was spinning now as the crowd moved around us. In the distance, the questioning "hoo-hoo" of a long-eared owl formed a chorus with the crickets. The local Druid, Bormag, began a chant that broke into melodic song, recounting the battles of generations of past; some of the words we knew, some he sang alone, his clear, high voice streaming into the night like a lark's song. I had that familiar feeling that my heart would burst, looking out onto the crowd of my friends and loved ones, the villagers that I had come to know throughout my life. It had been a hard life, but it would have been so much worse without the support I had from my village. I leaned back, enjoying the moment, never wanting to leave. *How had I ever entertained leaving?* I thought to myself.

And then I was instantly reminded. Ros's tenor rose to my right, above the deep voices encircling Aric on the periphery of the stones. One look at his ruddy complexion betrayed his intentions to me at once. He had come to start something with Aric if I wasn't prepared to leave with him. I had become uncharacteristically short-tempered lately. I said a quick prayer in my head and prepared myself to stand up from the stone on which I sat with Ray. He grabbed my arm and gave me a warning look that I was surprised to see. It was unlike him to get involved. Perhaps it was his bond with Aric, or perhaps it was our own connectedness, but he pulled me back as I tried to move toward the two men facing off now. I stared at him, as questioning as the owl, for a moment before my attention was pulled back to Ros, who was staring at me across the fire.

"I just need to speak to him for a moment, Ray," I said. "I'm not going anywhere."

"I've had a dream of him jumping off the cliffs into a fire, Ailsa. Whether that is literal or metaphorical, you cannot follow him into it, do you understand me?" he asked in a fatherly tone, glancing down at my small belly.

"I know the dream." I responded, nodding.

"You don't even know how to properly sail," I heard Ros muttering as I walked over to him. Aric and the other explorers seemed to be laughing, taking it in stride, and attempting to calm Ros, assuming he was drunk, which was making him even angrier. "You don't belong here," Ros said as he spat. Aric tracked my long strides as I made my way over. We made eye contact, but he didn't smile or interrupt me. He simply nodded a gentle, half-nod in my direction. He knew. And he was prepared to let me deal with my own mess.

"Your handler is here, Ros." a deep voice said across the crowd as I grabbed Ros's arm and glanced over at Rasha, sitting between her fiancé and Ros's, both of whom looked concerned. She gave me a pitiful, helpless look that angered me almost as much as her brother's ridiculous behavior. I pulled my hood up and covered my face, feeling like everyone around the giant fire knew, just as intimately as I did, what this was actually about. It wasn't unusual for drunken fights to break out between rivals at festival time, but if that happened, we weren't going to have the benefit of privacy for slipping away.

I snapped my hood up, "Is this your idea of slipping away quietly?" I pulled his arm, indicating he should follow me, and he did. Grandmother had gone over to speak to Aric, and Ray was distracted with the ceremony as I looked over my shoulder to make sure no one followed us to the shore.

I had run the decision over in my head one thousand times before I made it and one hundred times after. The outcome was always the same. I knew what I had to do. I took a deep breath. I was angry at him for acting out, but that wasn't the most important emotion at play here. What was it Ray always said? *Feel the feeling, but don't become the emotion.* We walked so speedily to the beach that I was losing my breath.

"I feel your fear," Ros said, holding my hand, our fingers interlaced tightly. "Cast it into the fire! The boat is ready, with sails. It's safe with plenty of food and water to get us to the southern isles."

The wind was not particularly strong, nor was the ocean rough, but the night was cold for Lughnasadh. He was right: it would be a safe crossing.

"I'm not afraid, Ros. Well, not of the crossing, at least."

"Then what is it, Ailsa?" he snapped. "You have the great unknown ahead of you. Seize it for yourself! We have an open journey and anything we can dream, like you said you wanted!" He paused, breathing heavily from nearly running away from the fire at the stone circle.

We had reached the walkway down to the beach from the shorter cliffs of the island. The sound of the waves rolling in seemed a calming roar compared with the madness of my best friend in front of me. He started to ease me down the steep incline that led to the beach. I heard the jubilant chanting from the fire far behind us and turned around instinctively.

"You know I love you, Ros, but I can't go," I said, and I felt his fingers slip out of mine.

He looked back at me, the open sea and the setting sun framing his pink face, his fire-colored hair, and the high arches of his blond brows and lashes. "It's what we said we wanted," he said in such an innocent manner that it broke my heart.

"I changed my mind," I said, placing my hand on his heart, a familiarity, I realized in that moment, I had with no one else. "It's not my dream anymore." I wrapped my heavy green cloak around me tightly against the night. "But it's what you want, and I want you to seize it."

"All I want is *you*!" he screamed, almost childlike.

"Ros, I know you feel that way now, but it's simply not true." He sank into the sand, head in his hands, elbows on his knees, and I knelt next to him, searching, praying for something to say.

"I could wring your skinny little neck, Ailsa. Don't tempt me." I backed away for a moment and took a deep breath for perspective.

"It's an adventure with nothing to tie you down, and perhaps that is closer to who you are than just someone who only wants me." I laughed. It was a tiny, amused noise, nothing more, but he glared up at me as I spoke. "That's never who you were when we were growing up, Ros. You've always dreamed too big for this island, and I loved you for it. You didn't need me then and you don't need me now. Look at your sail! It will take you where your soul leads." I gestured out to the moorings at his boat, which stood, shining and beautiful, lengths above the rest. He had poured his heart into it day by day, and I was shattering that same heart in this moment. I shivered from the thought.

"Is it love or *loved*, Ailsa? Because you've used both tonight."

I brushed the golden-red wisps of hair from his eyes and bent down, touching his forehead with mine. "I said both because I love you now and have loved you in the past, and I will love you forever."

"I should have known you would be afraid," he said in quiet disgust.

"I'm not afraid to go with you, Ros. I'm afraid to stay and fulfill the role I was born to. I'm afraid of what being head Druid will mean and how it will test me, I'm afraid of mothering and birth and how being a dowser like father will change me. And that's why I have to stay. It's the harder thing because it's not running away."

"And what of the child—if it is mine and I'll never see her or know her?" He thought for a moment, looking up into the stars for answers they could not give. *How many people had faced these same struggles before us? And how many more would across time?* I thought. I watched him for what felt like a long time and an instant. I watched the anguish on his face melt into something deeper; more sorrowful. Then he placed a callused, cupped hand on my cheek, and his eyes glistened into mine for what I hoped would not be the last time. "Tell her the stories of old; don't let her forget them. Tell her about our alder trees and my broken leg. Take her out on the boat. Make sure she knows that my heart is strong, that I was always true, despite enduring some difficulties and making mistakes." He pulled me to him. We shared one last, warm kiss, and then, holding the back of my head, he gently pressed my cheek to his so I could feel the hot tears burning tracks down his full cheeks and pointed jaw. "And sing her the songs we used to sing. You know my favorite one."

He began to hum the tune quietly and then sang, "Now wherever I roam I am not alone, you left me with something to hold on to." We rocked back and forth pressed together for a few last moments. Ros smiled at the kicks he could feel through my cloak on his thigh. "She's strong like her mother, aye?"

A lump formed in my throat. I couldn't think of anything to say. "Sing to her yourself, Ros. You can come back to tell us all about your adventures."

He nodded. "You told me to follow where my soul leads."

"Go, then," I said, "before the ceremony begins and Rasha and the twins come looking for you." He turned quickly to go and left without looking back.

As painful as it was, I forced myself to stay and look out over the horizon, watching him leave, sails pulled and bow uplifted in defiance of the breakers that challenged him before the promise of the still, open seas on the other side.

I thought about our different perspectives in that moment. Ros, facing those angry waves, focusing on getting through the rough moment, having faith that there was calm and peace ahead. And me, with the perspective of the gods, standing on the high ground above him, seeing clearly that there *was* peace ahead of him, if he could only push through the crashing waves.

CHAPTER 22:

MABON, THE AUTUMNAL EQUINOX

Edie

We made our way to the southern end of the beach in the gloaming; it must have been close to 6:00 p.m. by the time we had finally made both crossings, from Larne to Campbeltown and Campbeltown to Arran. The evening was sublime. It was warm for the coast on a September day, so we left our jackets on but hanging open, rather than having to bundle up with hoods and scarves against the cold. The crossing had been less than sublime.

We had gotten off at Campbeltown with Charlie and Colin and picked up a few of their friends to hop across the channel to the Holy Isle, formally called Arran, where Machrie Moor and the standing stones awaited us. We sat around the boat, shoulder to shoulder with other Campbeltown locals making the trek across the channel to the huge bonfire. The main conversation centered around the drink on offer by the festival hosts but would occasionally circle back to the stones themselves. Colin had introduced me as an "expert," so I felt everyone looking at me expectantly for an explanation as theories were thrown around.

"What did we agree to?" I whisper-yelled to Frank, who sat next to me on the fishing boat heading with haste across the open Irish Sea to the largest island situated in the Firth of Clyde.

"There's no way you're seasick in this little dinghy at full speed," he shot back at me. "If you are, it's psychosomatic, for sure." He made the international sign for crazy, staring at me and rotating his pointer finger counterclockwise next to his right ear.

I felt irrationally angry and, without responding, gritted my teeth, faced forward, and stoically lifted my chin into the wind whiplash of my hair battering my face, pulled out from my long braid. I was fighting against any uprising nausea, be it from seasickness or fear of capsizing. We reached the eastern coast of the island without incident in what had seemed like hours but ended up being more like thirty-five minutes, I was told. I stepped onto land, feeling like I could bend down and kiss it, but was immediately distracted by what lay ahead.

I looked at the lovely scene before me in my usual clinical way, which was more like an archaeologist and less like a twenty-something excited for a social event. The bonfire on the beach where everyone was gathered was actually below the stone circle, naturally protected from the fierce westerly winds by a large sculptural rock protrusion that seemed to feature a cave. I needed to check that for carvings later. There were some natural, rocky pathways up from the beach to the moor on which the stone circle sat, and I wondered when we would process up there. The sky was dark blue, not yet black, and clear with stars shining brightly down on the firelit faces of the local people gathered in an age-old custom. The fire was several feet above the heads of the folks around it and about twelve feet wide. The celebrants were scattered, some on logs around the fire, others standing in groups close to the kegs, and some venturing out toward the ocean or up on the rocks toward the cave. I estimated around 150 people.

"This must be the whole damn village," Frank said, impressed at the turn out. "Let's go get drinks and have a sit by the fire."

Frank and I headed over to share a large stump in front of the fire. "I wonder if they'll let me dance with them," I thought out loud, looking over at the young women, their hair hanging loose down their backs, with halo braids. They were barefoot, wearing flowing dresses, the picture of a Celtic fantasy, and I suddenly felt self-conscious in my jeans, wool sweater, and windbreaker.

"Don't you need the dance as a distraction for the rest of the group to take the measurements and photos you need in private?" Frank asked.

"You're right, I can't distract myself away from my own work," I said, a little disappointed.

"Let's take our drinks over toward that cave, where it's quieter. We can have a sit by the fire later while you tell me how I can help you record your data."

I smiled and nodded, but suddenly my work felt utterly out of place in the middle of this beautiful celebration.

As we made our way up toward the cave, I felt better about my outfit choice and was happy to have on my boots while navigating the slick rocks that led to the mouth of the cave. We found a nice dry spot at the opening to the cave where we could perch to watch the others around the fire.

"Feeling curious about the ritual?" Frank asked.

I nodded as I drank down most of my beer in just a few gulps from sheer thirst. "I'm more excited to experience it this time than I was at Beltane or the solstice, for sure," I said. "Do you think it will fit into the key with the rest of them?"

"I'm sure it will." Frank smiled at me and put his hand on my shoulder. "You're making new maps of the ancient world, Edie. It's going to be brilliant."

"Don't you want to be spending time with Colin now?" I asked. "We have an hour before sunset; I'll check out the cave alone and then come find you." I stood up and zipped my jacket. The proximity to the dampness of the cave had sent a shiver down my spine.

"I'd rather play it cool and see the cave with you," Frank answered, standing up and reaching down toward me to help me up.

Frank turned his phone flashlight on, and I used the mini torch on my keyring to illuminate the cave around us. We both gasped when we saw the carvings, ancient and modern, completely covering the walls and ceiling. Deeper into the cave, the ceiling opened up, becoming vaulted with stalactites, and a shadowy figure appeared on the walls. Frank grabbed my arm, but his fingers felt dead and cold. I heard his cell phone hit the ground, and all was dark, save the small blaze of my keychain. Had his heart stopped? No, he was alive.

"What the hell is that?" he asked breathlessly, but I was frozen. The shadow began to hum a familiar tune, and then we heard an Irish voice out of the darkness.

"Sorry to scare you." He appeared around the corner, smiling.

"What are you doing wandering around here in the dark? That's not safe," I said.

"Aye, I know it well in here; I'm safe enough, darlin'. Anyway, I had my phone, but it died."

"Oh," was all I could think to say.

"Was hoping you would message me back," he continued, brandishing his flip phone.

"Ohh," I said again. I had been keeping the secret of Michael's messages from Frank. He was close to us now, and I could see his patterned wool sweater and dark, windswept hair.

"Ahem." A muffled sound of Frank clearing his throat behind us reminded me that his phone had dropped somewhere onto the wet cave floor. I spun around, shining my flashlight on him below.

"There it is!" Michael called out, diving to help and crashing into Frank's head in the process.

"Thank you, Michael," Frank said, taking his phone and walking toward me with a serious look in his eyes. "I'm going to find Colin, Edie," he said, patting my shoulder. "You'll be fine here for a while." He nodded toward Michael and turned his back to leave. "I'll meet you up at the circle before sundown." And with that, he disappeared out of the cave opening toward the sea, and we were alone.

Michael pointed to the markings on the cave wall behind me. "We call it the king's cave." He walked toward it, put his hand up against an ancient handprint that fit him perfectly, raised his thick, black eyebrows, and looked back at me with a smirk. "They say Robert the Bruce hid out here after the Battle of Methven before he was crowned." I walked up to the wall where he stood so much taller than me I couldn't reach the handprint; I could feel his heavy breathing and the heat of it on the back my neck, since there was nowhere else for it to go in the shelter of the cave. He smelled sweetly of beer, wool, and some musky cologne, which must have become a habit from bartending.

I traced a nearby spiral with my index finger. "Art is so visceral. It's impossible not to want to touch it when you see it, to experience it fully."

"Aye, much of life is like that." Michael smiled in reply, and I felt him repress the urge to reach out and touch me. I was glad though, I wasn't ready.

"I was an artist before. I studied art history at university, but one of my archaeology professors told me early on that if I went on just one dig, I would see that holding dusty artifacts was more powerful than setting up glass and lighting to display one."

"Sounds like someone I'd like to have a beer with," he said, looking at the wall just inches away from me. We stood there in companionable silence another moment or so, and then he started laughing.

"What is it?" I asked.

"You made quite the impression on my grandfather," he said.

"What?" I didn't think I'd spoken to anyone but Frank, Colin, Charlie, and their young friends who had been our boat companions.

"He went to the bar on an undercover mission for me to see how the blockhead I hired to help me while I was off last month was doing."

"Oh, Mickey is your grandfather?" I asked, stunned.

"I'm his namesake, of course," he answered, winking at me, and I was reminded of how annoyed I was at myself for liking his ancient flirtation tactics.

"Of course." I smiled, nervously. I started to sweat a bit. Had I said anything embarrassing to his grandfather? Michael's fingertips brushed the edges of mine so lightly I couldn't tell if it was on purpose or not. The contact sent a feeling like an electric shock through my body, but I tried to remain cool on the outside.

"Don't worry. He just thinks we have a lot in common. Said you reminded him of me." Michael smiled again, turning toward me.

"Oh, did he?" Despite my bashfulness, I turned to look directly into his eyes, genuinely curious about this revelation.

"Yeah, well, he thinks it's nice to have common interests, you know. Something that ties you together, that you…" Michael had a habit of moving his hands wildly as he searched for words.

"That you inspire one another to greatness?" I completed his sentence with my own spin, I suppose, and the look of intensity he gave back to me, the fire burning in his dark blue eyes, was all the answer I needed. He touched my neck lightly, and my small fairy wing earring dangled over his thumb. I felt the lightest pressure of his large farmer's hand on the back of my neck and wanted to dive toward him when the drumbeat initiating the ceremony resonated within the cave.

Michael let out a snort of a laugh. "Is that my heart beating?" he asked, laughing.

"I have to go measure the stones before sundown. I'm sorry." I backed away.

"You're not doing the procession up from the beach with us?" he asked, indignant.

"No, sorry!" I called behind me as I ran out of the cave and took a sharp right turn to scurry up the side of the cliff.

"Edana!" he called after me. I turned around to look at him, and he stood there in his boots and jeans and Fair Isle sweater, sun setting behind his jet-black hair. He was perfect. "You should really relax and enjoy the ceremony. It'll teach you more than your measurements ever will. You should've done so at Beltane too. I let it slide then, but tonight you're not an archaeologist, for once. OK? Do the procession with me."

"I need the data, Michael. I'll see you up there."

Once again thankful for my footwear and gloves, I bounded up the cliffside. I reached the top in just a few minutes, but the sun was plunging quickly, and I needed the light for the photos and hand measurements. Luckily, Frank and Colin had the LiDAR tripod set up already. I could see them in the distance as I ran across the moor, waving madly.

"Drums caught you with your pants down, huh?" called Frank, his hands cupped around his mouth, camera hanging around his neck. As I jogged up to the stones, I pulled out my measuring tape, tools, and journal from my satchel bag. Colin peered around the LiDAR at me with his eyebrows raised.

"Not precisely," I said, throwing my bag down.

Frank laughed and lit a cigarette. He walked over to show me some of the photos he had captured—they were absolutely stunning, with the stones standing in the light of the gloaming.

"Wow," I said.

"Mmhmm," he replied, rolled cigarette in mouth, fingers maneuvering the zoom and arrows on his DSLR. I flipped to my stone circle drawings with a tracing paper overlay and began my hand measurements while the LiDAR took its own. Frank walked over to Colin to share a drag of his cigarette.

"Do you have true north on the compass over there?" I shouted. As I finished up the measurements, the result became clear. I walked to the north stone without them having to tell me which it was. I began the formality of the sketch, which wasn't necessary but seemed magical as it came together, illuminating my theory on paper, not in words but in the picture of the way the stones fit together, like the gears of a clock, but telling a different kind of time, a more magical one. I flipped up my tracing paper and watched the stones disappear and then fall back together again in perfect place when I dropped the pages.

"It's remarkable!" I said and looked up to see Frank and Colin quickly moving our things aside as the drums and singing got louder and the procession started up from the beach.

"Come dance with us!" they called as they meandered down to join the crowd.

"I will in a minute," I shouted over the music and chanting of the festivities.

Frank lifted his arms and danced off, looking as pagan as ever, and I jotted a few notes down before hiding my notepad in my jacket pocket. The procession reached Machrie Moor, and I started searching among the crowd for Michael to deliver the happy news. As I searched, the drumming and singing got louder and louder. I thought I had found him a couple of times in the densely packed crowd, but I had all but given up when I heard his voice—but in a high, shrill call I'd never heard before. I whipped around, eyes wide, to find him in the middle of the circle at the altar stone. He was calling the dancers like he had at Beltane. The memories of that night came rushing forward, and I pushed them back, unable to process anything more than what was right in front of me.

I stared into the light of the torches illuminating the stone circle, my eyes watering in response to the brightness and closeness of the flickering flames. I reached for my phone and noticed that it was at three percent. *"Damn it,"* I whispered. Discreetly, I started the audio recording as the singing began. I heard a familiar voice coming through the recording, and when I looked off to my left, I noticed Frank, Charlie, and Colin joining in with the chanting. It was a call-and-response led by Michael. Everyone was enraptured, but I felt myself on the outside of it all, unable to give myself over to it, a voyeur, not a participant.

Looking down at my phone for solidarity, I saw it had abandoned me too, with a briefly flashing dotted white circle spiraling in front of my eyes. My phone powered down, exhausted by the boat ride and cold wind, and no doubt by the sheer pressure I had put on it to record every second that happened so that I could absorb every detail at a later moment. I closed my eyes and breathed in a deep, cold, smoky gulp of air. Frank beckoned to me casually with his free arm; the other was around Colin. The singing and bodhran drumbeat was now so loud there was no chance of hearing someone unless they were yelling directly into your eardrum. I staggered over to him, pushing past people who were standing, and explained, weakly, that my phone was dead.

"So what?" he responded in my ear, shaking me by the shoulders a little. "What would Sully say?"

"To be here, in the moment. The experience is the research," I answered, pulling Frank's leaf crown and pulling out my braid, letting my waist-length hair fall free. I pulled off my sweater, glad I was wearing an oversized white T-shirt. I used my ponytail holder to tie the shirt up and slipped my boots and socks off, placing them with my jacket next to the LiDAR and other equipment.

While I did this, a huge fire was being built at the center of the circle from the torches people had carried up from the beach bonfire. The chill had left the air, and the standing stones came into better view, lit up like white giants as the night darkened. Declan, Michael's friend whom I had met at Beltane and who played lead bodhran, an ancient folk drum, stopped abruptly. The singing and other music died down, and for a moment there was complete silence, except for the hum of the wind over the nearby cliffs. I wondered where Michael had gone, and then the drums started again, and he was next to me.

"Are you OK?" he asked in my ear. I nodded. "Ready to dance with us like I showed you at Beltane?" he asked with a tilt of the head.

Just in front of us, the fire roared as Michael interlaced his fingers with mine and I felt the same jolt of electricity I had in the cave. Now, in the ceremonial dancing beat, the whole of the company came alive, me included. I looked around me and noticed that somehow no one looked as if they were from the twenty-first century. We had all transformed into part of a ritual, timeless bodies electric, light in the darkness. Declan raised his voice up above the sound of the hypnotizing bodhran, and the men joined in, while I was ushered into the back of the circle dance by some young women, some of whom were so giddy, it must have also been their first Mabon celebration.

I smiled across the fire at Frank, who was humming along with his new friend in perfect pitch, his crystal-clear voice recognizable to me and rising above the rest. I started to laugh uncontrollably as I stumbled through the dance moves, feeling the cool earth squeeze up between my toes, almost erotically. I knew from all my reading that these dances were supposed to induce a trancelike state. The music and atmosphere simply enveloped you.

The dancing movements were simple and repetitive around the stones. At some point we were all handed lanterns, which became an extension of our arms. Time seemed to vanish altogether, and I found myself no longer looking over to check on Frank and Colin, no longer looking to either side of me at the other girls to know what movement I should be doing, and eventually not even looking for Michael's electric smile. There was a lot of spinning and weaving in and out between one another, and I started to get really dizzy, like I was really drunk without drinking anything, lost in a vortex of vertigo. Maybe I looked like a total idiot, but I didn't care. And honestly, I didn't think anyone else noticed or cared. That's the beautiful part of being one small moving cog in the larger picture. It felt good to be unburdened in such a way, to feel as if my mistakes didn't matter so much. I had wisdom that was the missing piece to a puzzle. I had a purpose I was fulfilling. And beyond that, what else really mattered?

I felt a squeeze of my fingertips, my heartbeat quickened, and suddenly we were all holding hands, moving in a new pattern, closer to the stone. We moved in this circular pattern until we broke off from the circle with our partners. That's when he found me again. He held me so close, I couldn't tell the difference between my heartbeat, Michael's, and the bodhran. One of them was growing louder and louder, pounding in my ears. I felt my palms start to sweat, my body tingling with heightened sensation. Everything else seemed to stand still, like the stones, even though we were still spinning—and then, with a kiss, it all went white.

CHAPTER 23:

BY THE LIGHT OF THE DARK MOON

Everyone had either erected their tents on the beach and crawled in for the night or, like Frank and Colin, had languidly propped themselves on logs and rocks by the beach bonfire like a Dionysian dinner party. People played guitars, told stories, and many came up to Michael to chat with him as we sat by the lapping tide, alone together. I had wrapped myself back up in my jacket but left my hair down, twirling it around my fingers nervously.

"I love when the fire festivals fall on a new moon," he said. "When it's this dark, you can see every single star." I nodded. "We see them how people saw them every night before all the pollution and buildings and light blocked them out," he added.

"I couldn't agree more," I said. "I love new moon energy. It feels like the beginning of a new chapter."

"I like that," Michael agreed, shifting closer to me.

"I still can't believe I fainted." I laughed, a bit embarrassed still but focusing on more important emotions.

"Yeah, I couldn't decide if it was a compliment to my kissing style or maybe a bad sign," Michael joked, flashing his white teeth with the lovely little space in them. It may have been dark out with no moon, but I could still see the important parts under the light of the stars. "I've never had a girl faint when I've kissed her before, though I have heard I'm not terrible at it," he said, clearly fishing for some absolution.

"I think I was just overtaken by the ceremony as a whole. I really lost myself," I said, leaning back to rest on my elbows and get a better view of the stars.

"I'm sorry for surprising you like that. I lost meself in it too, and I lost my ability to, uhhh, you know, restrain my desires." He looked down bashfully and handed me back the tin mug of tea we were sharing. "I hope you're feelin' better now." he added. I sipped and thought. Unafraid of the silence between us. Apparently Michael didn't share this courage because he quickly piped up. "Frank seems quite smitten over there, which is nice. I've known Colin for a while. He's a nice bloke. Often drives the lorry that delivers new kegs to the bar. And so what did your measurements and alignments tell you up there on the moor?" he asked without taking a breath.

Was Michael getting nervous and thus chatty? I wondered, amused that this ultraconfident leader of men and women, and pint slinger no less, could be nervous. "I feel confident about my thesis," I continued since he seemed relieved I was doing the talking now. "The book will discuss the monument complex throughout the Northern British Isles, their alignments, and thus when they would have been used for festivals, as well as the distances between them and how and why ancient people would have traveled between monuments to celebrate the wheel of the year with a broader community."

Michael nodded. "Sounds like you may have learned something from the modern festivals as well as the ancient monuments." He nudged me with his shoulder playfully.

"I did. Truly. And Sully would be so glad," I answered earnestly, looking into his eyes a moment too long and losing my train of thought as he bent closer to me. "Your grandfather told me what you do for the locals in August at your farm," I offered, changing the subject. "Hosting them for weekly bonfires, free beer, music, and stories so they get a reprieve."

He nodded, gaining the courage to peer over at me out of the corners of his eyes. "Aye, it's a beautiful thing, community," he said in a soft voice. "You Americans are so determined to be independent and self-sufficient, I think you forget you need people sometimes." He reached out to place a hand on my knee. "Do you know what the ancient meaning of Mabon really is?" he asked gently.

"It's derived from Welsh and means triumph over the darkness." That made him laugh, and I wasn't sure why.

"Yes, love, literally." he sniggered. "But the meaning of the ritual and in coming together, is to remind ourselves that we need one another to overcome the darkness." I sighed a deep, guttural sound. "The darkness of the winter months ahead." he clarified. I nodded. " Edie, I'd love for you to come to the farm for a wee stay, see old Mickey again, meet my animals. You'd love it there." I nodded again, looking out over the sea. "I'd say you could excavate anything you like there, but your mind seems so far away, I'm not sure I can reel you back in, even with that." His thumb moved back and forth over the outside of my kneecap in a reassuring rubbing motion. He was trying very hard to act in a courteous, platonic manner, but the restraint was written all over his face.

"I never really had the approval or the love of my father," I said. Out of the blue, into the universe, there it was. Michael's hand stopped rubbing my knee, and I felt him hold his breath as I continued. "I guess I went into academia to prove something to him. Maybe that I was smarter, or better, or just worthy of admiration." Now I was on a roll and I blushed. I hadn't shared so much of myself in a long time.

"Mmmm, that's hard." Michael said soothingly, urging me to continue. He was gentle with me like I imagined he was with the animals on his farm.

"I wanted strictly academic admiration, but Sully gave me something more. It was a fatherly love I'd never had before. I took it for granted, I ran away, and then he was gone. And all the emptiness I had felt as a child came back, but worse this time."

"I understand," he said. "And that's why you're working so hard on your wee book and why you're determined for it to be perfect. You owe it to him."

"Yes, that," I admitted. "And I think it will be the thing that gets me a research professor position at the university. And that's where I need to be to make a difference like he did."

The admission hung between us in the air for a moment, and once again Michael broke the silence. "I don't mind ye living three hours from me if that's why you're pushing me away, Edie. Reason doesn't matter o'er much where love's concerned."

I laughed out loud. "You can't love me. This is the third time we've met." I laughed some more, looking into his serious eyes.

"But I *could* love you is what I'm sayin'," he said defensively. "So don't overthink or hold back because of Dublin. You do what you need to do."

"Will you go with me?" I blurted out, and he went a little pale, speechless. "No! Sorry, I just mean—will you go with me to Dublin and Newgrange for the winter solstice? We can do some Christmas shopping in Dublin and be back by Christmas Eve?"

"Ahhh, of course, love," he said, relaxing, knowing that I had not asked him to uproot his life and move with me to some gray apartment at Trinity for a professorship I didn't even have yet. I didn't correct him for calling me "love" this time. I let it lie between us, so it could become what it wanted to, and I think this gave him some comfort too. Like I might let him in. He reached for my hand. "I'm sorry your heart has been broken." he said, simply. We interlaced our fingers, and he asked me, "Didn't you say your pa was Irish? From Donegal, when we were there for Beltane?"

I nodded. "Yep. O'Connors we are."

He ran a finger across my clavicle where a smattering of freckles covered my décolletage. "Catholic too?" he asked.

"Oh, yes," I answered. "Saint Catherine of Siena is my patron saint."

"Ahhh," he said, looking into my eyes, "Mines an Italian too." I loved how Irish people said Italian like "Eye-talian." "Too many Irishmen carry the weight of their ancestors. Pain from deprivation and years of injustice, especially Catholics living in the Northern Republic like your pa." I nodded in agreement. "I'm not saying this in defense of him, mind ye," Michael continued, reassuring me, looking away to find the words. "I'm sayin' it so you know I understand that you've suffered, as many of us have." He looked at me, searching for something.

"Thank *you*," I said. "Not only for recognizing me, but for wanting to understand me." I set my tea down, finally, and took his hand in mine, rubbing the knuckles.

Then his coy smile. "When you're feelin' more tethered to the earth, Edie O'Connor, I'd like to kiss you again." He tilted his head and narrowed his eyes in a gentle question.

"I feel…I feel so rooted to this ground, I don't know if I can ever get up," I said blissfully, with tears in my eyes.

"Weeeell, that's good enough for me." Michael smiled into my eyes as his fingers smoothed my hair and pulled my chin toward his for our second kiss. This time we both sank into the earth together, and the waves lapped at our feet, and the bodhran music played by the fire, our friends' voices lifting into the perfect fall evening.

CHAPTER 24:

SAMHAIN, AGAIN

Ailsa

"What makes you wake at daybreak and lay your head down at night?" Jord asked.

"I know the answer to the second one is wine," answered Ray, smiling in his broad, frog-like grin that stretched from ear to ear. He and Jord had set out across the hills to the moor just before dawn. Preparations for the eve of Samhain were underway, and my rounded belly was finally peeking out from my heavy green cloak. It was colder than usual and had already snowed once. Last Samhain, I had walked home from the smokehouse with Ros wearing my cloak only, but tonight I was wearing fur underneath my Druid's cloak, as well as a thick wool dress under that, and I felt a bit like a round hedgehog plumping up for winter. Three moon cycles had passed since Ros left, and while some days, like today, it felt like I thought of him constantly, other days passed peacefully with no reminders of him at all, as Aric and I prepared for the arrival of the baby and the Druids searched for answers in the stones, awaiting the prophetic arrival of the messenger from the south that Ray called *the stranger*.

"The crack in the stone," Jord said, his eyes drifting to the tallest stone.

"I've examined it several different times," I said. It appears that the crack happened where the veining is most concentrated, and inside the veins, the rock shimmers; when set aflame, it melts."

"How did you get up that high to look?" Ray asked, astounded.

I smiled knowingly. "Aric lifted me up."

Jord said, bashfully, "I'm sure he was happy to do it for you," and we all had a laugh.

Ray's eyes were wide. He had been in a jovial mood that morning, but as the time of the ceremony grew near, I could tell something was on his mind. "I have dreamed about this night," he said. There was a long silence as he seemed to be deciding something important. Jord and I waited with our breaths held. "It's the night of the fire," he said finally. Jord and I glanced at one another. There was always a fire at the stones on Samhain. "He comes tonight," Ray said, gathering his things.

"Who, the stranger?" I asked.

"I'll be back here by nightfall for the ceremony," Ray responded, answering my question without actually answering.

Jord and I looked at each other and bade farewell to Ray, watching him as his short legs carried him to the king's cave with haste. He turned around abruptly.

"Tonight you will call the fire, Ailsa," he declared.

"But I call the dancers now," I protested.

"Spirit tells me that you will be in childbed for the winter solstice ceremony, so I need Jord to practice calling the dancers once before then."

Jord smiled down at me. His eyes were dark pools, like the black of the deepest part of a lake. "Do not fret, 'twill be all right, child. I feel your parents here with you on this most auspicious day the ancestors descend to earth." I looked up and saw their reflection in his eyes, which were so dark the pupil could not be distinguished. "Let us go and prepare the village for the procession," he said. I gently brushed a spider from my cloak, and Jord helped me to my feet.

"He's a funny little man, changing the ceremony at the last minute," I said, mostly to myself.

Jord agreed, adding, "I wonder who this stranger is."

Jord gave me his arm for the long walk across the moor and through the oak grove back to the village and I thought it peculiar that as close and Ray and Jord were, Jord was still clueless about the intentions of the stranger. "What's the answer to your riddle, Uncle Jord?" I asked as we walked, but he looked confused. "About waking and laying your head down?"

"Oh. It wasn't a riddle. Just an observation about the sun's power over us all."

I shook my head and smiled up at him. "I always felt like you embodied the calm that falls over the land at this time when the veil is most thin, Uncle."

"I thank you for that, Ailsa. I am particularly thankful for the wisdom of the ancestors tonight. It is most needed at this time."

We walked through a light drizzle of rain, and I pulled my hood up, happy to reach the oak grove where we were covered. As we crossed the river on flat rocks, I heard a voice call to me. "Did you hear that?" I asked Jord. He shook his head, continuing toward the village. I told him I would catch up to him after I stopped by the great oak for a prayer before the ceremony.

As I made my way there, I heard footsteps following. No one can sneak up on a Druid in the woods in autumn. The leaves were crunchy, and the light drizzle had sent all animals and their sounds inside their dens and nests for the moment. "Who's there?" I demanded as I approached the great oak. Someone grabbed me from behind, and I screamed. I instantly regretted that—and hoped Jord hadn't heard me—when I spun around to find Aric's giant face grinning down at me. The time between Mabon and Samhain was the Nordic New Year, so he had been home with me all this time, in celebration with the few other Norseman in the village. This, combined with the imminent birth of his child, our growing affection for one another, and Ros's long absence, had left him nothing less than jubilant the past moon cycle. In this moment he looked a little crazed, though.

"Are you here to kill me?" I asked through short, jagged breaths. I was rebutted with a long and hearty laugh from Aric, who nearly doubled over with hilarity.

When he finally regained his breath, he responded, "No. Do you know where we are?"

Looking around, I felt the rough, three-foot-wide trunk of the tree that I had flattened my palms against for support. "We're in the oak grove, at my tree." He opened his mouth to respond but instead just glared down at me intensely, willing me to understand. And I stared back at him, blank, remembering the time Ros had followed me out to the old oak grove to tell me about his plan for Lughnasadh. I stared back into his eyes, creasing mine into an almond shape, and suddenly I saw exactly what he wanted me to see. "How do you know about my tree?" I wondered out loud. "Do you follow me?" I asked, near frustration.

"Yes. And no," he responded, holding up his hands to keep me from interrupting him as he continued. "I came here, in grief, to be alone, when you were just a child and my wife had died. And I saw you. I watched you like something ethereal. You didn't seem real."

I stared up at him in disbelief, afraid of what he had seen since then and what he could know, afraid of a part of me being laid bare without my knowledge. "So you sought out the old gods of the oak grove to heal you after Iona died, when the gods of your home didn't show up for you?" I asked.

He looked at the ground, the oak's woven roots, which seemed to entangle us as we stood there, rising up between his feet and as high as my thighs. The ancient trees started to crawl from the earth like that. He was as still as night, and then there was a small, gentle nod followed by a tear that fell to ground around the roots in offering. "But I found healing from you instead." His words floated up to me, and he lifted his gaze to mine and continued, more impassioned now. "This child, who I knew had lost everything but who nonetheless seemed so full of life and happiness, was my teacher. I wanted what you knew about grief, your secret to surviving it."

"There's no secret," I said, feeling in that moment the full weight of my father's grief, which had pulled him under.

"I saw you here, at this tree, and I felt like I knew your soul, like I had seen it here, and so when I did love you, *after we were married,*" he emphasized, "I knew exactly where to come when I was looking for you and exactly what you'd be doing when I found you here. I couldn't ever disturb you in what felt like both your work and your pleasure at the tree, but I felt that if I could be a part of what you were doing, a voyeur of your ritual, then maybe I would be closer to you, understand you better."

Some incredible feeling bubbled up inside of me, and I couldn't stop it from trickling over my lips and bursting into fits of laughter.

I slid down the trunk of the tree into a crouched position, scratching my back like a bear on the way down, feeling comforted and at home in between the large roots of my tree, where I rested my arms and continued my fits of giggles, laying my head back against the trunk and inhaling the smell of the sweet black earth beneath me and the musky man, my husband, looking very perplexed.

"What on earth is so funny, my dear?" he asked.

After a few more seconds, I got myself under control and lifted my arms to him in embrace. He crouched down with me, nestled in the roots like a pair of rabbits. "Nothing," I said, resting my head safely on his shoulder and closing my eyes, thinking to myself that whether life was all free will or destiny or a mixture of the two, it had somehow aligned. I had been so mad at Ray for dismissing Ros, for forcing the connection with Aric, and for leaving me in the dark about it for so many years. But Ray hadn't forced anything. He had merely seen the truth, from a different perspective, and he had let it play out as naturally as possible, hopefully with as little pain as possible. I said a silent prayer for Ros's happiness, as I often did when he sprang to mind.

Normally, Aric wouldn't have let me get away with something as dismissive as "nothing" when I broke into one of my giggling fits, but the sound of the dancers bringing up their voices in procession to the stone circle sent a shiver up my spine and pulled us both away from our moment.

"Oh no, I'm late!"

Aric stood up and pulled me into his arms. "I'll carry you up to the moor; it will be faster." I wrapped my arms around his neck for stability, and he patted the trunk of my tree. "See you soon, old friend," he said to it and ran off through the woods.

The last of the ghostly procession arrived at the top of the cliffs just as I joined the Druids and Jord began calling them, their lanterns floating across the moor toward the rest of us at the stone circle. The dancers approached from all directions, long white dresses dragging behind them as they carried lanterns with them up the path from the beach. They wore veils as well, thinly woven to show their faces through the silvery white fabric. The veils were held in place by flower crowns made from juniper, lavender, ivy, and jasmine. I had helped Rasha and Reina with theirs, and we had stayed up late, talking about Rasha's new husband and silently hoping for Ros to return home for Samhain eve, but he hadn't.

The sound of the Druids' humming eased a knot in my stomach that I didn't realize I had been carrying until then. I had expected Ros to come home, even just briefly, this week for his birthday and favorite festival. I took a deep breath and strode toward the light of the huge fire, leaving Aric behind me with one last squeeze of his fingertips. The sound of my heavy breathing and heartbeat faded as I got closer to the drums and the song and story that called the dancers around me. I stood in a circle with the other Druids, looking for Ray with no luck. Was he with the stranger? I wondered.

The drums stopped; the dancers froze. It was my turn. I stepped up, prepared to call the torches to the great fire at the center of the circle, but I never called the fire that night—or ever—because a greater fire than any of us had ever seen before had just arrived on the island.

Ray's voice rang out in the stillness, and when I carried my torch to look down the beach toward the cave where he had disappeared to, I saw the fire that he had described in his dream: wild, out of control, and consuming the boats moored on the beach.

"Ray!" I called desperately, following Jord to the path that led down to the beach. Then Ray appeared, seemingly out of the mist, walking toward us on the moor.

"You must go alone, Ailsa. In haste." He spoke directly to me, but Aric stepped in.

"Are you mad? She's with child."

I quieted him. "I'll go," I said.

I walked across the moor, handed my torch to Ray, illuminating his sooty, sweaty face, and made my way down to the beach.

As I came closer to the cave, I recognized Ros's beautiful crab claw sailboat as the kindling of this great fire. I gasped and ran as fast as my legs could carry me, calling Ros's name. He stood on the bow of it, and when he saw me, he picked up one of the flagons of strong wine he had packed, took a long, deep swig of it, then threw it into the ship with a satisfying smash as the shards flew everywhere. I shielded my eyes, thankfully, because in one instantaneous *whoosh*, the fire went up, hot on my face, and the ship disappeared in flames in front of us.

"Ros, are you ok?" I ran to him where he had jumped off into the water just in time. His face was flushed red from the heat of the fire, and I saw the reflection of it in his eyes. I waded out in the water to my knees, but he pulled me out farther and kissed me sweetly until I was immersed to my shoulders. He tasted like salt: his sweat, tears, and the ocean mingling on my lips. "Why did you scorch your beautiful boat, Ros?"

"They're after me," he said, out of breath, kissing my cheeks.

"Who?" I asked. "And firing the boat is a little attention-grabbing if someone is pursuing you, don'tcha think?"

He smiled at me with the huge, wily grin that had captivated all the girls of our youth, and I saw then that he had returned to his wild and unpredictable self. "I made it down to the south isles and decided to go over to the mainland. I met some men from the south to trade with, and they asked me about ye." he explained. "How?" I asked, perplexed. "They wielded strange weapons, Ailsa, sharp as sharks' teeth, but bigger, more formidable. They threatened me more than once with them." I wondered why Ray hadn't mentioned the possibility of violence from the stranger. We had simply been look-ing for messages about the stones, not expecting battle, I thought. "And they had all kinds of jewelry and breastplates," he continued. "I've never seen anything like it. I was worried for you since they were asking after you, so I sent them off track, far north, but as I was coming back here for Samhain to warn you all, I saw them sailing into the eastern harbor, and they shot one of their silvery weapons at my boat."

He was out of breath from telling me, so I held his head in my hands to calm him. "I'm OK," I said. "*We're* OK." I smiled.

He pulled me to him, and we embraced. "I'll take my fishing boat so they don't recognize me and leave in the middle of the night so I can go up to see everyone at the Samhain festival for a moment."

As he spoke, he started off toward the cave where his fishing boat was moored. He spared a scarce glance at me over his shoulder, and in that moment, a falling star streaked downward across the sky. I gasped and pointed up, but it was too late; he had missed it. *Blink and the magic is gone.* I let the thought float in—and out just as quickly as the light had appeared in the sky.

I ran after him, struggling in my heavy clothes, removing the wet fur from under my cloak. Ros looked over at me, standing at the mouth of the cave as he prepared his small fishing boat inside, heaving in what was left of the furs, woolen blankets, and leather bags full of soaps, herbs, dried jerky, fruit, barley and medical necessities. I brought him my warm underclothes, he smiled and nodded. Last, he pitched in his flint tools. He had spent more time on a boat in his life than on land, perhaps, so it was no surprise that he worked swiftly and effortlessly. He pushed his boat out of the cave onto the runners that dropped it down into the deeper waters that surrounded the cave opening. The same one where Aric had washed ashore nearly twenty years ago.

He extended his hand to me. "Let's walk up to the Samhain fire and tell them not to worry about my fire," he suggested, holding up a dry cloak for me.

I laid the wet green Druid's cloak in his boat, assuming I'd walk him down with his sisters when he left, and I wrapped the indigo-dyed wool around me. "This is beautiful," I said.

"I got it for ye in the southern isles," he answered, looking pleased to see me in it. "Don't tell Rasha and Reina, though," he joked. "Never did think the green favored you much."

We held hands and walked past the fire, tamed by the wind and waves somewhat, toward the steep pathway up to the moor from the beach. "The tide's going to change soon." I pointed out. He raised his eyebrows, kissed the back of my hand, and motioned me up the path in front of him. "I'll be back in time." he answered.

I looked for Aric's face first as we crested the hill to the moor. Ros ran over to his family, resistant to part ways with me, but I saw Ray's concerned face through the jubilant crowd first and walked straight to him, the heartbeat of the bodhran pounding in my ears. "Don't worry, the fire is dying down and he's leaving after—where's Aric?" I interrupted myself.

"He's here, Ailsa. The stranger from the South. Aric took some of his men to meet his boat at the eastern coast."

My heart leaped into my throat. For Aric, for Ros, and finally for Ray and myself. "What are they going to do?" I asked.

"My intuition and experience tells me they mean no harm, but speaking to Ros today has led me to believe they can easily make enemies, and they clearly know who you are."

"Why do they know me, Ray? You're the head Druid. You're the one with the visions."

Ray gave me an abashed look, but before he could reply, someone yelled my name from across the darkness.

"Ailsa!" I heard Aric's voice and went to meet him, sprinting up the moor. "They saw us coming and turned south to go around to the other coast."

"Why would they do that if they meant well?" I glanced at Ray, who had joined us, and noticed Ros watching us over the crowd as well.

"Ros!" Aric yelled. "The tide is going out and taking your small boat with it!"

Ros hugged his mother and walked over to us casually so as not to frighten his family any more than they already were. "Are they here?" he asked Aric.

"They're coming around to dock on this side of the island," he answered.

"Best you go, Ros," Ray said. "Aric says they don't seem friendly."

Ros looked at me. I looked at Ray. "She'll be safe with me here," Aric said. "No need to worry." I was, as always, thankful for his kindness.

Ros nodded, said goodbye, mostly to me and mostly with his eyes, and made for the quickest way down. We three watched him, solemnly, yet no sooner had his head disappeared in descent than it popped back up again. "They're down there by the fire!" he yelled, pointing and running toward us.

"How'd they get here so fast?" I turned around, looking at Ray, Aric, anyone who could explain.

"I told you they've some sort of sorcery," Ros said. "My boat's gone past the breakers; I can't get to it. I…" Ros looked at me, defeated.

"Ray, please!" I grabbed his hands urgently, "Can you go talk to them and make sure all is well?"

"I'll go with him," Aric said. "Can't send the old man by himself." He rubbed Ray's shoulder and smiled his sweet smile at me, eyes creasing into triangles.

Ray nodded solemnly and reached for Ros's hands. He held them in his own, and I saw tenderness pass between them for the first time. What had they talked about on the beach before they set the fire? I wondered, watching them. Ray reached up to hug Ros, and I heard him whisper, "You know what you have to do."

Ros nodded and patted Ray's shoulders. There was shouting in a foreign language down on the beach. Aric kissed me goodbye and reassured me all would be fine. I looked at the stone mace and ax he carried, and the ceremonial mace that Ray carried, and felt better. "Be careful," I said as he turned to lead Ray down to the beach.

Ros had left to walk south in the direction of the cliffs where we had met so many times. His pace was quick, so I had to run to catch up with him. "What were you and Ray talking about? What do you have to do?" I asked, barely able to breathe.

"Go back to the stone circle, Ailsa," Ros said without looking back at me, still walking too fast for me to catch up in my condition.

"Please!" I yelled. My heart was thumping so hard with my exertion and fright. "Please don't jump like my father! Ros, tell me you wont!"

At this, he turned around. The edge of the cliffs was in sight, and I fell to my knees in exhaustion.

"I have to," he said, walking over to me and lifting me up. "But I'm going off the south cliffs, where there are no rocks below, only the one craig that I can swim to if I don't catch my boat. But I will, don't worry. I'll dive for it– I've done it before, just not so high up." he laughed. He walked with me a bit closer to the edge, and the wind blew the new indigo cloak he had given me up around us, whipping my hair wildly. "See, it's just there. I can make it if I jump now."

The edge of the cliffs hid the fire and Ray and Aric from our view to the west. I closed my eyes and said a prayer that they were safe. "You don't have to go like this," I pleaded, looking down at the swells of the sea below, spying his little fishing boat fifty lengths from the shore.

"Tell the foreigners I went south again to the traders," he said, looking down at the ocean below, searching for the best place to enter the water. "I'll be long gone in the other direction." He winked at me, silently telling me that if I ever needed him I could find him in the North, the lands of pink and green night skies and ship builders. He pulled me in for one last, long kiss. "Tell my story, Ailsa. The Samhain eve that I flew down from the cliffs into the sea."

He laughed with excitement in his ocean blue eyes, his huge ear-to-ear grin visible across the moonless night. How many times had we laughed together? As young children we had played games in the meadow, hiding from his parents and rolling in the dirt with his dogs. As older children we had found humor in almost everything, especially anything serious. All the ceremonies and festivals at which we had planned pranks, snuck off, made jokes, or laughed at the serious behavior of the adults flew through my mind all at once, and I managed to laugh through my tears. I held the underside of my belly on the steep ascent to the very top of the cliffs, the place where it had begun, where he had first kissed me under these very same stars, with different promises. "It's time." he said.

We backed away from the edge of the cliffs together, holding hands. Once we were well enough back, he looked at me one last time, took a deep breath, and took off running full speed. When he reached the edge of the cliff, he pushed off hard, put his arms out, and dove into the sea with the grace of an albatross. I ran to the edge, where I saw his boat bobbing, straining to see a small head pop out of the water. "Please!" I begged out loud.

I cried for him and collapsed on the grassy cliff, just inches from where we had dangled our feet as children and then challenged our individual destinies as adults, coming together as one for the first time. Sheer physical and emotional exhaustion had pulled me back from the stars to the earth, though. Through my hazy vision, I could see Ray coming into focus at the corner of my eyes, hunched over me, checking my breathing and palpating my stomach. I felt the familiarity of his small yet strong and knobby hands and the way in which they could deeply probe all of the inner organs; he knew exactly where they should lie and how they should feel.

"Did he make it?" I whispered, grabbing his forearm as much to reassure him of *my* strength as to get him to stop prodding and poking me.

"Shhh, Ailsa." Ray laughed in his fatherly manner, a deep rumble in his chest. "Ros and Aric are both safe, but you're fevered; let's get you home."

And somehow, for the second time, Ray lifted a person one and a half times his size and carried them to safety.

CHAPTER 25

Between My Finger and My Thumb, the Squat Pen Rests

Edie

"Somehow, rain is just not quite as festive as snow," I said with my head pressed up against the hotel window, one hand holding a glass full of whiskey, etched with "Season's Greetings," the other clutching the remote, which had been scanning through Christmas programming on hotel cable channels.

Frank lay splayed on the bed, tie loosed and mouth agape, and then after some time said, "I have no idea how you're still drinking. I'm so full. I can't believe they eat Christmas goose outside of Dickens's novels."

"I don't think you were supposed to eat the whole goose." I laughed.

General moaning came from the direction of the sleeping alcove as I tapped on the glass and drew spirals with my finger in the condensation left by my breath. "You know what," I called over to him, "after all this time, I'm going to give you the bed and take the couch for myself."

"Why?" Frank sat up earnestly. "Is the couch really good here?"

I rolled my eyes. "No. I'm just thankful for you. For this journey you went on with me, for being there for me as I navigated all of this, and most of all…" I walked over to him, sat on the bed, and smoothed his fine brown hair away from his forehead. "I'm proud of you for quitting."

"Oh, the smoking?" he asked. "It's hell. I'm only doing it because Colin—"

"No. It's for you too," I protested, cupping his perfectly angular chin in my glass-chilled hand.

"Well, if it's time for Christmas sentiments already, then I'm proud of you for quitting too," he said, propping himself up a bit.

"Well thanks, but I only smoked in solidarity with you occasionally," I contested.

"No, Edie, I mean the whole 'I am an island' lonely wanderer bullshit. I think that we've both successfully escaped real commitment in relationships by depending on each other, and I'm proud of both of us for embracing a new kind of love."

I snorted at this. "You may be pushing the holiday sentimentality a bit," I joked.

Frank blinked at me, crystal sapphire eyes framed by dark, thick lashes, serious as ever. "It's OK to love him. It doesn't make you weak," he said.

I returned to the large Georgian window of our hotel room, which looked out onto Saint Stephen's Green. We had come to Dublin to celebrate my book—mine and Sully's—being done. Frank went to pour a bit of whiskey from our Jameson bottle on the desk and joined me at the window. There we stood, looking out onto the lights of the city.

We had just had a big, ridiculous Christmas dinner downstairs in the Shelbourne, next to a Christmas tree with all the trimmings. We sat at a round table, Michael on one side of me, and Sully's wife Mary on the other side. She had whispered her praises to me over the research I had done, squeezing my hand, eyes filling with tears at everyone's toasts and the news that I would be the new visiting professor in Neolithic Archaeology at Trinity the next semester. Michael's grandfather Mickey sat next to him, excited for a trip down south for the holidays, and Frank next to Mickey. They had become fast friends. Sully and Mary's daughter, Caitlin, was away at school in America still, not returning for the holidays this year (a new boyfriend was the rumor), but their son Cian was next to Frank. Cian and Michael had recognized each other from school in Belfast a few years prior, and Michael had cleared his throat in an intimidating way a few times when Cian had had some pointed questions about the research.

I was patting his thigh next to me, letting the red wine flow, answering with ease. I was happy Cian was invested. His towering height reminded me of Sully, and I wanted him to feel he had a voice. I had him make some cover suggestions since he had studied graphic art, and Mary rubbed both our shoulders as we leaned over her looking at the publisher's mock-ups. Her eyes gleamed with the joy of having family home for the holidays. I imagined she had been lonely for the past year, and I vowed to visit her regularly as long as I was in Dublin. Everyone was in a blissful holiday mood, and we finished the night with a round of pass-the-parcel with a gift Mary had bought and wrapped six or seven times, laughing and humming along to the Bing Crosby Christmas music that was piped through the dining room.

Around eleven o'clock, as the day before the solstice drew to a close and Mickey and Frank were falling asleep at the table, we decided to call it a night. Cian ushered Mary out to their car after a few tearful hugs, and the rest of us trudged upstairs to our two rooms; Mickey and Michael in room 102, Frank and I across the way in 103. "Silent Night" played as we kissed cheeks and bade farewell until the morning, when we would make the forty-five-minute trip to Newgrange. I could tell that Michael wanted to linger outside the door for a moment after Mickey went inside, but I felt so fuzzy and warm inside from all the red wine, Christmas cheer, and toasts of congratulations on the book that I was a little afraid of what I might say or do. He saw me backing away and gently pulled me to him, rubbing my nose with his.

"Sleep in heavenly peace, my Edana. Thank you for bringing me and the old man with ye for this wonderful weekend." I felt the cadence of the next three words he wanted to leave his lips. But he felt me pulling away and just kissed my forehead instead.

"You're welcome," I answered with my hand on the door, which Frank had left slightly ajar. "I can't wait for you to see it!" I said as I slipped inside.

It was just half an hour after that awkward farewell that Frank and I stood there at the big Georgian window, whiskeys in hand, comfortably silent for several minutes, as only best friends can be, with the *Doctor Who Christmas Special* playing loudly on the TV in the background, staring at the people down below running around to meet friends for a holiday pub party or running back home into the arms of loved ones.

Finally, I made my confession to Frank and to everyone below. "Look, I know I've been impossible, treating this whole dogged process of research and writing and finalizing Sully's book like it's sacrosanct…or like I'm Robert Langdon or something." We laughed and sipped our whiskey. "In a way, it was a grief process for me, and I needed it in order to—to escape having to feel all the sadness again, having to relive the huge loss of it all. I didn't think I could do it again. Lose another father."

I took a sip of my whiskey, breathed on the window glass, and traced another spiral with the tip of my pointer finger while Frank looked at me, his eyes turned down in sadness like he was a loyal Labrador, standing by me as he had for the last decade, as I continued. "It saved me. I want you to know the crux of it. This whole cycle of the year, observing the ancient Celtic calendar, following the pagans around, learning the dances, visiting every functioning stone circle from here to the Hebrides. It brought my joy back because I realized my job is my vocation and I can do it with seriousness and joy, simultaneously. You and Michael helped me to see that. And Sully," I added. "Sully used to say, 'You can't do a good job if your job is all you do.'"

Frank nodded, with a knowing smile that I knew meant he had the perfect literary quote at hand. "'Are they dead that yet speak louder than we can speak, and in a more universal language?'" he said, raising his glass to clink mine.

"Who's that?" I asked.

"An American like you," he answered. "It sure has been an epic adventure." He laughed.

"You know, I'm happy for you and Colin. I like him. He can use a LiDAR really well."

"He is very useful; I will say that." Frank giggled, the sweet sound of effervescent love bubbling up. "I don't have to tell you how much I like Michael or how perfect he is for you." He raised his eyebrows.

"I think it's so unfair that the bargain we have to strike for loving someone is the possibility of losing them. I don't want to lose anyone else, but I think you're right. It's too late for me now, anyway." I smiled.

"What do you mean?" Frank asked.

"He asked me to come to stay over from Christmas to New Years with his family. Apparently on Christmas Day, the whole village gathers at their ancient farmhouse and Mickey dresses up as Father Christmas." Now it was my turn to giggle.

"That sounds incredible!" Frank said. "I think Hogmanay is bigger than Christmas on the Scottish Isles, so I'll be up that way. We should do something together in the New Year. Maybe a boat ride and a bonfire?" I nodded and squeezed his hand, giggling. "We'll always be soulmates, no matter who we fall in love with along the way," Frank assured me as he finished his last sip of whiskey and made his way back to the bed.

I had gone to the mirror to remove my earrings, humming along to "Christmas in Killarney," when I heard a light rap at the door. I slid across the carpeted floor in my stocking feet and received a light electric shock when I opened the door to reveal Michael, dressed in full-length coat, gloves, and hat.

"The rain stopped, and I wondered if you would mind joining me for a walk?" he asked, hesitantly smiling and rocking back and forth in anticipation.

"Isn't it midnight?" I asked.

"Yes. I wanted to ring in the solstice with my favorite archaeologist," he offered, eyebrows raised in supplication.

I got my coat and shoes, and we headed downstairs and past the giant Christmas tree, out onto Grafton Street. The shops were lit up still, and lights stretched across the cobblestone road, illuminating the night like the stars had on Mabon when we first kissed. We walked hand in hand, stopping to peer into pretty windows, tip buskers, and grab a walk-up coffee. I got a decaf, hoping I might sleep for a few hours before we left for Newgrange at 5:00 a.m. Michael got his usual cappuccino.

Before we knew it, we had reached the gates of Trinity College, where bright lights were cast onto the buildings nearby, dressing them up for the holidays. "Do you mind if I give you your Christmas present early?" he asked, reaching into his pocket. He pulled out a small box wrapped in gold paper. There was a small, folded paper on top that simply read, "to my love."

I opened it very carefully, revealing a wooden box carved with a spiral. I looked up at him, smiling. "Your handiwork?" I asked.

He nodded. "Keep going." Inside was a single silver bangle bracelet that was inscribed all the way around, "Be who God meant you to be and you will set the world on fire."

"You remembered." I said, deeply moved.

"I want you to know, Edie, that I'm endlessly proud of ye and I'll support you whether you teach at Trinity or in Timbuktu. I just want you to know how much you deserve to be happy."

My eyes filled with tears, and the drizzle that had picked back up in the last few minutes turned to tiny, fluffy snowflakes that landed in our eyelashes and hair. They covered my red wool gloves, and I pulled his face down to mine to kiss him. We were excited by the snow like little children and ended up walking around the city for the rest of the night, up Clare Street to the old Viking docks, over to Phoenix Park, and then back to O'Connell Street and up to the M-1 to catch the 5:00 a.m. bus to Newgrange. I don't think I had ever talked that much in my life, but the conversation and kisses flowed ceaselessly as we walked for hours in the falling snow.

I didn't arrive back to the hotel room until noon the next day. Frank had risen, ordered breakfast to the room, and was sitting at the table in the hotel bathrobe surrounded by waffles, bacon, coffee, and orange juice when I entered, sopping wet, exhausted, and absolutely electrified. We had seen the light as it snuck into the passage tomb, illuminating the altar wall. It had been one of the purest moments of joy in my life, and Sully was there, so vividly, in every moment of it.

"OK, sit down, have a waffle and some coffee, and tell me everything," Frank said.

I laughed and slid down the door onto the carpeted floor. My feet were aching, and I needed to sleep. I covered my face. "You'll never believe it," I said.

"Wait, what?" Frank asked again, sitting up, even more interested.

"First of all, the passage tomb lit up even though no one thought it would this year with all the rain!"

"That's great," Frank answered, "but I feel like there's more."

"I told him I loved him," I whispered, still not sure it was real. I hadn't ever really felt it or said it to anyone before, so I was unsure of what I was supposed to be feeling.

"How?" Frank asked, mouth agape.

"I don't know," I said. "He said something to me, and then it was just like dawn at the passage tomb: There was a small crack that the light could enter, and it did, despite all the clouds and dismal forecasts. And all of a sudden I was just—"

"Illuminated?" Frank asked, smiling beatifically.

"Precisely," I said as I crawled over to the bed.

"So what did he say, Edie? Don't leave me hanging!" Frank got up, following me to the bed to tuck me in.

"He gave me this bracelet," I said, extending my arm before closing my eyes to get some much-needed rest before our trip north to stay with Michael's family for Christmas.

"And?" Frank asked as I dozed off.

"And he said...wait, let me remember exactly." Frank laughed, sitting patiently at the end of the bed. "He said, 'I have something to teach you about love. It's not some fragile thing that shatters when we walk through something hard.'"

CHAPTER 26:

A Winter Solstice Nativity

Ailsa

This is how I found myself in my grandmother's house on the day after Samhain again, a year since I had cuddled around the fires sharing stories and sinking into bliss together with Aric and Ros. I had told my tale of the stones, why they were built, and what magic lay inside them. The thought of telling stories gave me a pang as I awoke, still wondering about Ros; how he had the courage to cliff jump into the night sea like that was more than I had ever expected from him. I was surrounded by a pile of soft hides, furs, wool blankets, and feather pillows, yet I felt myself suspended in the air as he had been.

Grandmother waddled over to me by the hearth, her softly rounded form slightly hunched. She felt my head with her long, graceful fingers and looked into my face with bright eyes, humming a tune with as much mirth as a new mother. Her hair was nearly all silver and hung straight down her shoulders cascading over her back; she flipped it back and forth as she worked, grinding grain on the quern for bread, deflowering herbs, and drying and cutting up her medicines. She sat on the floor now, legs folded beneath her as she brushed out my hair, equally long but black as night like my father's and full of knots from the ocean wind.

Grandmother's brush didn't go through my hair quite as smoothly as it did her own. "Your hair must be coarser than a boar's, Ailsa."

I took the tea and drank, the heat of the liquid assaulting my senses, along with the camphorous smell. "This tea is nectar, Grandmother."

She smiled and fixed my blankets around me. I gazed into the crackling red-gold embers of my grandmother's hearth fire. These days we kept the fire going all day long so that we could sleep at night, blissfully warm under a pile of furs, a goat's stomach filled with warm water at our feet for extra heat. The longest night was approaching, just a little over one moon away now. Ray and the rest of the Druids felt sure the baby would arrive then and that she would be marked to be a Druid like me, my Uncle Jord, my great-grandfather, and my ancestors who built the stone circle.

"You should go back to sleep, darling; you've been through much," Grandmother said, finishing my plait and kissing my forehead. "I'll tell Aric you're feeling better. He's out pacing in the barley field with worry. Thank the gods we cut it last month, or he'd have stomped it all to death." She laughed, rising slowly, bones cracking, and went out the hide door.

But I couldn't sleep, wondering where Ros was, if he had let either the sea or his sadness, or both, swallow him. "Love is not some fragile vessel that shatters when the fire is hot." I ran his words from last night through my mind over and over again. But I never questioned my decision. "This is blood sport," he had also once told me, talking about love. Ros burned so hot, it was hard not to catch a few of his sparks for yourself. He knew that as much as I loved him, I couldn't go. He knew before I did.

Aric ducked in under the hide of my grandmother's house and made it to my bedside in one stride. Grandmother stayed out, surely to give us some privacy. He kissed every inch of my small face. I felt a little like I had been greeted by a loyal hound instead of my husband.

"Hello," I said weakly.

"Oh Ailsa, Ray said you would be fine, but I couldn't help but worry while you slept all day."

"How is *he*?" I asked.

"A bit sore from carrying ye to me so I could whisk you home, here." He laughed. "But he's all right; he's with the *hapiru* in his home."

"The stranger?" I asked.

"Yes, and he's very strange. I saw them gathering stones this morning." Aric smiled, looking into my eyes and tucking my hair behind my ear. "But he's not here to hurt anyone," he continued. "Ray *is* currently trying to talk him out of sending one boat full of men south to find Ros who beguiled them and caused them to lose a good sail and rudder, however."

"I don't think they'll catch him," I said, smiling, finishing my tea and laying my head back to a more comfortable reclining position. "Gathering our stones?" I asked. "Why?"

Aric's eyes widened and lit up. And I began to think he was acting giddy for more reasons than just my apparent health improvement. "You should have seen it, Ailsa. Last night on the beach, he broke off pieces of the boulders with the white and silver veins—you know, the ones at the cave's entrance? And he melted them in the fires of Ros's ship. The fire burned hot enough to melt stone, and he said this melted substance, combined with the blue and green veined stones in the circle, is what their weapons called *bronze* are made of." He smiled at this thought. "Those weapons and breastplates, and jewelry, he can teach you to make it all."

"Me?" I asked.

"Yes, he calls you 'the dowser.'" I looked away from Aric into the fire. "He's traveled so far, Ailsa. He speaks of his homeland in the south, where there are great cities and huge buildings, taller than trees, more people than you could imagine."

He placed his hand on top of mine, which lay on top of the furs. I should have been sweating, but I felt a cold chill run down my spine and a ghostly presence. *Was it my father? Still here for Samhain, trying to warn me about these strange visitors.*

Aric continued, "He says he needs you to use your dowser ability to help find the stones that contain the magic substance when you are well."

A snow blanketed the entire island for the first time since I was a girl, and similarly, a sickness had fallen over the village in the last fortnight, both making the days more silent than anyone would wish. Everyone was keeping to themselves, by their hearths, under blankets, but occasionally neighbors would venture out to check on one another, exchange children who weren't sick so they might play a bit, and take their minds off the slow passage of time as the days became shorter and the winter weather and illness kept us all inside by the fire.

Ray was going around from house to house, checking on the weaker and older patients. Two elderly women, friends of grandmother's since childhood, had passed away, and one baby and two small children were very ill. I worried to the point of obsession about spreading the illness to my grandmother, but as second Druid to Ray, I felt the need to accompany him on most of his visits and to relieve him of his duties when he had been working around the clock. Grandmother and I also helped however we could from home, boiling extra water, steeping willow bark to make tea for body aches, steeping inhalations of peppermint and eucalyptus leaves to help relieve congestion. The children, adults, and elderly could drink the tea, and I would dip a rag into one of the bowls to saturate the end and then wring it, drip by drip, into the infants' mouths as grandmother had done for me when I was a mewling sickly babe. It was easy to busy myself around the house when I was there making the medicines, heating stones for those with the chill and heating the inhalations. I held children, swept floors, comforted the grieving, and felt light on my feet until the end of the day. We went on like this for an entire cycle of the moon.

During this time, Elijah, the stranger, or *the hapiru,* as most called him, had worked tirelessly at the stone circle and around the coastlines, gathering what stones he could and teaching Jord how to increase the heat of the fire. He asked me to help lead him to the stones that contained the metal and taught me how to use and amplify my dowsing abilities. I talked with him about the stones, recounted the stories of my ancestors, and listened as he explained the science of alchemy, but I felt like I was most needed by Ray and the village at this time. Peculiarly, Elijah had no fear of the sickness that had struck the village down. He appeared immune to it, in fact. That was honestly something I had even more interest in than the bronze.

We spent most of our days and evenings in Grandmother's house. I trusted Aric to keep her safe and warm by the fire, well-fed, and hydrated with marrow bone soup. I made several huge batches of the soup with all the bones from Aric's hunts, and once the sicker patients could drink, I replaced their sipping tea with pitchers of the healing and nourishing broth. I looked forward to coming home to the two of them at the end of the day. We would all cuddle up by the fire as we sipped soup and discussed the welfare of the sick and the work the Druids were doing to keep the illness at bay for the long winter ahead. Then we would distract ourselves from the sickness, telling stories and singing so the baby could hear our joy for her impending arrival. This was how the last few nights leading up to the longest night of the year were spent, and despite the hardship the village faced, I hadn't felt so safe and content since I was a girl and I had fallen asleep to the sounds of my father and grandmother talking.

In the morning I would wake at dawn and head to Grandmother's house to check on her and prepare my needs for the day. The day before the longest night of the year, I woke up early. *What am I forgetting?* I thought, and grandmother replied promptly, "Take the ground dandelions to mix into the teas as well, huckleberries for those who can manage to eat a few, and perhaps—" Instead of finishing her sentence, she started to push herself up from her low seat by the hearth. "If you look in my smallest reed basket, you'll find a clay vessel full of mistletoe."

"Are you sure?" I asked. Mistletoe was a potent herb, and only the Druids were supposed to use it, but Grandmother was a renowned healer, and I trusted her.

"Just one little needle ground into the tea of the old ones, darling. It will help. And let Aric help you carry everything, please. I'll stay put, I promise."

Obediently, Aric pulled his cloak over his shoulders and began to lace his over-the-knee snow boots by the door. I had organized everything onto wooden pallets that were easy to stack and carry or pull with leather straps across the fresh-fallen snow. Aric followed me outside dutifully, showing the most subtle of smiles as a hint of his amusement at being my apprentice. "Maybe we should get you a dog for this," Aric jested as I passed him with long strides, kicking my cloak and skirts up in a flurry of snow as I walked with intention toward the houses that needed care.

"I had a dog." Falcon was really my father's dog, and he had left me not too many years after my father had, gone to die by himself in the woods. His body had been torn apart by vultures and foxes before Ros and I could find him. "He was in quite the state when I found his body, but I made him a funerary pyre at the cliffs after we found him in the oak grove near that moss-covered fallen log that crosses the river under the canopy," I explained, remembering that awful day, silently replaying it in my head.

"He's a *dog*, Ailsa," Ros had said, balking under the fifty-pound weight of Falcon and trying to keep up with me as I walked toward the cliffs.

"He's a coward," I had choked out between sobs. And Ros had been stunned into silence, having never heard me cry before. "He didn't have to die like that. I could have been with him. Coward."

The rest of the walk to the cliffs had been silent. Rain pelted us, mingling with tears on our faces. Ros, then a boy of fourteen, rarely given over to emotion anymore, felt his throat thicken at the black, silky touch of Falcon's ear as it flopped against his left hand. Ros had stayed with me through the night, watching me stand, without fear or exhaustion, as the six-foot pyre burned all the way to embers. He knew it was not Falcon that I called a coward—it was my father, not his dog that I was unable to forgive in my heart, for who could not forgive a creature with love as steadfast as a dog's?

Aric paused at the door to the house we were visiting to tuck the loose hair behind my ear. "I'm sorry you weren't with your dog, Ailsa. I'm sure you wanted to hold him by your hearth and kiss him as he departed the world." He kissed my forehead.

"He was partly tame but still a bit wild. He needed to die alone in the woods like an old, sick wolf would, and I couldn't begrudge him that." I rubbed the small of my back, which had begun to ache as the day's labor wore on.

Aric chuckled through his nose as we entered the house. "No, I don't suppose you could begrudge him. He sounds just like you."

"You're not a bad apprentice," I told him later as we walked on to the next home, where two sick, elderly women lived together. He laughed and massaged the top of my head with his hand, broad fingers spread across my skull within the hood of my new indigo cloak. I hoped my old green Druid cloak was keeping Ros warm on these long, frigid nights, but knowing him, he had someone else keeping him warm.

"Where do you think Ray ran off to, anyway?" Aric asked, returning me from my thoughts.

"He had to go prepare for the winter solstice with the other Druids," I answered as I kneaded the back of my hips with my knuckles. Aric saw the furrow of my brow and put his larger, stronger hands to my back, where he pushed harder. It felt good, but the pain would not abate. I looked into his face and saw the worry. I must have looked worse than I thought. "Let's get back to Grandmother's house quickly," I said, my clammy hands grasping for his.

He picked me up swiftly, a swirl of cloaks, and ran for home, calling for someone to fetch Ray.

"Red hair." It was the first thing I heard after I awakened. Ray was there, holding my daughter over me. As he lowered her, a halo of light appeared to follow in her wake, and when she touched my chest and felt my heartbeat, her crying ceased. After Ray's face and my daughter's face came into focus, the next face I saw was my husband's.

"Like my mother's hair," Aric said, smiling down at me. It was a simple, innocent remark. But what it held was an understanding, a union, that we maybe didn't know we had until that moment.

I saw him swallow. It was audible, and I knew the hours that had passed had not been easy on him. Somehow Ray had saved me, holding my life in his small, glowing, strong palm, yet he had not been able to save Aric's first wife Iona. The baby had been born breathing, but my own breath had stopped and then come back again, just like Aric's had that day by the sea. I didn't understand but knew it was part of a design I was never meant to understand.

"Did you have a name in mind?" Grandmother asked.

"Did you, *Mamai?*" Aric asked, using the simple, sentimental word for mother, and it took my breath away, so shocked and touched I was to consider myself in the leagues of this precious word I had used for my own *mamai*, a word which I hadn't uttered aloud in so long.

"I do have a name in mind," I replied, and my voice felt shaky and not my own as I spoke it out loud. Ray smiled and ducked out silently.

The furs and hides were piled high in the main room, where the sunlight spilled in through the doorway and windows. We were close to the hearth, and the warmth of Aric's body and the furs he had brought for the baby kept us warm. He sat, naked, legs spread in the bed, with me squished between his thighs and the baby alternately suckling and asleep at my breast.

"Two years married tonight," he whispered into my ear, leaving a wet kiss on my cheek.

"This is happier than I thought I could ever be two years ago," I said quietly into the sweet smell of my baby's russet and ginger head. "I hope I make you both proud of me," I whispered.

"I think she's smiling," Aric said. I took the pearl that Rasha had given me, which had been concealed in the leather purse full of herbs and seeds that now lay next to our bed. I waved it back and forth in front of her big blue eyes, which looked too big for her head. She cooed, her gaze reaching upward toward the stone, her eyes crossing to focus on it.

"A beautiful black pearl," Aric commented, stopping my hand to observe the iridescent colors—green, blue, violet, indigo, gray, midnight, and pitch black—as they undulated across the dark surface between my fingertips. "You're lucky to find one of such beauty. I've seen strings of them, but no single pearl so beautiful as that."

I smiled. "Rasha gave it to me one morning at the river when I caught her practicing her ritual dance. I thought I had lost it, but I think I understand better now what it means to do the rough work to make a pearl."

Aric laughed. "Shall we sing to her?" he asked in his tender and deep voice.

"Yes, I know just what to sing," I replied.

Some days later, my grandmother, her brother Jord, and Ray were gathered around the hearth on the other side of our house from where I was reclining with the baby. They had brought gifts of herbs for us. Lavender and calendula from Ray's garden for my aches, wild chamomile picked by Grandmother for my rest, and lanolin from the sheep's wool for cracked, sore nipples from breastfeeding, harvested from Uncle Jord's sheep. They smiled into their earthenware tea bowls, then grinned over at us with pride.

At the moment I saw her, I knew we had been souls intertwined for eons. There she was, smiling up at me, smelling as fresh and new as a ewe in spring, but she was eerily familiar. "Where have we met before?" I asked her as I kissed her light blue fingertips. She nestled into me, and I kissed the soft orange fuzz on her head. It had an earthy smell, mingled with my own musk and the new and special scent that was just hers. "I thought she would be a stranger when we met, but she's not, is she?" I asked.

Grandmother went to her work kneading my belly to make sure everything had come out over the last few days. "Och, no, lovely. She's been here all along, just waitin' for you to be ready. Watching you as ye climbed your trees, as you lost your parents and found your Druidism." She searched deep within my womb to be sure everything was out, found something she didn't quite like and distastefully discarded it, then settled herself to a bit of a push and pull of realigning my hip bones.

"And now she's here in my arms, and the moon is new, and so is life," I said.

"It's actually quite old, what you're doing, love, but I get your meaning. It's new for you." Grandmother kissed my forehead, and, exhausted, I fell asleep to the sound of her humming and rocking our little light-bringer, Sorcha. There were also the deeper sounds of my uncle Jord, my husband Aric, and his adoptive father Ray laughing and talking across the room. My family was whole for the first time since my own birth, and I could rest now, but not for long. Just ten days after the solstice, after Sorcha's foretold birth, Ray disappeared.

CHAPTER 27:

SORCHA

ay passes to night, and night becomes day again. Winter becomes spring, eventually, when the light-bringer comes. Time passes, sometimes steadily and slowly; other times it's as fleeting and as magical as the glow of a firefly on a summer night. However it passes, you can't hold onto it. Like everything that is good and precious, you have to let it go. Once I plucked a beautiful orange oak leaf from my tree and set it, like a boat, tripping down the chilly freshness of the river that runs next to the grove. I watched it float and spin, bumping into rocks and logs, until the river took it out to the sea and it disappeared forever.

Time whisks away every single thing we love until it is just a memory. We let precious things go so that the next can come to us. What reward can we possibly gain from holding on so tightly? I learned all of this through my life experiences, through my meditations at the stones, and now I looked down at the light-bringer I held in my arms and wondered if I would ever be able to apply the knowledge in this circumstance. How could I ever trust the world enough to let her go? For the first time, I feared my own death.

I thought of my own mother's funeral pyre. A sight I wasn't old enough to remember but an event I had imagined over and over again throughout my life, anytime I beheld another pyre or looked deep into the flames of the festival fires. I had let her go into the ether at the tender age of the babe I held in my very arms, and somehow I survived. I imagined my father's funeral raft, fashioned in the way of his people, drifting off to sea, and the flint arrows of fire raining down on him until, *whoosh*, the whole raft was alight and his body disappeared into the smoke. I had not been brave enough to go down to the shores that day, but I had imagined it over and over. How had I gone on all these years after that? And yet I could and did find happiness in each passing day.

And finally, I thought of Ros. I thought of how he might look in the vast sea from the flight of an albatross or another great seabird, his bright red hair against the gray-green ocean as he expertly navigated and steered his little boat through the waves and tides of the northern islands. I didn't fear for him because I knew he maneuvered that boat as if it were an extension of his own body. I knew the open sea was where he belonged, and that made the letting-go easier on my aching heart.

There she was in the sunlight, walking toward me. Hair on fire from the sun, an amber color I'd never seen before: red, gold, cinnamon. Aric still said it reminded him of his mother's hair, and I realized how little he had spoken of her before Sorcha was born. She was an only child. But of course, so was I, and so was Aric. She danced in the woods on tiptoes, calling to the birds. She named the squirrels and rabbits, played with Grandmother's goats more than the other children, and fell asleep by the hearth with puppies in her lap. Life was changing in the village with the development of the forge and the search for copper and tin minerals. We traded some out but kept most for ourselves, in the king's cave, where they waited to be alchemized into a new life, like I had been in the days leading up to our visit from the stranger.

I was head Druid now, since Ray had vanished, and so much of my life was dedicated to others, to the fire festivals, to the village, and to building relationships with the forgers, tradesmen, and metalworkers new to the village. Ray had left me as a young Druid. "Come back to me, Ray. Come back to Aric. Come back to Sorcha," I prayed at the stones every festival and every celestial event. Only Jord and Elijah had been at the stones with him the day he vanished. The great spiral stone had hummed, they said, and he was gone. Jord had moved in with grandmother to help take care of her, and we stayed up by the hearth many a night, telling stories about our best friends who had disappeared, hoping for their welfare, waiting for the day they would return with stories of their adventures. I smiled to think that maybe their paths would cross at the gathering at the large henge to the south or maybe where all the greatest boats and priests converged: Orkney.

We continued the work of pulling out the green veins from the standing stones, chipping away at the massive blocks without destroying them. So few places had both the green veins and the silver ones needed to create the perfect alloy. They didn't naturally occur in the same type of stone. We had the silver veins, which occurred naturally on the glittering stones at the mouth of the cave, the stones that Aric had washed up on as a boy, the stones that had burned in the hot fires of Ros's boat and melted in front of Aric's eyes on the night Ros jumped into the sea. And because our ancestors had moved stones from another island to erect our stone circle, we also had the green veins. Elijah said it was unheard of to have both types of stone so close together, and this gave me the uncomfortable feeling that we would have many more visitors in our future.

And just as intuition had warned me, late in spring we had an unexpected visitor: a traveler who brought news from the northern isles in a ship with a crab claw sail. When he appeared on the coast, I had been at the stones, and I ran down in excitement that it might be someone else. But he was a northerner, much like my father: tall, with a leather bag and dark brown cloak lined with wolf's fur; long, pointed features; and handsome dark eyes shining down on me.

He was trying to explain something when I summoned the Druid elders, Elijah, and my apprentice Griff, the youngest new Druid, down to the cave. "These stones are from my land," he said in our language, handling the pieces of the standing stones that we had harvested for their blue-green veins. "Our villages used to be one, many years ago, after the ice receded, but the Druids left to inhabit this island and build a new stone circle, similar to the one we have."

Jord came to look over my shoulder at the stones. "It's just like Ray dreamed," he whispered.

"We must start a fire now. I have bellows to harness the heat and melt the stones. I will show you." The new man said.

I looked up at Jord and looked back at Elijah, his mouth agape.

"Uh, how have you come to this knowledge, friend?" Elijah asked him.

"And why have you come to share it with us?" I asked, pointedly.

He darted his eyes around, looking for an explanation. We all waited, staring, a united front with a peculiar feeling about this man. "This Ray you speak of," he began, and Jord's eyes opened wide, filling with tears, as Griff's small hands squeezed my arm tightly, "he has spoken to us as well. He brought this boat to me, together with a ginger man, and bade me come share the news with you." The man clearly hoped this information would gain our trust. "He wants you to know that he lives still." The man extended a palm full of the spiraled shells that Ray collected in his meditations on the beach.

Jord gasped, his long, bony fingers covering his mouth. Elijah let out a short cry of utter shock and happiness. The northern man smiled when his news brought joy to us and reached with a long metal poker into the fire to retrieve the rocks.

Griff hugged Jord in glee. "They're both alive!" he exclaimed in a voice cracked with emotion and adolescence, looking over at me.

Yet I was still unsure. "What else did they say?" I asked. "You're holding something back." I needed the full truth in order to trust this new man, whether Ray did or not.

The man was focused on his craft, though. He poured the melted rock into a four-sided container he had pulled from his bag, and we all watched, holding our collective breath. Elijah rejoiced when he saw the copper fall like warm honey into the pointed mold. After a moment of intrigue, questioning, and chatter, the liquid cooled, and the man looked up into my eyes, opening the mold to reveal to us our first shining spearhead.

"I don't want it." I said reflexively, staring at the weapon that reflected my muddled likeness.

"It's not for you." the man answered quietly. And now seven pairs of eyes stared at him across the growing fire as our shadows danced on the cave's wall, foretelling what would come.

"Ray also said that he and Ros will be back to help fight the war that is coming when you are gone, Ailsa, and Sorcha has become head Druid and alchemist."

ABOUT THE AUTHOR

C.E.L. Delafield, a North Carolina native, is a seasoned archae-ologist with degrees from The University of North Carolina and The University College of Dublin. Her expertise in Prehistoric Archaeology breathes authenticity into her historical narratives. A former high school English literature teacher, Delafield is also a passionate hiker, doula, and dog rescuer. She is the acclaimed author of the Wheel of the Year series and a recipient of the Sam Selden Prize in Playwriting. Her writing, rich in relationships, excitement, and romance, is deeply rooted in historical accuracy. Delafield resides in Pittsboro, NC with her husband and two daughters. Her stories bring the vivid and unforgettable landscapes of modern Ireland and ancient Scotland to life, a love story to West Ireland, the home of her heart and The Isle of Skye, where she was married.

COMING SOON

Wheel of the Year: The Age of Alchemy

Wheel of the Year: The Age of Iron

Milton Keynes UK
Ingram Content Group UK Ltd.
UKHW030746071024
449371UK00006B/491